# DESERT SIREN

# Desert Siren

## WES SMITH

DREAMWIRE PRESS

Physical editions printed by IngramSpark.
Printed in the USA.

First Edition.

ISBN 978-0-9994703-0-5 Hardcover; 978-0-9994703-1-2 Digital

Library of Congress Control Number: 2018908092

Jacket Design by Brad Holten

To Brad

For our crazy lifelong journey

Alexandra Stirling was floating. Her world fell out from beneath the soles of her feet as a sensation pulsed through her chest like the anticipation before a roller coaster's first drop. In the back of her mind, she knew she should fear what was happening, but her instincts kicked into overdrive, hellbent on the solitary thought of self-preservation.

*Brace yourself,* her inner voice screamed.

Beside her, Alex's captain—the goliath woman Ghaoithe Loinsigh— gripped the sides of a chair with enough force to turn her knuckles white. Throughout the bridge of the *Cloudkicker,* her crew did the same as best as they could. Objects hung suspended in the air around them. With what little rationale Alex had left, she hit the floor and followed suit, catching the bolted legs of her captain's chair just as the scabbard holding Excalibur whistled by and crashed into the wall behind her.

Time caught up and screamed forward as their vessel tipped, replacing the sky in the observation windows with ridges of glittering sand. The items that escaped gravity for but a moment zipped past Alex to join Excalibur at the back of the room. A mug shattered against her arm, and she cried in pain as she resisted the urge to loosen her grip. The *Cloudkicker,* that impossible, invincible airship, plummeted towards Egypt.

As the prow collided with a dune, it skipped upwards like a stone across a placid lake. The glowing protective runes that marked the *Cloudkicker*'s hull no longer kept it aloft, but they protected the ship from the force of the impact. Inside, however, they held no sway as the inhabitants were thrown about like pick-up sticks. Alex's fingers slipped. She remembered flying upwards, then backwards, and finally hitting her head on who-knows-what. Her vision blurred and eventually left her altogether.

Alex swam, trapped in a tidepool of dream and memory. She thought she heard someone yell emergency orders, but the garbled voice faded into the murk that surrounded her. She turned her head. The movement took eons in her water-trance state. In the distance, a speck of light appeared and grew until it encompassed everything in her vision. She stepped into the brightness and entered the elegant Osiris suite she had only just escaped. White lights bounced off white carpet and into ebony furniture. Outside the glass walls, scattered lamps of mountain villages glittered among a rugged landscape.

"I was wondering when you would show up," said a man's voice. In front of a large glass table with a fire blazing in a center pit stood a gangly figure in a tailored suit. Though his back was turned towards her, Alex could never mistake the languid drawl in his voice.

"Ethan?" she called in her head.

"You're a long way from home, Alex," Ethan replied without turning.

Alex shook her head, trying to contain thoughts that flitted in and out of her head like butterflies. "I watched you die," she said.

The image of her beloved Ethan, down on his knees with a gun to his head flashed by. She heard Deacon pull back the trigger. Her breath hitched in her chest.

Ethan remained looking towards the distant lights of the villages beyond his business towers. "Never trust in the concepts of life or death in this realm," he said with a slight, knowing chuckle. "This world of relics and ancient magic doesn't like following the rules of logic we try to place ourselves in."

Alex strode to Ethan without thinking. Just as she was within arm's reach, he turned. The warm face Alex knew no longer existed. His right temple had disintegrated, blown apart by a bullet from the other side. What little of his smile remained clung to his jaw by precarious strings of sinew. Yet Alex did not recoil. Somewhere in her subconscious, she knew that she was in a place beyond her scope of knowledge.

"You need to go," he said without moving his mouth.

"Can I really live without you?" Alex asked. It was not the trembling heartache she expected. She was asking for permission.

"You've already started to."

The room shrank around them. Behind Alex, screaming cut through the air. The shouts warbled and shifted, molded themselves into solidity.

"*Alex!*"

She shot up and drew air into her lungs. The bridge of the *Cloudkicker* buzzed around her. She steadied herself against the dizziness affecting her vision. Something wet and sticky trickled down the back of her neck.

Beside her, Ghaoithe stared with a wide, dazzling emerald eye. The captain placed a hand on Alex's back to keep her still.

"Don't move. You're pretty banged up," said Ghaoithe.

Alex dared not test the order. "What happened? Where are we?" she asked. She felt a warm cloth press behind her ear followed by an intense throbbing that left her crying out.

"Hang in there," Ghaoithe comforted. "Sorin stole our extra flight crystals. We crashed. You got clipped by the desk. I'm going to assume you have a concussion."

Alex winced, as much from the name of the Ghaoithe's former first-mate-turned-traitor as from the pain in her head. She should have guessed Sorin would have made off with the extra fuel that kept the *Cloudkicker* afloat. In front of her, the crew scrambled about the bridge. A few others were lying on the ground. Those who were awake assessed the damage to the ship. Glancing from the corner of her vision, Alex spied a pair of heavy, worn boots beside Ghaoithe's crouching form.

"We're checkin' out the rest of the hull, Captain, but we're really exposed out here. Nothin' but sand on the horizon," said a gruff voice above the boots. It was Fleet, Ghaoithe's aged quartermaster.

"Get a ward around us, Fleet. Our first priority needs to be hiding this ship," Ghaoithe ordered.

Fleet grunted. He leaned in front of Alex and beamed a quick smile through his salted beard. "It's just a scratch. Tough little minnow like you has seen worse," he said before launching himself down the ramp from the captain's balcony.

The throbbing in Alex's head worsened, and she let out an involuntary groan. Ghaoithe slipped her free arm beneath Alex's legs.

"Hold the cloth as hard as you can against your head and let me know if anything hurts where it's not supposed to," she said.

Alex raised her arm. It took all of her draining strength to keep the cloth held in place. Ghaoithe lifted her up without effort and cradled the girl as she would an injured bird. They rushed through the ship's decks, past disheveled sailors, towards the personal quarters. Alex barely registered the organized chaos around her, focused entirely on the bandage at her head and the warmth of Ghaoithe's protection.

Once they reached Alex's room, Ghaoithe stopped outside the door. She glanced down at Alex. "What's your name?" she asked.

Alex scrunched her nose. "Uh, Alex?"

"Where were you born?"

"New Delta, Missouri. What are you doing?"

Ghaoithe let out a relieved sigh. "Making sure you'll stay conscious on me. Think you can stand long enough to get inside?"

The pounding behind Alex's ear refused to let up, but her initial nausea upon awakening subsided. She nodded a slight affirmation and another wave of dizziness struck. Ghaoithe braced her with a firm hand as she got to her feet. They entered the room, and Alex eased onto her bed. Ghaoithe took the cloth from Alex. It was covered in crimson, but far less than Alex had expected. With nimble fingers, the captain combed through the blonde curls covering the wound.

"Yeah, that's going to leave a mark," she explained, but Alex could sense a bit of relief in the words. "Looks like you didn't lose much blood, but you'll have a headache for a good couple of days."

"Better than stitches, I guess," grumbled Alex.

"Wouldn't be a part of my ship without a few battle scars."

Ghaoithe crossed to the side of the bed. She brushed her fingers alone the runes along the wall. Alex squinted as the outer wall of the room switched to its windowed mode and gave the two a look outside. Fleet and several others etched giant patterns into the sand with long poles. The sigils, the sweeping language that powered their ancient world, did not shift with the rest of the sand around them.

"I need to go help. We're vulnerable," said Ghaoithe. She squeezed Alex's shoulder. "You should be fine to get some rest. I don't think you're that easy to get rid of."

"Aye, aye, Captain," Alex smirked with a slight salute before she allowed the darkness to take her.

As she drifted off, Alex wondered at first if the entire sequence of events had been part of her imagination. She remembered being in New Delta, Missouri at one point, working as an intern for a newspaper. The *Cloudkicker* appeared outside the local hospital one day, while Alex was visiting her ex-boyfriend, Ethan. Captained by The Sky Thief Ghaoithe, a master relic hunter in search of the world's lost artifacts, the crew kidnapped Alex. There was a map, Ghaoithe said, hidden in a movie poster in Alex's possession. Unhappy with her dead-end Missouri life and sensing no real danger from the captain, Alex chose to stay on board against Ghaoithe's wishes. There was a whole time-lost world out there where Earth's myths were real, powered by ancient writing that glowed blue. Alex needed to see it for herself. They were searching for Pandora's Box.

There was the lost city of Roanoke before it was burned down in a surprise assault. Something about a rival. The Illuminati? No, it was... Osiris. Yes, Osiris was the right name. They were a powerful conglomerate with eyes everywhere, and they wanted Pandora's Box too. Ethan had been a part of them all along. He used Alex to get close to the map, and she needed to find him for answers.

The *Cloudkicker*'s search led them under the ocean. A city—not just any city but Eden itself—hid under Bimini Road in the Caribbean, but Ghaoithe was too late. They were after something there, something big, something related to Pandora's Box. Whatever it was, the Osiris leader Deacon took it before they arrived.

They chased him to Osiris headquarters in China and were taken prisoner. Ethan was there. Alex recalled that clearly even in her scrambled thoughts. He was there with Alex's best friend and a plan to leverage her for Alex's cooperation. It turned out he was a plant, Ghaoithe's secret contact within the Osiris Corporation. He helped the crew escape. They searched the Osiris base for the object Deacon took from under the ocean but it wasn't a relic; it was a girl. A young girl named Ellie.

*That's right.* Alex's thought pierced the darkness around her. *We have to protect Ellie.*

But things went terribly wrong. During the escape, Deacon was a step ahead of everyone. He shot Ethan. Alex saw it happen. She could hear the gunshot through the pulsing of her head. Ethan was dead, and Alex was alone and scared in a world of myths. The crew managed to escape China and were now trapped in the Sahara Desert en route to a trade city called Dilmun.

That could not have all been a dream, could it? No, that had happened. Alex's boring Midwestern life had been turned upside down by the Sky Thief and a flying airship and a deadly game of tag.

When Alex woke, the usual gentle bounce of the ship was absent, and the dull ache behind her head was all too real. She sighed and stared at the panels on the ceiling of her room, not wishing to return to the trouble that awaited her. In her old life, she could have rolled back over and slept for a few more hours of peace before returning to monotony. She briefly considered feigning indisposal. No one would blame her. She could stay right here in her room and wait for Ghaoithe and Fleet to return from wherever they were going, repairs in tow with Osiris none the wiser. She would spend a few days catching up on her book of artifacts and enjoying a hot meal or two.

However, she knew she would regret it, that she would let down not only the crew but herself. She made her choice and it was time to see it through. With no small amount of effort from her stiffened neck, she turned to check on the progress outside.

Sunlight beat down on the desert landscape. It caused the sand to sparkle and glare with blinding force. The looping swirls drawn in the sand had been completed, and nothing inside its inner circle had so much as a trace of wind to dissolve its protection. Fleet was no longer barking orders, but a scant few guards patrolled just inside the sigil wall.

Alex remained content to lay and stare. She wanted to enjoy the relaxation she knew would not last much longer. Sure enough, no sooner did she begin to drift again did a knock come at her door.

"Come in," she groaned. She pulled her legs over the side of her bed. Her boots had not even been taken off her feet, and the strange pressure of being over-worn itched at them.

Damian pulled the door aside. He peeked into the room through the crack in the doorway, fearing for Alex's modesty. When she motioned for him, he strode in as if the room were his own. Alex was happy to see that the man who saved them from Osiris looked no worse for wear after the crash. He was a drifter like her, no more than a stowaway who weaseled his way onto the ship and somehow made it more cheerful in the process. Alex connected with Damian in a way she could not with the others, a long-haired boy from Los Angeles, kindred threads to the life they used to live.

"You look like you ate a batch of bad grapes or something," he said with complete earnesty.

"I wish it were just a hangover," Alex replied. She rubbed the tender bump and winced.

"Not going to be much time for drinking from here on out, I'm afraid," Damian said. He reached out a hand. "Captain said she could use you on the bridge but only if you're completely up for it."

With a groan against her better judgment, she accepted Damian's hand and the pain in her head. He helped her into a sitting position and waited as she fought off the dizziness that spun the room.

"I never thanked you..." Alex started.

Damian shook his head and flashed another devilish grin. "No need. It's nice getting one over Ghaoithe. Doesn't happen too often."

With that, the two embarked through the quiet halls of a shipwrecked *Cloudkicker*. By the time Damian and Alex entered the bridge, Ghaoithe had already unfurled several parchments across the lightweight table usually used for poker games next to her seat. Beside her stood Fleet and the dreadlocked woman named Tory that kept watch over the ship when both Ghaoithe and Fleet were away.

Ghaoithe noticed the two newcomers and waved them over to the table.

"You doing ok?" she asked Alex with an arched eyebrow.

"Don't suppose there will be much ice on this trip for the bump on my head?" Alex asked.

Satisfied that Alex's joke signaled a return to form, the captain returned to her papers. Most of them were maps. A supply checklist of a few meager items poked out from underneath them. Ghaoithe pointed at a detailed cross-section of Egypt.

"We are somewhere around here," said the captain. Alex glanced over her arm to see their location. Very little surrounded them but the expanse of the Sahara in every direction. Ghaoithe moved her arm in a sweeping arc eastward and landed on Cairo. "We need to get here."

"Cairo? Isn't that going to attract a lot of attention?" asked Alex. She imagined the looks Ghaoithe would receive strolling into a modern city with her sky blue, rune-etched armor.

Fleet leaned down onto the desk. "Trust me, lass, we will not be the strangest thing you'll see there."

"Not like we have much choice, either," Ghaoithe said. Her gaze turned to the sand outside the bridge windows. "We're just asking for trouble until we get this girl back into the air."

"Our circle will hide us for now, but they won't stop anyone from driving right into us," Tory spoke up. She ran a calloused hand over her sunburned face. "Not going to take long for Osiris to start combing through here."

"Where are we going?" A child with stark white hair popped up between Ghaoithe's arms. Ellie's appearance at the table gave the crew a start, including a string of expletives from Tory. Alex could not recall seeing the child on the bridge when she had entered with Damian.

Gathering her senses, Ghaoithe placed a hand on Ellie's head. "You, little lady, aren't going anywhere," she said.

Ellie tilted her head up at the captain. "What do you mean?"

Tory regained her composure. She knelt down to meet the child face-to-face. "You're stayin' right here, miss. Aunt Tory will keep an eye on you while Cap's away."

The rogue's charm came off as cannibalistic more than helpful, all scissor teeth and gunpowder. Ellie stared blankly at Tory before looking back at Ghaoithe.

"Why would I stay here? You'll need me," she said simply.

Ghaoithe and Fleet exchanged glances. "What do you mean 'we'll need you?'" asked Ghaoithe.

Her question seemed to go unheard; the young girl's attention was already on the maps. "Do you think we'll see any camels?" she asked with excitement.

"Of course," interrupted Damian, "and I bet we'll see the pyramids, too!"

Damian shot an understanding glance at the others. With a nod of the head, Fleet gathered the adults of the table over to a corner of the captain's platform, careful to keep Ellie in his sights. She was absorbed in some tale Damian wove for her.

"What do ye think, Captain?" Fleet asked.

"Of course she's not going. Until we know more about her, she stays on this ship," Ghaoithe replied. She lacked the usual decisiveness in her tone.

Wherever Ellie came from, it was clear that she held more sway than any normal child. When she spoke, her words made perfect sense to the listener, as though it was silly to question them in the first place. Alex had experienced it before, in the *Cloudkicker's* galley, not long after they escaped the Osiris complex in China. She wondered if it was simply the emotion of the time, but as the next days passed, Ellie's influence over those she spoke to became apparent. That the child had somehow been kept for millenia in the city of Eden underneath Bimini Road raised questions no one dared to ask. Everyone on the ship simply continued on as though her presence were completely normal.

"She sounded pretty certain she was going," stated Alex, "and her cryptic messages don't tend to help."

Tory rubbed her nose with her sleeve. "Not gonna lie, Cap'n. That kid gives me the creeps. I can watch her if you say the word, but I can't be sure on anything actually keeping her here. You seen how she jus' pops around."

They paused for a moment. Given the trouble they had just finding Ellie, she was too valuable to Osiris to risk losing her on a trip to Cairo. Ghaoithe clearly did not like the idea of the child leaving the ship, but even she had enough doubt to wonder about Ellie's strange premonitions. She groaned and tugged at the leather straps of her armor.

"Tory's right," Fleet broke the silence. "We can keep her here, but that kid is unpredictable. The way she goes around this ship… it may be best to let her have her way on this."

Ghaoithe pursed her lips. "And risk losing her in Cairo?"

"If Osiris finds this ship, we're done for either way. At least we'd be able to keep an eye on her," Alex reasoned.

Tory wiped her hands on her frayed pants. "No hard feelin' if you wanna keep a personal eye on her, ma'am. Not after Sorin." She sneered at saying the traitor's name.

Rubbing a hand through her crop of fire hair, Ghaoithe let out a frustrated grunt. She weighed down the options one last time before turning to Fleet. "Where you go, she goes and vice-versa. I don't care if she walks up to the gates of Hell itself, you do not let her out of your sight."

"That's that, then. When's launch?" Tory asked. With Ghaoithe and Fleet gone, she would once again be in charge of keeping the *Cloudkicker* safe from harm.

"As soon as the sun goes down and we can star chart our exact location."

With that, they broke their circle and prepared for the desert ahead.

# II

Though she'd often read about the desert's bipolar extremes, Alex was still vastly unprepared for the cold outside of the *Cloudkicker*. Even with the sunset only a short time ago, the scorched sand had already cooled. Alex dug up her modern clothes from her old Missouri home in the hopes of blending back into a modern city. They were comfortable and durable but did little to combat the chill that seeped into her bones. She pulled her jacket tight before hoisting Excalibur onto her back.

The others fared better. Damian and Fleet focused on assessing the packs on the ground. Ghaoithe stood beside Tory, pointing at the brilliant array of stars in the sky as they plotted their exact spot in the wasteland. Ellie ran through the sand, oblivious to the crew's plight as she rolled down dunes with sheer joy. Though the moon was little more than a sliver in the sky, its light bounced off her figure, creating an unsettling glow with her white hair and the gown she refused to replace.

Once satisfied with their star chart, Tory raced up the gangplank. With a final wave, she disappeared into the ship. The hull, normally dazzlingly bright with swirling blue energy, sat as little more than a dark monolith in the night. Alex shuddered. The ghost ship look did not suit such a lively bird.

Ghaoithe gathered the group. "We have maybe a few days at most before Osiris pinpoints us. The wards we placed will keep the ship hidden from anything that doesn't walk directly through them, but we're going to have to travel hard to Cairo."

Fleet hoisted a pack on to his back. "What are we waitin' fer, then? We got a solid day-and-a-half ahead of us," he huffed.

With silent agreement, the small team moved into action. With their supplies on their backs, they began the trek across the desert. Alex had been given a smaller bag than the others, but it shifted uncomfortably over Excalibur's scabbard as they started. She began to doubt her insistence on bringing the sword with her on long journeys.

They crossed the wards in the sand. Ghaoithe halted and looked back. The *Cloudkicker* was no longer there, invisible among the desert landscape as though there were never a wreck at all. Ghaoithe circled their location and inspected every angle around the ship. To the uninitiated, she might have appeared to be a strange bird bobbing for insects in the empty sand. When she returned to the rest of the crew, she nodded in satisfaction.

"Solid work. You'd have to practically bump your nose on the ship to realize it's there," she said as she patted Fleet on the back.

They turned eastward, guided by some innate intuition through the stars. No one spoke. Even Ellie, with all her restless energy, succumbed to the quiet travel. She eventually ended up on Fleet's back. He did not seem to mind; the man looked incapable of tiring under such light weight even in his age.

As they walked, the chill abated, thwarted by the movement in her limbs. Alex, for her part, enjoyed the stars. Though she grew up in rural life, her home was just close enough to a college town to suffer from light pollution. In the desert, however, the Milky Way cascaded overhead with uninterrupted magnificence. Though the group was in a rush, nothing distracted them from the heavens that watched over their every step.

"Do people in Lost Earth believe anything is up there?" Alex asked.

"You mean like a religion?" replied Ghaoithe. They spoke with hushed voices, as if the sky would shatter if they made too much noise.

"In a way," Alex said, struggling to put her question into proper words. "We're so focused on what's real in our legends and myths here on Lost Earth. Do you ever wonder what's beyond the sky? What put all that here in the first place?"

Fleet hummed in thought. "Some do. Most of our folk just like enjoyin' the moment and leave what's after that as a new thing to explore when the time comes."

"So you never think about the stars? Other planets?"

"Not so much. We leave that to your world. We may not agree with all your technology and whatnot, but that don't mean modern society don't have dreamers, too. They just focus on different things. What y'all do to learn about space... well, it's incredible alright, but that's your journey."

Alex adjusted her pack, her head down in thought. Finally, she turned to Ghaoithe. "What about you? You don't seem like the spiritual type."

"I believe in the power beneath our feet," Ghaoithe replied quietly after a moment. Even her armor seemed dimmer than usual, as if it understood it was not meant to outshine the lights above in that moment. "I believe in the wind and the ocean. I think there is energy in the earth all around us, guiding us in its own way."

"So you're a witch?" joked Damian.

"No," Ghaoithe said sharply. She caught herself and spoke again, softer, "Witches believe they can control the spirits and energy around them. Outside of our sigils—which we don't even fully understand—I don't think nature is something so easily contained. But I do believe it has power. There are places in the world that are outside even a relic hunter's understanding where ancient energy draws people to them."

15

The conviction that Ghaoithe spoke with surprised Alex. "I never would have taken you for being religious," she said.

Ghaoithe stopped in her tracks. She stared up at the Milky Way above with her one good eye, as if she had spotted an old friend in a crowd after several years. "Some people use religion as a source for community, and that's fine. I think belief is a much more personal and private matter, though," she said.

"Careful. The captain's getting all sentimental on us," Damian jeered.

Ghaoithe gave the stowaway a hard shove, knocking him into the sand. "There are over two hundred different religions, and you're going to the same place in all of them."

The group laughed. All except Damian who, straddled with a heavy pack, struggled to right himself from the sand.

Despite the jokes, Alex noted Ghaoithe moved solemnly after their discussion. She never considered the captain a spiritual person, but there was no denying something was different about her. When she looked at Ghaoithe, she saw more than the captain's size and unmistakable attire; there was an ethereal quality to the way she moved and carried herself, like she balanced between this world and something greater. Something mystical and unknown to mortals.

That Ghaoithe believed in something ancient made perfect sense; she *was* an ancient creature, something from a place well beyond Alex's understanding.

The conversation also sparked a conflict within Alex. Since her parents' deaths, she had struggled alone and without much faith in anything. Not her friends, family, or any kind of higher being. But in this world where Thor's hammer was real and she carried a blessed sword, she no longer had the same conviction against powers beyond humanity's control. Her world had been altered and molded by something in the undercurrent of every action she took since she first saw Ghaoithe, nose-to-nose, in a rural Missouri hospital. Alex could fight it if she wished, but she was not entirely sure she wanted to.

With her thoughts to occupy her, Alex lost track of time. She was aware in the back of her mind that the constellations moved across the sky, but she had little intuition for reading them the way Ghaoithe and Fleet did. They walked seamlessly over the sand, stopping only to stare above at points or right their coordinates among shifting dunes. By the time they called for a break, the moon was in a far different spot in the sky than Alex remembered.

"We'll stop here," Ghaoithe declared. "Four hours. I'll keep watch."

The team lowered their packs with relieved groans. Ellie stirred as Fleet lowered her to the ground, yawning the sleep out of her system; at least Ghaoithe would have company on her watch. Within moments, they had their shelters set up, consisting of little more than lean-to's made of a couple thin poles and a cloth overhead. They had traveled light, not expecting any prolonged delays.

"Just enough to keep the sun off ya," explained Fleet. Given how short their rest would be, Alex doubted sun would become an issue.

She laid down on a blanket over the sand. Not ready for rest, her head tossed and turned and soon her body did the same. The air was too chill or the sand too uncomfortable. She could not find a position to ease the knot on her head. She worried about snakes coming out before the baking sun. She thought about Ethan.

With the past few days, insomnia had become a part of her regimen. When she did sleep, she was more often than not troubled by nightmares like the previous night, replete with images of Ethan calling to her from his grave.

She was also full of hate. She hated Deacon for taking Ethan from her, hated that she would never know his complete story, hated being stuck in a desert at four a.m. She saw Ethan's body slump in front of her eyes, the carpet stained red just as his heroism came to light. Fear, disgust, and anger boiled together until she wanted to scream every time she stopped moving. If not for her friends aboard the *Cloudkicker* to prop her up, Alex knew she would have unraveled. She had lost too many people to circumstances devoid of any measure of sanity. She worried about whether her best friend Becky was safe, if she had been notified of any of the events surrounding the night in the tower.

Frustrated, Alex sat up and left the mock privacy of her shelter. Ghaoithe and Ellie sat side-by-side on a ridge facing a brightening sky. Ghaoithe was deep in telling some grand story, occasionally gesturing to the sky or making wide arcs with her arms. The girl beside her was entranced.

It was a sight that made Alex smile. Since their escape, Ghaoithe had the least contact with Ellie out of the entire crew, locked away in her captain's quarters to research the strange girl's origins. Alex had no clue how the captain would handle letting a child aboard the ship, even an odd child somehow linked to Pandora's Box. It was as though Ghaoithe was not only put off by children, but that she was in some way scared of Ellie and purposely avoiding her.

Alex rose from her shelter and made her way over to the two. At her approach, Ellie ran down the dune to greet her with wide eyes. "Ghaoithe was just telling how the sun rises!"

Alex smiled and took the girl's hand as they walked back up the dune. "Oh really? And how is that?"

"There's a man and a chariot and he drives these big fiery horses…" Ellie went on.

Alex looked at Ghaoithe with a wry smile. The captain shrugged and then turned back to face the sunrise while Ellie recounted all that she had learned.

Before long, the rest of the party woke up as well. By the time the tents were squared away and a light breakfast of fruit was eaten, the sun started to slide above the horizon. The chill in the air subsided and the temperature spiked rapidly.

"We need to hurry," Ghaoithe reminded them as they packed. "It's going to get hot."

# III

Humidity dripped through every inch of the Open Road Inn. It seeped into the thatched roof and down the bamboo walls, into the fabric of every scrap of cloth. Despite an open-air entry and a fan that rotated lazily overhead, nothing escaped the sticky sweat of the jungle. Outside, another storm threatened the skies as they did every half-day like clockwork.

A single woman sat at the bar, tended by a rugged man who wiped down glasses behind the counter, though there were rarely enough customers to warrant such cleaning. He did not speak with the woman. No one ever spoke to her. She kept to herself as she sipped languidly on a brandy watered down by ice long melted. She pulled open the top buttons on her tan huntsman shirt in case a breeze swept in to cool the shine on her skin, but it did not work; she was simply too soaked to care anymore.

The sound of expensive heels entered the bar with no attempt at stealth. The rhythmic thump of a cane accompanied them. They stopped at the seat next to her and waited. Peering from beneath a leather outback hat and strands of ebony hair, she gave the suited gentleman next to her a once-over before returning to her drink.

"Only two kinds of idiots would wear a Brioni suit in Uganda," she said, voice oily even after extended disuse, "those who have a death wish and those who grant them."

The man beside her dug into his jacket pockets and pulled out a cream handkerchief. He used it to wipe the steam off his gold-rimmed pince-nez. With a cunning grin, he returned them to the tip of his nose.

"I admit that this may not be the most appropriate attire for the heat, but business is business, Ms. Vargas," he explained.

"Jessie." She downed the remainder of her drink and signaled the bartender for another. "I don't do formalities."

"I expected nothing less from your reputation," said the gentleman. He took off his own bright fedora and fanned himself in the heat. "They say the famous Desert Siren enjoys the life of a vague wanderer, after all."

He noticed the faintest of sneers cross Jessie's chapped lips before they sipped at the drink before them. He'd made an impression. Impressions were good.

"You got something to tell me or you just gonna be a pain in my ass all day?" Jessie snapped. She wanted the rain to come, to give her an excuse to leave for solitude.

"No need to be rude... Jessie. I came here to employ your services at a premium."

Downing the rest of her drink, Jessie whipped around and leaned back in her chair, all legs and smoke and sex. The kind of woman men would kill for only to discover they had to survive *her* afterward. And she was grumpy. She wanted another brandy.

The man next to her, however, made her balk. He was older, rail thin with stark white hair and a pointed goatee. Worse yet, he displayed not even the slightest hint of fear or caution towards her. She didn't like doing business with men who weren't either trying to get into her pants or nervously looking to high-tail in the other direction.

The calm, quiet ones were the most dangerous.

Jessie leered at him. "No doubt you can afford me, but I'm not taking offers right now."

"Oh, but you will for me," he replied, his toothy grin unflinching.

"Really? You going to give me an offer I can't refuse? Please do. I could use a long-term vacation."

"I was thinking of giving you the Sky Thief instead."

Jessie sighed and rubbed her eyes with a trembling hand. She was too tired for this. "Look, you need a brawler for that. It wouldn't be the first time Ghaoithe's been my target, but nothing I've got is getting through that armor of hers. My advice is to leave the nice lady alone to search through her musty old dungeons in peace."

"She's not the target. She has two girls with her that I need. The younger one alive," said the man. He swirled the glass in his hands, clinking the ice together, but did not drink.

A creeping shiver ran up Jessie's spine. She stood, no longer wishing to stay under the watch of the stranger before her. "I don't know who you are, but you'll have to hire a different freelancer."

"You know quite well who I am," the man hissed through his calm, "and I know about Venezuela. I know about your estranged daughter Maxine. I know about your debts. I know about the celebrity you left behind. You are the one I want for this job."

Jessie's eyes went wide, and she lost the facade she carried for years. "No!" she shouted. "I don't deal with your company! Get out or I might break our agreement."

It was the man's turn to stand. He did not press upon her or grimace or swing. He only stood, put on his hat, and leaned on the polished cane in his possession.

"I am aware of our treaty. However, I'm afraid that circumstances have called for an amendment to our arrangement," he calmly explained.

"Then kill me. Get it over with if that's what it takes," Jessie snarled. She moved within inches of his face, hoping for a response.

Deacon did not so much as flinch. "I have no intentions to kill you," he said.

"What, then? You have nothing else over me."

"We do, Ms. Vargas. Or have you forgotten the ones you left behind? We can expose them. We can bring all of our media and lights and helicopters wherever they try to go. They will not sleep without photographers outside their window. They will not move without a press junket following them. They will have no privacy, no personal life, no safe haven. They will be our playthings for the masses to consume just as they did those years ago."

Jessie backed away. Her skin paled as she fought back a scream. Options and variables ran through her head, each more desperate than the last. They all ended in one of two ways. Neither were very appealing. Outside, the patters of rain bounced off palm fronds.

As the storm picked up and Jessie remained quiet, the stranger fumbled with the brim of his cap.

"I'll take your silence to mean we have a deal. Don't worry, madam. After this, you will have a nice, lonely little place of your choosing and you can rid yourself of this unpleasantness for good," he said in a chipper tone to console her.

"Where's the lead?" Jessie asked, deadpan.

"Northeastern Egypt. Likely headed to Cairo. We will send someone with equipment. If you need anything more, simply ask for Deacon."

With nothing more, Deacon was gone. He strode out of the doorless bar and into the rain. Jessie grabbed her brandy glass and launched it against the nearest wall, frightening the barkeep and sending a spray of glass throughout the room. She stomped outside. The Open Road Inn was little more than the bar and a small grouping of tiki-themed huts used as guest rooms. For weeks, Jessie had been the only customer. Resorts had short lifespans in a region torn by war and constant thunderstorms. It was exactly the kind of place she had come looking for.

As she burst into her room, she halted. Standing in the dark, she absorbed the rain that dripped onto the roof and out of her clothes and into the floor. She wept. She cried about her poverty, her loneliness, her drunken state. Mostly, she cried because Osiris won for the second time in her life. They would never stop winning.

When she had dried herself out, she regained her composure, shook off her frustrations, and turned on the light in her one-room hut. Stripping herself of her clothes, she laid them out to dry and began assessing her possessions. The Desert Siren traveled light, not out of want but necessity. She rather liked having things, but her lifestyle rarely afforded the stability for that luxury. Ultimately, her room consisted of little more than a bed, a nightstand with a meager offering of cracked books, and a few toiletries in a restroom off to the side of the building. All that she owned fit into a compact suitcase she kept near her door at all times. She filled it with a few spare clothes and zipped it shut. Near the bed, she pulled out the drawer to her nightstand and opened the bottom panel. Rolls of U.S. dollars hid inside.

Lastly, she crouched underneath the bed and pulled out a large, hard case. She popped open the latches and stared at the contents. A sleek, onyx machine as long as her arm span with a telescopic sight mounted on top. Barrett M82 .50 Cal.

She lifted it and stared through the sight for smudges. It swung through the room, effortless in her hands despite its weight. Focused and trained, she ran through a checklist in her mind, a mechanic scouring every inch of the tools under her control for malfunctions. She found none. Whatever issues she had with Osiris, the jungle, or her past were forgotten. She concentrated on her job and only her job. She could deal with her own guilt when she was resting for the remainder of her short life on an island of her own. Her mind buzzed, partially from alcohol, partially from the anticipation of travel. Facts, figures, routes, and more swam through her head in rapid fire pace. She would need supplies, transportation, maybe even a small team from Osiris. Kidnapping was not her forte.

She could barely remember starting her life again. The case and its contents were all that she had known for years with no time to reflect on what brought her to Africa until she found herself in bamboo-constructed taverns in the middle of the rainforest. Then, she did everything she could to forget again and move to another. Whatever happened to her, she could not return to her former self, all style and entourage and intrigue. This was her home now.

Satisfied with her inspection, Jessie placed the gun back into its case and locked it. Throwing on her still-sopped clothes, she rushed to the door. After a moment's hesitation, she returned to the dresser. On the inn stationary, she wrote a quick note of thanks to the bartender and apologized for the broken glass. She slid $100 underneath it and made her way outside, ready to replace the downpour with the desert she knew by heart.

# IV

With the chill of the night evaporated, Alex wrapped her jacket around her head to prevent burning to death. She was thankful for the long-sleeves and loose clothing protecting her skin but little else soothed her as shimmering bands of air rose from the top of every forthcoming ridge.

"Almost there," Ghaoithe encouraged. But she had encouraged with those same words for hours.

They had water. Supplies were no issue for the adventurers. However, the sun melted their pores and their minds. Their captain, stalwart as ever, went through the motions of tracking the sun, but they could see even her experienced frame slumped with fatigue.

The lack of sleep hit Alex in full force. She spotted things in the heatwaves of the dunes, figures silhouetted that should never have existed. She shook her head, told herself she was hallucinating, but she continued to feel ill. After toppling over in the sand, Damian took to her, never out of arm's reach and providing plenty of water from their flasks when he noticed her fading.

The only one among them without issues was Ellie. She bounded up and over ridges like a white kangaroo. She bugged the group for attention less and less as they walked, seeming to know the dire straights they were in. It didn't diminish her enthusiasm, though, and she appeared on top of every ridge as a bright, excited beacon towards their goal.

They were close. The only break in their trudge through the vast desert came when Alex spotted an airplane overhead, transporting passengers to Cairo without any awareness of the *Cloudkicker's* plight or existence. Its appearance enthralled Alex, not because of her former life or the sign that they neared the Egyptian metropolis, but because its seemed so primitive. Planes were limited by jet fuel and cramped seats. They didn't have an entire galley inside or private sleeping quarters. They didn't feel alive like the *Cloudkicker*.

Technology had not been completely forgotten to her. The crew's circumstances were less-than-accommodating when they were captured by Osiris. Yet Alex relished part of their captivity. She secretly enjoyed working elevators, florescent bulbs, and Ethan's luxurious suite. The world she had left behind had become a novelty. She thought of the so-called "modern world" and was utterly confused by its existence. She stood captivated by the mere existence of the airplane overhead for several minutes, ignoring the calls of her companions. How could mankind accept an archaic steel tube when something as magnificent as the *Cloudkicker* flew right under their radar?

She snapped out of her daze when Damian began shaking her. "Hey, you ok?" he asked, eyes wide. The other crew members stared at her as well, worry plastered on their faces.

"There was a plane. How silly is that…" she began. Realizing nothing she could explain would make sense to anyone but her, she stopped and shook her head.

Damian hoisted one of her arms around his shoulders. "Alright, you're using a crutch the rest of this trip," he said.

Alex moaned a complaint but otherwise gave no resistance. Her head swam only just above consciousness. She daydreamed of what kind of giant, fluffy beds the sultans of the Middle East enjoyed.

The group picked up their pace with Alex's legs on autopilot. Beneath their feet, the ground began to level off somewhat. The dunes shrank and transformed into rocky earth. It could have been Mars as easily as the Sahara: scorched, barren, and lifeless. Had they not known the area was already home to ancient civilizations, no one would have expected people to flourish in the area.

Ahead, Ellie leaped up another ridge. As she breached the top, she let out an ecstatic shriek. She turned to the weary travelers and jumped up and down.

"We're here! We're here!" she shouted.

The others climbed the ridge to meet her. Beyond them, three triangular peaks rose above the flattened earth, a sprawling city as their backdrop. Tour buses and their patrons weaved among palm trees. Beyond, cutting through the heart of Cairo, the Nile flowed among towers and history. The city spread like a puddle on concrete, stopping with a hard edge as it touched the desert underneath a thin veil of smog.

The sight pierced the veil of Alex's thoughts and gave her a renewed, if somewhat disjointed, focus. Slack-jawed at the sprawling metropolis, she eased off of Damian's shoulders. She could already feel the city's sway, the subtle force that called people to it. There was something magic held in that place.

"This is like some kind of explorer's mecca," Alex mused aloud.

"Used to be," Ghaoithe said. "It's one of the few places the modern world took interest in, so most everything's been found. It still holds a few secrets, though, if you know where to look."

"Not gonna to have much time fer explorin' anyway," huffed Fleet. He had taken their trip in stride, but the sheen on his face betrayed his bravado. "We need to get to a safe haven immediately."

They were exposed and stood out blatantly on the ridge to any passing vehicles. At the very least, they needed to get among people, to blend in among the throngs until they could disappear from prying eyes.

"Swing south. Avoid the pyramids. We'll head to Samir's," Ghaoithe ordered.

Alex and Damian shrugged at each other, not informed enough to understand the captain's reasoning. Alex resigned to staring at the landmarks from afar. Around them, cameras glinted and tiny figures buzzed like bees around a hive.

"I thought they'd be bigger," said Alex as they turned away from the landmarks.

"You're used to the Gateway Arch. A lot of famous buildings can fit under that thing," Damian explained.

Alex momentarily forgot that, like herself, Damian was not originally from the world of ancient relics. She knew only a few details about the stowaway's life, but she soon realized that he was likely just as fascinated by Cairo as she was. He took in the surroundings with ravenous eyes that recorded every instant, every brick into memory. Under his laissez-fair attitude hid an extremely sharp observer. Alex wished she had asked him more questions about transitioning from a normal life to one of skyships before they crashed.

As the five of them continued to walk, their environment changed sharply from a desert to a worn, bustling city. Fleet had been right: they were far from the strangest or most exciting thing in Cairo. All around them rushed cars from nearly every era, obese vacationers in fanny-packs and sunhats, and locals in all varieties of fashion. Women covered in traditional hijabs gawked at designer stores full of color. Men in elegant white robes crossed paths with teens adorned with soccer emblems. A military guard shaded himself under an archway with a rifle slung across his shoulder, a reminder of the turmoils that plagued the country.

Ghaoithe navigated all of this uncomfortably. She knew where she needed to go, the map of the city second nature like every other map stored in her head. Their route took them by squat grey buildings, mosques with detailed carvings in stone, and shining glass shops. What made the captain nervous was the modernness of it all. Her eye shifted nervously at every vehicle that came too close, every cellphone in the grip of a Versace-shaded teen.

In a city of wonders, she was out of her element.

They were not completely alone, however. There was nothing so obvious as Ghaoithe's armor, but hints of the division between worlds poked through the technology. A spark of blue light in an open window, a knowing glance at Ghaoithe. Such was the allure of Cairo, a convergence of old and new alike.

*At least*, thought Alex, *we'll have friends if Osiris does show up.*

The city also took a toll on Alex's energy. After her initial wonder faded, Damian fed her a ready supply of snacks to keep her from becoming delirious again. Bars of oatmeal and fruit kept her going but only on fumes as the humidity rising from the river slammed into her with full force. The others were not much better off. Even youthful Ellie calmed down. She stuck close to Fleet as she had been told to do when entering the city.

Turning down a tranquil avenue, Ghaoithe slowed her pace. Nestled along the street were palaces with towering gates and ornate fountains. Palms lined the sidewalks with picturesque utility. It recalled movie sets of Beverly Hills, The Hamptons, Dubai. The sweat-and-sand covered sailors felt entirely out of place as they caught glimpses of wealth through high, protective hedges. Halfway down the avenue, Ghaoithe stopped at the gates of a wide beige mansion. A circular drive wrapped around a fountain molded with the visages of a tiger, an elephant, and a monkey turned towards the sky in unanimity. Columns guarded the entrance. A crest depicted a pouring chalice in the faded stone above them.

Damian's eyes darted across the manicured carpet of grass before them and then back to the empty street. "We shouldn't be here," he said.

"Calm down. Just give me a second to work this thing," Ghaoithe said. She hunched over a small box beside the gate, working out the system of buttons on its face in timid curiosity.

Nervous and impatient, Damian crossed to her and pressed a round button at the top of the box. A voice filtered through, *"Name?"*

The sound caused Ghaoithe to jump. Composing herself, she shouted into the box, "GHAOITHE LOINSIGH!"

The speaker hushed for a moment before a hearty bout of laughter boomed through. *"Get in here, Cavewoman!"*

A click and the gate buzzed open, scaring Ghaoithe a second time and raising stifled giggles from Ellie and Alex. From the front of a mansion strode a large man in a pristine white galabeya. He towered over everyone but Ghaoithe yet the bright smile beneath his black, wild beard showed no trace of the natural intimidation that emanated from the captain. This was a man naturally built for hugs.

"Samir!" Ghaoithe shrieked. Her girlish tone took her crew aback, as did her leap into Samir's arms. He returned her embrace wholeheartedly with a cheery bellow.

As he eased Ghaoithe back on to the ground, Samir placed his hands on her shoulders and sized her up. "Still every bit the wanderer," he said. Then, he turned to her companions. "Now, you must introduce me to your friends, my child!"

The captain went down the line, introducing her crew. Fleet was first, outstretching a hand in greeting. Samir looked at it, swept it aside, and wrapped the quartermaster in tight arms.

"I do not do handshakes!" Samir laughed. He did not spare any of the others from his welcome.

Once finished, Samir put his fingers between his lips and let out a sharp whistle. Men in crisp suits streamed from the mansion and assisted the *Cloudkicker* team with their backpacks as Samir walked them through the front garden. Without the extra weight, Alex rubbed her cramped shoulders, though she refused to allow Excalibur to be taken from her. Inside the gates, the front drive expanded beyond her expectations. Tall shrubs bordered paths of poppies and irises. To the right of the mansion, a drive ended with an eight-car garage. A caretaker washed a mammoth Bentley outside. Throughout the complex, cameras mounted high on the perimeter fence watched every inch of their domain.

It was not, in any sense, the kind of environment Alex thought of when the captain came to mind. "I never expected Ghaoithe's friends to be so modern," she said.

"There are a few of us who like to dabble in both worlds, my fair lady. Though Osiris controls much of the world's wealth, they do not control all of it," Samir explained with a wink.

"We can go into that later," added Ghaoithe. Her eyes sagged for sleep, but the rest of her glowed with enthusiasm.

Inside the palace, cool air washed over the weary nomads. It filled their bodies and erased the dread that had spurred them through the desert. The *Cloudkicker* was not forgotten but at least the emergency team—and especially Ellie—were safe for the time being. A grand staircase welcomed visitors with a faded red carpet. Throughout the foyer were extravagant displays of wealth, though not in the way Alex had expected. She imagined in her mind a collection of urns or possibly a sarcophagus or two. Instead, the halls were filled with medieval suits of armor, cherry wood bookshelves with frayed bindings, and large oil paintings of English noblemen.

Samir sensed their confusion. He said, "Welcome to my home! This was once a British estate in the early days of occupation. As you can see, I have gone through great pains to preserve it this way."

"So you're friends with the British?" asked Damian. Samir flashed a wide grin.

"I wasn't," he said, "until these pieces became worth a great deal of money."

He hurried the group upstairs as fast as their legs would take them. Once at the top of the grand staircase, they took a long hall to the right. Samir spread his arms wide at the array of doors that awaited them.

"These will be your rooms! Please rest and clean as you need. I will have my servants assist you with clothing and linens."

"Aren't you going to even ask why we're here?" asked Ghaoithe, raising an eyebrow.

"I never ask for a reason to see you," he said. He patted her arms.

"We shall talk when you do not look like you fought a car."

Ellie pulled on the host's robes. "Are you the captain's dad?" she asked.

"No, little one. Allah praise any man who had to deal with this terror as a child!" he roared. He leaned in to Ghaoithe, kissed her on both cheeks, and dashed down the stairs in a flurry.

"You heard the man," said Ghaoithe. Everyone's eyes lingered on their boisterous savior as he left before making their way through the hall. No one spoke, each silently choosing one of the many rooms available at their discretion.

Alex slammed her door shut, more to ensure she was actually capable of closing it properly with her sapped strength than from any particular mood. She tore the scabbard off her back and tossed it onto the floor next to a four-post bed drawn with orange silk. She barely registered the color before passing out on top of it.

Blaring sirens snapped Alex out of her slumber. They warbled outside the curtained balcony of her bedroom. She pushed her hands over her ears at the surprise, and ran into the hallway. Damian, two doors down, peeked out as well. Ghaoithe strolled out of her bedroom near the staircase fully prepped for the day in her armor. She noted the bystanders and waved.

"Morning call to prayer. You'll get used to it," she said.

Alex nodded and shut her door again. Once the initial shock of waking wore off, she could hear the song in the blaring. Badly cracked speakers obscured the original recording, but there were words in there. She pulled the balcony entrance closed and the singing reduced to a dull muffle.

In the morning light, she felt highly aware of herself. A full night's rest did wonders for her and her headache, even if it still stung when she grazed the bump on her head with her hand. She could feel the sweat, dry and sticky, embedded into her skin. Her hair tangled itself into a blonde web bordering on dreadlocks.

Since joining the *Cloudkicker*, Alex's concept of personal space had changed drastically. Though its runes enlarged the spaces below decks somewhat, it was still very much a cramped ship. By contrast, there was so much room in Samir's palace that it took Alex several moments to orient herself among the fluttering curtains, paintings, and hand-carved wardrobes within her room. When she did find the bathroom, it was no less extravagant, with marble counter tops and gilded faucets. The shower had more buttons than her old car, and she timidly pressed them at random until she figured out their purpose.

She bathed with a renewed appreciated for what a shower, a *real* shower, could do for a person. In the sky, Alex had rarely stopped breathing long enough since Roanoke to give them much thought. While the airship had the same conveniences as modern bathrooms, the water always felt fake, like an alien's poor imitation of what water was supposed to do after having it described. It was always tepid and never quite rolled off her the way she expected of a shower. Here, she had soap, shampoo, three kinds of bath scents, two body washes, facial scrubs, and an array of brushes of all kinds, including a long, curved spongy thing she dared not ask about. She forgot about Osiris, Ethan, and Pandora's Box. She almost convinced herself they never happened and that she was still a journalist in her Missouri home writing about a business sale.

But she did remember. She remembered that she wanted to remember. She did not want to forget Ethan or Ghaoithe or Fleet. If she had not been taken aboard the ship, she never would have held Excalibur, talked with people in the lost city of Roanoke, or taken a shower in a palace in the shadow of the Great Pyramids. She could slow down one day, but that would not be arriving any time soon. Not while there was still walked within an entire world of unexplored places.

Rejuvenated, she slid open the shower door and breathed in the heavy steam. She dried herself with a fluffed towel that could have been made of clouds. On her bed, Samir's servants had already swept in to press her clothes and sheets. They even polished Excalibur's scabbard, much to Alex's delight. Clean and clothed, she made her way into the mansion hallways.

The other rooms were already open and redressed with no sign of her companions. As exciting as exploring the building would be, her stomach gnawed with displeasure. Finding breakfast in an urban jungle would have to be her first priority. Her boots bounced through the empty hallways as she admired the paintings and antiquities that lined the way. Once she found the stairs, her nose sensed the unmistakable aroma of batter. She followed it almost by instinct, slowed only by the understanding that the polished floorboards were likely expensive and should remain unmarred by hungry relic hunters.

When she did eventually find the source of the smell, she expected to find the camaraderie of her captain and Fleet. Instead, she found only Samir, his head buried in the over-sized pages of a newspaper. He was alone at a large, darkly colored dining table. Two plates waited on top, along with cups of steaming coffee in black mugs. A television droned on behind him, a recap of the previous night's rugby match displayed on the screen. There were no traces of sigils or Lost Earth anywhere in sight. In fact, the scene was so astonishingly normal that Alex bit her tongue to ensure she was not still asleep. The scene remained, and she entered the dining room.

At the sound of Alex's footsteps, Samir lowered his paper. He flashed his wide smile. "She stirs after all! I was beginning to think I would be dining alone this morning."

"Where is everyone?" Alex asked.

"They have already come and chat with me. Ghaoithe and Fleet had matters to attend to about the city. Damian and Ellie are currently ravaging my library. Please, sit. I shall call for our breakfast."

As Alex sat, Samir reached beside his mug. He lifted a small, shining bell and gave it a ring. Within a few seconds, a host arrived with trays of French toast, bacon, eggs, biscuits, hashbrowns, and everything in between. It was more food than two people could possibly finish, though Alex's stomach was eager for the test. Still, unsure of proper manners in such a home, she waited for Samir's reassurance before digging in. It was not quite what she expected for breakfast in Cairo, and she felt an underlying sense that Samir had chosen their menu for her sake.

They ate in silence, Samir with his newspaper and Alex's head reeling with too many questions to pick from. Once they finished, her host took the initiative.

"I thought I might like to show you the grounds," Samir said. It was more of a demand than a question, and his eyes glinted with that similar kind of mischievous knowing Alex had seen so many times in Ghaoithe before.

Thinking it would be improper to refuse, Alex agreed. Were it any other man, she might have been hesitant to spend time alone with a stranger. Yet despite his burly exterior, Alex felt no apprehension towards Samir. She could not explain it, but she innately understood she was sitting beside a friend. He reminded her quite a bit of Fleet in that way. This was a man who had the potential to be a devoutly loyal companion or a terrible foe, and Alex was pleased to be situated among the former.

Samir led Alex outside through the front door. Properly hydrated now, Alex was able to fully appreciate the scale of his wealth. His manor was much larger than she had realized from the previous day, spanning several acres of manicured lawn. They conversed in minor chitchat with Samir doing most of the talking, explaining the meaning behind this statue or the significance of that bed of flowers. Every word was gentle but with an underlying current of something more that remained unsaid. Alex's concentration floundered with questions that went politely unasked. They strained the air and made Alex giddy inside like the few minutes before Independence Day fireworks. She caught Samir glancing at her and smiling often, as if she reminded him of some inside joke resurfaced from long ago.

Finally, as they made their way behind Samir's mansion, he stopped. A worried expression crossed his face. He tugged at the sleeves of his long robes. "Ghaoithe said you were quite the inquisitive one, and yet you have been so far restrained! I hope your stay is to your liking?" he asked.

The sudden accusal caught Alex off guard. "Yes, it's lovely. There's just a lot to take in is all," she managed to eke out.

Her feint was poor, and she knew it. Samir stood, silent and judgmental for a moment. Finally, he clapped her hard on the back and let out a warm guffaw.

"It seems we are both elsewhere in search of answers! Let us skip the tour. Today is a special day, and we'll both feel better if we cut to the chase, as the English say. Come. I have something to show you," Samir said.

Alex relaxed a little. She'd been so worried about her questions for Samir that she never considered he would have some for her. Alex was, after all, the stranger who appeared out of nowhere alongside the woman Samir had apparently known for some time. Ghaoithe would have gone over the basic details of their arrival, sure, but how much beyond that? Alex doubted even Samir could crack the vault containing the captain's thoughts.

They circled around the back of the mansion to a wide garden with tall hedges along the pathways. Sprinklers misted the air and mixed with the pleasant scents from flowers to cut down on the Cairo heat. As they walked along the pathways through the hedges, a low building appeared. It looked like a mausoleum with accented pillars and a pointed roof made of stone. It was to this building that Samir took Alex without a word. When they were close, she could see the entrance shimmer with thin sigils. This took her somewhat by surprise, as she had not yet seen many traces of Lost Earth in Samir's home.

"Ghaoithe tells me you are from America. From the city with the arch," Samir said. He pulled out a long key from within his robes. Sigils wove around its length.

"Yes, although I'm a couple hours away from St. Louis. It's mostly farmland where I live," Alex said.

"Cairo must be quite the shock for you then," Samir said as he unlocked the door.

"That's one way of putting it."

"What do you think of the captain and our little world?"

Alex balked. She sensed something more to the question. Not malice, no, but a type of protectiveness regarding her answer. She thought suddenly of her dad and how he had sounded when she announced without fanfare that she had found her first boyfriend, Tyler, in middle school. Her dad disliked Tyler at first and hounded her ceaselessly with interrogations about his character. Eventually, he came around to trust Tyler, though Alex herself moved on after little more than four months. Her dad sounded as Samir did now.

"It almost feels like a fairy tale. I keep thinking I'm going to wake up soon, and that scares me more than anything Osiris can throw at us. I don't know what I'd be doing if Ghaoithe hadn't taken me aboard, but I don't think I would have liked it as much," Alex said. It was the truth, and it was all she could offer.

Samir eyed her seriously for a moment more before he softened. He opened the door to the building and said, "That is good. Dreams are powerful things in Lost Earth. After all, Aladdin would have no story if he did not have wishes for the djinn."

This made Alex feel better, like she passed a critical exam for her future. She said, "Knowing Ghaoithe, she probably found the magic lamp."

"Alas! She did not. That was found before her time. I hear the djinn works for a start-up in California now."

"Of course he does," said Alex as she rolled her eyes, mostly at herself for not seeing the answer coming. "What is this building anyway?"

"My little vault of memories," Samir said. He stepped to the side and motioned for Alex to enter.

The dark space lit up as Alex crossed the threshold. It wasn't the sigil light of Lost Earth, just a regular motion sensor that warmed the interior with an amber hue. She stood in a single room that took up the entire interior of the building. It was a cozy study, with leather-upholstered furniture and rugs accented in earthy tones. At the far end, a massive desk was neatly arranged with paper, a small laptop, and an assortment of inkwell pens far beyond the budget of her last salary. High shelves lined every inch of the walls, their contents encased within locked glass. She gasped as she took in their contents. A few shelves contained leather-bound tomes, but the majority of the cases held artifacts from eras beyond measure. Ancient vases, knives, unbound scrolls carefully placed under protective lighting, and portraits both vibrant and faded welcomed her to their abode. Some were dull while others glistened with faint sigils across their surfaces.

"You just have all of this just sitting in here? Out in the open?" Alex asked as she gawked.

"This building is safer than the marble and stone let on, but yes. This is my most precious collection," Samir said.

"These must be worth a fortune!"

"They were gifts."

"Gifts? From who?" Alex asked. At Samir's expression, her mouth went agape. "Ghaoithe found all of these?!"

Samir nodded. "Every one."

"There are so many! It must have taken ages."

"You make Ghaoithe sound like an old caned professor, child! She is only a few years older than you," Samir laughed.

Alex bit her lip. She never so directly confronted questions about Ghaoithe's past. All too often, Alex had become used to viewing Ghaoithe as an ageless, irrepressible force of nature. Having Samir around reminded her that the captain was still a human being with an upbringing of her own. There, among the relics she had found, Ghaoithe was grounded. Alex was unsure if it was ok to approach her in such a vulnerable state.

Staring past her reflection to look upon a staff carved out of whalebone, Alex asked, "How long have you known Ghaoithe?"

The side of one of the leather armchairs creaked as Samir sat on its armrest. He rubbed his beard as he counted and hummed. "If I had to guess," he said, "about twenty years now. It is hard to know for sure because she always feels like she's added a few years of stress on top of things. She was just leaving the cusp of her childhood when she barged onto my doorstep, though. So, yes, about twenty years."

Alex scratched out "immortal" in her imagination's biography of Ghaoithe and replaced it with "early 30s." She tested another step forward as the journalist instincts within her rose ever cautiously. "You practically raised her, then?"

"Oh, there was no raising that child. I fed her, gave her a home, taught her the proper ways of relic hunting, but she had already raised herself by the time she came here."

"How did she end up with you?"

Samir's eyes stared at her, but they did not see her through the memories that played there. He moved to sit fully in his chair. Alex did the same in the chair opposite from him, across a low glass table.

"She was brought to me by one of my associates. Ghaoithe was not much different then than she is now: fearless, restless, and with her eyes on bigger things. She did not have her armor or that ship of hers yet, only a few coins and a bundle of maps in her bags. She ran into trouble a few times trying to get a crew of her own. Nothing she couldn't handle, of course. If I were to say it plain, she likely scared off half of those interested and she was too sharp to fall for the other half that wanted to fleece her.

"I had a bit of an artifact trade back then. Nothing so grand as what she sought, but I had contacts keeping an ear out for unusual news. One of them came across her and saw something the others couldn't. He sent her my way. She had barely stepped past my gates before demanding information about this and that. It was as though a wolverine had been loosed in my house."

Alex snickered. "That sounds like Ghaoithe all right. Did you tell her anything useful?"

"Not at first, no. I honestly did not know what to do," Samir continued. "I never married, you see. I have no way with children, let alone headstrong ten-year-olds in search of lost cities. I turned her away, but she kept coming back. She'd leave for a few days, then return with some new lead she wanted to corroborate, and eventually she came to stay for good.

"From then on, I taught her what I could, played along with her little search for myths. When she first started trekking out on her own, she would come back with a new bauble or a handful of trifles. Nothing big, but something. Little by little, she earned the favor of travelers. I thought nothing of it. I had very little faith in her ability, but she grew on me like a daughter. If this was what she wanted, who was I to keep her from it so long as she stayed out of trouble?"

Alex said, "Staying out of trouble does not sound like Ghaoithe's strong point."

Samir rose from his seat and made his way over to a shelf behind the writing desk at the end of the room. A simple tea set sat next to a faucet, and he filled the pot. He turned on the hot plate beneath it and waited.

"No, it is not," Samir said. There was a tremble in his voice. He leaned on the back of the office chair at his desk. "In fact, she started getting hurt. I thought she was getting into fights in town, but no. She was entering more and more dangerous areas and had so little regard for her own health in the search for knowledge that she would shrug off injury so long as she took home the prize.

"The first time she came back bruised, I must have yelled at her for hours. I forbid her from leaving without my approval from that point forward. I withheld any information I could from her. Yet she managed to slip beneath my eyes time after time. Her injuries did not stop as she ventured in search of her legends. Spears, jets of fire… she must have run into every trap ever invented. I was powerless to see to her safety because I did not know what to do. In hindsight, she was stronger than I gave her credit for. I think her scars bothered me more than her, but I had come to love her dearly and no amount of assurance can allay that bond."

The teapot whistled. Samir stayed quiet as he poured two cups and allowed them to steep. When they were done, he brought them over on a tray and handed on to Alex. It was a sweet, black tea with hints of honey and cinnamon. It was the perfect drink for a day full of storytelling.

Samir sat back down and slowly sipped on his own as he recounted his story. "Soon, she was leaving for weeks, and I worried for every moment of them. This went on for some time. I thought maybe she might have found another home, and maybe she did. But, she always returned eventually, her bags full of trinkets."

Alex could only imagine the pain Samir must have gone through. Her own parents were protective, but lives in the modern world were far different than those of Lost Earth. A child could not set off on her own one day to make a life for herself like they did here.

"How did you cope with that?" Alex asked. "Did you just stop trying to raise her?"

Samir tugged at his beard. "I never gave up, no, but I came to understand that storms could not be stopped by a whistle. I knew the moment she was no longer mine. She was a young woman by then. This time, she had been gone for months, not weeks. Some part of me knew she was alive, but it was a hard time filled with doubt. When she finally reappeared at my gates, she carried a case nearly her own size. She looked as though she had not slept for her entire journey. The way she stood, I could tell she was different than before. She was grown, mature, but also sad, as though something important had been forced from her very soul. I held her and begged her never to do such a thing again. Then, she said she had something to show me."

Alex sat on the edge of her seat, her tea going cold on the table. She knew that Samir would tell her the story in his own time, but the extended silence gripped her.

"She took me to her room and opened the case. Inside was the most brilliant leather chestpiece I have ever come across. Blue as the waters of the Maldives and runes that danced about like the sands. I asked her where it had come from, but she would not tell me no matter how hard I pressed. And then she asked me to shoot her."

Alex squeaked in shock.

Samir's body quaked with a laugh. "That was my reaction, as well. I refused, and she insisted. Eventually, she said that if I did not do so, she would run through every bar in America and start fights until someone else did. I was left with little choice. She put on her armor, and I shot her. As you can guess, it did not leave so much as a mark on that armor, and that was her farewell."

"She left you? Just like that?" Alex asked. It did not sound like something the immensely loyal captain would do, even in the heat of her teenage years.

"Not fully, no, but she was no longer mine to protect. She was free to explore as she pleased with or without my say. All I could do was guide and support her. She would return here to rest, but this was no longer her home after that. She belonged in the clouds."

Sitting back, Alex mulled over a young, headstrong Ghaoithe and the heartache Samir must have felt. It was a story oddly familiar to her. It came to her whenever she thought of her parents and the loss she had felt once they were gone. There, in the heart of Cairo, it was that heartache that brought her kinship with Samir.

"What was she looking for? Did she find it?" Alex asked.

At this, Samir grinned wide. "Of course she did. She left again not long after bringing in that suit of hers. This time, she was gone for many months. By the time she showed up again, I had already received word about Atlantis's discovery and knew it must have been my Ghaoithe. Everyone started to call her The Sky Thief after that, but I knew her true name: Ghaoithe Isabel Loinsigh. My little explorer."

He said these words with such pride that Alex could not help but smile as well. It was the same effect the captain had on others. Not a magical one like Ellie's, but a genuine determination that brought out the best in her crew. It was that aura she had that kept Alex going despite everything that had happened.

As he looked at Alex, Samir said, "You know, you have that same expression she often had. That impassioned gaze that sees no barriers."

Caught off guard, Alex looked away and hid beneath her curls. "I wouldn't go that far."

"You do, and if you seek wisdom, then it is this: do not let go of that gaze. Ghaoithe has shown me that intelligence and talent are powerful tools to have, but they are nothing compared to motivation. If you want my blessing, then continue on this path with her and you shall have it. Protect her where I cannot. She needs you even if she will not admit it to herself. I can see it in her when she talks about you."

Alex nodded and picked up her tea. She did not taste it.

Even through all the talk of Ghaoithe, Alex did not see the captain again until the next day. The morning call to prayer blared at Alex just as before. She was more prepared for it, however, and bounded out of her room with a spring in her step. At the bottom of the central stairs, laughter echoed faintly through the foyer. Alex sought it out, winding through luxurious rooms of oddities until she finally reached the dining room. She saw her companions laughing over mugs of coffee. Ghaoithe, Damian, Fleet...

"Roy! Kirk!" she yelled. Across the room, two familiar faces leaned against the wall, their conversation halted as she entered. Roy, the tavern owner she had met her first night in a real Lost Earth city, had disappeared once word of the fire broke out in order to safeguard its citizens. No one knew what happened to Kirk, the twiggy, brusque scientist that made the *Cloudkicker* fly with his wealth of knowledge about sigils. She had worried over them since leaving Roanoke.

"I heard you've been causing trouble since our escape, little Minnow," Roy said, referencing Alex's nickname among those aboard the ship. The bartender opened his dark arms wide as she ran in for a hug. He looked just as he did in his bar in Roanoke and no worse for wear after the fire.

Kirk, gave her a nod from the corner of the room. A few new scars cut through the ink on his arms. She returned his nod with a quick smile. She did not expect him to express joy in much of anything, but she was glad to see the runic architect was safe.

"How did you guys get here? What happened in Roanoke?" Alex chirped. Roy held up a palm and passed her a warm cup of brew.

"You're far too curious for such an early morning," he said.

Alex blushed and distracted herself with a sip. The coffee was thick and bold, more so than she had ever experienced. She welcomed several more gulps before returning to her newly-returned companions.

"Sorry," she said. "We were just so worried."

"Nothing we couldn't handle," sneered Kirk. "Can't say the same for everyone in the city."

Roy nodded solemnly. "Aye. There were tunnels dug into the mountainsides in case of emergency. We tried to help as many as we could, but…" his voice trailed off.

"Point is we made it, and we're pissed," Kirk intervened. His brows furrowed at the memory of his lab under fire. "Didn't know what had happened to the *Cloudkicker* until you waltzed right into Osiris. Fortune had it that we've been holed up here for a few weeks trying to scrounge up information on Pandora's Box. Not many better places to find out about relics."

"I found them laying low after searching damn near every Lost Earth tavern in the city yesterday," Ghaoithe said. The captain sipped from her own coffee. Alex looked at her with a new light, imagining a younger, wilder version sitting in that same chair. The wonder must have been written on Alex's face, as the captain was quick to deflect the glance and stare out the window across the room.

"I think you just wanted to take advantage of Egyptian hospitality," roared Samir. He entered, overhearing the tail end of the conversation. His laugh brightened the atmosphere that stalled in the room.

"Something tells me you can afford a few extra nomads," poked Ghaoithe.

"Indeed! The truth is that it is nice to have friends in empty rooms," said Samir. He placed his hands together as he addressed them. "Unfortunately, I must bring business into this happy morning. I bring news."

The party sat straight in their chairs at the prospect of serious conversation. Only Ghaoithe and Ellie relaxed, picking at a plate of nuts at the center of the table. Alex wondered if Ellie even understood the situation they were in. The girl seemed oblivious, drawing on a piece of paper with a set of crayons between handfuls of food.

Samir continued, "I have discussed your situation with the captain. My staff are en route now to the ship. We shall return you to the air within two days."

The team released a collective breath. Only Kirk remained sour from his corner spot.

"You may trust your servants, but can we?" he asked.

"If they are with Samir, they are with me," said Ghaoithe with firm decision. "His team can do more than make a perfect cup of coffee."

Kirk shrugged, but he showed no other signs of being convinced. Or maybe that was just how he was born looking. Even if the scientist remained suspicious, however, the news was a relief to Alex. She had no doubts to Tory's ability to wrangle the crew or fend off anyone who stumbled across the *Cloudkicker*, but she worried about a repeat of the last boarding. Damian would not be able to help them escape a second time.

"I put my household through rigorous tests of loyalty," said Samir with a wave of his hand. He glanced at Ellie as her face glowed with satisfaction at the scribbles that constituted her work of art. "As to our other question, I have sent out feelers to seek information."

Alex wondered what research a man like Samir would have access to. Cairo's history and wealth of historical resources was staggering. She would be lying if she said she wasn't at least slightly interested in taking a peek at the troves of secrets at Samir's beck and call.

"Then it's settled. We rest fer a while and keep quiet," Fleet decided. No one objected at the idea. No one but Alex.

She shifted in her seat. "So, we need to stay inside?" she asked innocently enough.

"Cairo may seem exotic to you, but it's no place for a lady on Osiris's watch list to be walking around," said Kirk.

"You can't bring me to a city like this and not let me actually enjoy it," cried Alex.

Fleet crossed his arms. "Kirk's right, lass. It's too dangerous out there right now."

The disappointment on Alex's face was palpable. The Egyptian stepped in.

"Many people dream of seeing Cairo." Samir said. He placed an arm around Alex's shoulder. "As long as this beautiful lady is in my city, she is protected. Surely explorers such as yourselves will not deprive her of such wonderful sights?"

Ghaoithe frowned. "You've always been too arrogant where Osiris is concerned."

"Because they have yet to prove me wrong," Samir huffed. "There is a souk nearby, a gorgeous one with lots of life. I need to purchase some honey and a few other things. At least let her accompany my guards there so that she may see the real Cairo."

"You're being awfully adamant."

"Egypt has had many struggles lately, and while I will always help you, I must also help my country. It is important to show outsiders that we are not all riots and tear gas. Besides, I have quite taken to this young woman. She reminds me of someone I do not see nearly often enough," Samir said with a wink in Alex's direction.

The prospect of visiting an authentic market riveted Alex. She turned to Ghaoithe and Fleet and pleaded at them with the most wounded eyes she could conjure up. "You said yourself that his people could be trusted," she whined.

"Absolutely not," argued Ghaoithe.

"We've been cramped up in the *Cloudkicker* for so long, though. I'd be miserable here," Alex lied. She was certain that even two days would not be enough to fully explore the palace, but that was best left unsaid.

"You aren't going to drop this, are you?"

"I'm a Missourian. No, I will not."

The captain eyed Samir and then went around the room. She had work to do with their host, and Fleet needed to keep an eye on Ellie. Neither Roy nor Kirk were much use in the way of fighting, and Damian was better at stealth than being a bodyguard.

"Fine," Ghaoithe relented, "but you stay with Samir's men at all times or I authorize them to knock you unconscious to carry you back here."

Alex squealed and jumped out of her seat to embrace Ghaoithe. Samir patted the two of them on their backs.

"It is settled, then. You can meet at the staircase in five minutes," he declared.

Alex wasted no time in rushing back to her bedroom to prepare. Ghaoithe watched as she fled the kitchen before turning to Samir.

"Why did you have to do that?" she asked, clearly annoyed.

Samir's smile did not leave his face, but his eyes hinted that his thoughts were not in the present. "You never stopped wandering when you were asked to stay in place. Neither will she."

Ghaoithe stayed quiet, choosing to distract her tongue with another drink instead.

In the mansion entryway, Alex fidgeted, ready to burst until two men in gray suits arrived. They were both clean-cut with precision-shaved beards and buzzed hair. The shorter of the two reached out a hand. Alex noticed the black matte of a firearm underneath the opening of his jacket.

"I am Mohammed. This is Abdul. We will be your escorts," he introduced.

Alex returned their handshakes, and they made their way outside. A Range Rover awaited them in the circular drive in front of the complex. The fountain sparkled with the morning light, throwing liquid diamonds into the air. Abdul assisted Alex into the rear while

Mohammed hopped into the driver's seat. The spacious leather interior was foreign to Alex after her time in the skies, and she felt slightly claustrophobic in the modernity of the SUV.

"You must stick with us," explained Mohammed as they left the mansion gates. "We have been instructed to let you go where you please without time limits, but we must accompany you."

Alex placed Excalibur across her lap and leaned forward between the front seats. "I can live with that. What else should I know when we get there?"

Abdul turned and smirked at her from behind opaque sunglasses. "How to haggle," he said.

In her town of New Delta, Alex frequented the local mall throughout high school. She liked the contrast of it during the adjustment period after her parents were gone. Despite being a public place, she could walk around fairly unnoticed as shoppers darted from store to store, paying attention only to what was in their bags or what else they wanted to charge onto their cards. It was people-watching at its finest. New Delta's mall was quiet, though. It was mostly a hangout for bored teenagers with nowhere to go after school or elderly speed-walkers doing laps through each wing in the morning. A shabby arcade was built into a dark corner of one of the wings, the goths went into stores full of band merchandise they were too young to really understand, and one of the lone chain bookstores in town consistently saved the mall from extinction. It was a slow mall that reflected a rural lifestyle.

If New Delta's mall mirrored its down-home roots, the souk showcased Cairo's history as a crossroads of worldwide trade.

Before she even stepped out of their car, Alex heard the clamor of the shopping district. Throngs of eager patrons eyed vendors of fruits and produce before heading between high buildings draped with fabrics. Making her way onto the street, Alex breathed in spices and citrus and the faintest whiff of salt from the sea. The main part of the souk was a grand central market beneath tall arched ceilings. There were no individual rooms but rather a festival-like row of stands piled with goods where shop owners called out to nearby patrons. No sooner had Alex and her guards entered the stalls did the shopkeepers begin calling out to them, some blocking their path in order to show the visitors their wares. Mohammed and Abdul politely waved them off as they passed.

"Stay close. It will be crowded and the salesmen are persistent," Mohammed said. He walked in front of Alex while Abdul brought up the rear, forming some semblance of protection for their charge.

Alex paid no attention to her bubble, too awestruck by the trinkets, food, rugs, and sheer number of people surrounding her. The market atmosphere made Black Friday seem like a cakewalk by comparison. She could also understand Ghaoithe's reluctance earlier. With so many stalls and turns, Alex could not have navigated the market on her own, and she could disappear into one of the darkened side alleys far too easily without anyone noticing.

A stall of designer handbags caught her eye, each embossed with glinting letters of gold and silver. Alex could not help but stop, caught between gawking at the opulence of custom leather and thinking of how much the bags reminded her of her best friend Becky.

"Are those real?" she asked her guards.

"Most likely, yes," said Mohammed.

Alex stepped up to the stall, running her fingers over a small tote with emerald skin. Over the clasp, a golden sphinx roared, wings unfolded in all their glory. She never owned anything so marvelous, sticking to worn out bookbags and a frayed canvas purse she bought from Wal-Mart. Still, she liked looking as much as the next person.

Mohammed hailed the owner. They began chatting back and forth in Arabic. After a heated, animated discussion involving a flurry of hand gestures, Mohammed pulled a wallet out of his jacket and handed a few bills to the shopkeeper. Reaching across, he took the handbag from the rack and passed it to Alex.

"A present from Samir Nassar," Mohammed smiled.

Alex accepted the gift with her jaw open in shock. She choked out a meek thanks, unable to come up with words. He had given her the bag as though it were as simple as purchasing a gallon of milk, yet it was one of the most extravagant items she had ever been laid eyes on.

"Just for you. Only one," grinned the stall owner. He said a few more words in Arabic to Mohammed.

"He says it's unique, that all of the maker's bags are handmade to be exclusive," the guard translated.

Alex blushed, slinging the bag over her shoulder as best as she could with the scabbard at her back. A small paper fluttered from beneath its flap. She reached down to pick it up just as the wall above her shattered in a cascade of stone.

# VI

If given a thousand years, Jessie would not have been able to explain why she missed her target. She justified in her head that the blonde girl ducked at the wrong time. Fate conspired to save her with a falling receipt. However, the fact of the matter was that Jessie never missed her targets.

She. Did. Not. Miss.

Cursing, she placed her foot on the rooftop ledge and braced herself for another shot as she peered through the rifle's scope. It was too late; the girl and her guards vanished behind a wall and out of view. Panic set in around the souk as realization set in that shots had been fired. Jessie could hear the yelling even from her perch several hundred yards out.

"Well?" asked her impatient handler, a stocky brute of a man that could have been born in gray fatigues.

Part of her deal meant having Osiris watching over her back, partially to provide transport for their second target when the time came but also to ensure success. His tone highlighted exactly why Jessie preferred working solo. Clients that watched over her backs rarely understood the amount of time and patience required to do the sharpshooter's job. In their line of work, most mercenaries craved action and excitement, which stood at the polar opposite of Jessie's meticulous scouting of rooftops for days on end for vantage points in all possible scenarios.

Jessie missed a golden opportunity when the blonde girl unexpectedly left Samir's compound. The mansion was a fortress with no clear shot, just as the Osiris report had told her when they speculated that the Sky Thief might return there. The souk was a different story. Jessie should have had no issue from their position above a busy market square, even with a hasty set-up...

"She's on the move. North out of the market," Jessie curtly directed. She tried to stay short and to the point, matching the tone of her watchdogs as if her shot were on purpose. If she played it right, she could say that she was simply navigating her target to a better location away from civilians. She lifted her rifle off its stands. Osiris would be moving in on the girl, and there would be no police presence so long as they were involved. Jessie was in no rush to disassemble and move to the next vantage point. Slowing down was her way of getting on the brute's nerves, and she enjoyed every second of it.

In the marketplace below, Alex rushed between stalls. Mohammed guided her with his left arm, his free hand over a bloody cheek grazed by shrapnel. They lost Abdul among the crowds, but nothing suggested he couldn't take care of himself. Around them, the crowd jostled to escape the narrow walkways between the stalls and buildings.

Finally, the two reached an open street. On either end, waiting for them, were black SUVs. Alex went pale as she noticed the logo on each of their doors: a sketchy circle containing a sprouting tree. Osiris. Men armed with long assault rifles and thick vests poured out of the cars at the sight of Alex. Mohammed drew the pistol from within his jacket and fired a quick shot at the closest van as he pulled Alex back into the market alley. A bullet from their pursuers whizzed by, striking him in the leg. He went down hard into the nearest stall.

"Run!" he yelled. Alex pulled Excalibur from its scabbard and rushed to Mohammed's aid. He shoved her away and pulled the market stand onto its side, creating a barricade. "I'm not asking! You have to hide!"

Alex pursed her lips but said nothing. She placed a hand on Mohammed's back before turning and darting into the alleyways of the souk. She did not follow any direct path. She wove between stalls and down random walkways with the sole purpose of losing the Osiris mercenaries. Her sides burned as if they were shredding apart with every step.

As she rounded a turn, she found herself in a parking lot filled with cargo vans hauling goods to the market. Uniformed men chatted behind the truck closest to her. Just as she started to slink backwards, one of them turned and shouted as he spotted her. They reached for the weapons strapped to their shoulders. Alex looked to the van next to them and swung Excalibur. The padlock on the back gate sliced apart and a mound of watermelons toppled onto the surprised men.

Alex used the opportunity to duck past them and into a tight alley between residences. As she ran, she spotted a metal drain pipe that crawled up three stories to the rooftops. Having gotten nowhere on the ground, she sheathed her sword and began climbing.

*It's just like the rope walls at camp*, she thought. The rope walls, however, did not shudder and bend the way the pipe did. She only released her breath once she reached the roof.

The low roofs of Cairo provided a clear view to help assess her location. The arched halls of the marketplace were to her right. Directly ahead, the grassy lawns of the mansion district some miles away poked through the sand and smog. Peeking over the edge of the roof, people moved about steadily below, the uniformed Osiris warriors spread out among them in pursuit. The streets were no longer an option. She hoped Mohammed and Abdul managed to resist long enough to escape. Beside her building were several similar residences built together in close fashion from a time when cars were not the norm.

She knew she could not climb back down to the streets with the soldiers on her tail. She also knew she could not park herself on this lone roof. She needed to get back to Samir's. Looking at the irrigated lawns of the distant mansions, she started counting the rooftops in her head and, more importantly, how far apart they were from each other. Without much choice, she psyched herself up in her mind for what she knew she had to do.

*This is insane*, she thought as she gained a running start towards the closest edge. She leapt and floundered through the air without grace or style. She told herself to roll, like they did in the movies, but she fell forward more out of mistake than purpose and scuffed her arms on unpolished sandstone brick. She stayed in her landing spot for a moment, absorbing the sting in her elbows and the sun on her chest before regaining her composure.

With experience under her belt, she made the next two rooftops far more easily before shouts called behind her.

"O-53 in pursuit overland. Converge on my location!"

The helmet of an Osiris mercenary poked over a ladder on the roof behind her. He climbed over the edge, his eyes never leaving hers. All around, similar guards appeared from the streets below using ladders, pipes, and even their own devices to scale the apartments. They swarmed about like wasps around a nest, every roof covered with black-armored figures. The ledge of the rooftop brushed against the back of Alex's leg. She scoured the horizon for any safe route and found none. The only objects within sights were the muzzles of Osiris assault rifles daring her to move. Trapped and without an easy exit, Alex did the only thing she could think of.

She fell.

The sensation of careening towards the earth did not seem nearly as terrifying when she couldn't spot the ground below. Instead, she saw only the pale, cloudless sky above and the edge of the building men would surely peer down from shortly. For a moment, her descent slowed, buoyed back upwards before a rip signaled her return downward and red-and-white canvas stripes obscured her view. The ground knocked the air out of her, a solid punch against every inch of her back. Still, she thought in the back of her head, it hurt less than her ill-advised jump earlier. And it certainly beat a bullet wound.

More shouts cried out and the shuffle of heavy boots pounded on the rooftops as the Osiris gunmen scrambled back to their ladders. Alex untangled her limbs from the canvas, happy to note that more drapes fluttered above and prevented an easy shot at her prone body.

She retreated into a narrow alley. Sunlight failed to pry its way into the narrow passage. Wooden doors were inset at irregular intervals, most of them very solid with small, barred windows looking in. Alex tried the nearest one to no avail; it would take an elephant to break inside. She ran down the path towards the closest intersection. Plaster dusted her face as a bullet struck the wall next to her. She ducked into another alcove as more shots rumbled through the air around her. She heard the whistles as they flew by.

Alex tried the door behind her with the same result as the first. Briefly, she considered darting down the alleyway and hoping she could fly fast enough, but the back of her mind knew it was a hopeless endeavor. She was trapped under the archway, waiting for an impending execution by Osiris hands.

Pulling Excalibur out of its sheath, she was not going to go down without a fight. She thought of Becky, her parents, and Ethan. She wondered if she would change anything, if all of her life's mistakes would flash before her as a final dying outcry for a different outcome.

They didn't. All she felt was love. Love for where she had come from and where she ended up. Love for her second life and the captain who gave it to her. She was going to die in a gunfight in Cairo, which was more than she could have imagined a few short months ago when the most exciting event in her life was writing about a chain grocery store opening in her hometown. She raised her head toward the sky, relishing the clear blue above that took her throughout the world. Only then did Alex notice the woman standing high on the roof of a nearby business complex, a lady with raven hair that billowed from underneath a sad excuse for an Australian outback hat. She brandished a monster of a rifle that pointed straight at Alex.

"Hold on!" a voice chirped.

Alex jumped in her boots. Whipping around, a pair of crystal blue eyes stared at her. They were surrounded by a child's face so pale it was almost translucent.

"Ellie?!" Alex shouted.

The child did not respond. Instead, she grabbed Alex by the waist of her pants and pulled. The door behind them, the wooden monstrosity that withstood a hundred wars, swung wide at Ellie's caress and they tumbled inside. It slammed shut behind them, trapping the two in darkness as the sensation of falling once again overtook Alex.

The ground did not come as quickly as she expected. She drifted for several moments, Ellie's hand never leaving hers. When they did land, it was not with the thud Alex had become used to on her market trip but rather with the strange impression that she was little more than goose down wafting about in a breeze. They arrived at the bottom of an underground tower. A staircase lined the outer wall of the spire. At the top, her pursuers threatened to break in as pounding shook the walls. However, the door held, the faint glow of sigils etched upon its back visible even from the bottom of the well. The only other doorway was before them, an arched entry cast in a flickering amber light.

Sitting up, Ellie glared at Alex. Alex squirmed like child caught stealing from the cookie jar. The girl's patronizing stare projected something profoundly honest that Alex was not quite sure she had the capacity to deal with after narrowly escaping death.

"That was stupid," Ellie proclaimed, putting words to Alex's feelings.

"How did you get here?" Alex deflected. She tried to sound matronly, but the child's appearance shook her.

"You were in trouble," Ellie answered. She said this as if it were the most obvious answer in the world, which did not help Alex's already rattled nerves.

"But how did you get here? How did you get out of the house and past the guards? How did you get us into this building?" Alex rambled. Questions streamed out of her as logic slipped away the more she grasped for it.

Ellie just shrugged. She jumped to her feet, dusted off her white gown, and marched toward the light ahead of them. An exasperated Alex shook her head and followed.

An immense chamber sprawled out in every direction. Long candles along the walls illuminated countless rows of high shelves. Upon each layer were stacked books upon books, scrolls, parchments, and loosely bound papers that sagged their shelves with their weight. Alex choked as she breathed in dust and the faint smell of trapped lumber. Nothing stirred, including the air, and a fine layer of undisturbed dirt covered the floor. Beyond the reach of the candles, the shelves continued down countless rows into a cavernous void.

"Where are we?" Alex wondered aloud.

"A library," Ellie stated earnestly.

Alex waved off Ellie's quip. "It smells so dry in here. How has this place not burned down yet?"

The two started to wander between the rows of books, but the light from the walls quickly dissipated among the shelves. Returning to the entrance, Alex grabbed a candle from its sconce. She tilted it to let the wax drip only to be astonished when the candle resisted melting. She rolled the light in her hands, searching for sigils written into the mold but it resembled nothing more than a plain candle.

"Try this," Ellie offered. A tattered sheet of parchment drooped in her hands. Curious, Alex looked it over but the words were so faint as to render the paper useless let alone somehow contain sigil writing.

Alex cautiously held a corner of the paper over her flame. For a moment, the candle's smoke intensified before returning to its normal state. The paper remained intact. Letting the parchment flutter to the ground, Alex raised the candle high to provide more light to the chambers. Books continued well into the darkness beyond her vision.

Their only marker was an inscription in the stone above the entryway: *LOCO PRO REMEDIUM DE ANIMAE.*

Thinking briefly of turning back towards the stairwell, Alex decided against it. Even if Osiris left, the door would be watched. Their only way out was to find another exit, if one existed at all.

"Stay close. No telling how long we'll be in here," Alex ordered. She took Ellie's hand as they made their way into the sea of scrolls.

Though she followed Alex's lead, Ellie's head darted back and forth between bookcases as they walked. The shroud of darkness in the room didn't bother her like it did her adult counterpart. She eagerly tried to read the bindings they passed. Many of the writings were frayed or bound with cracking leather, their ink often faded beyond the point of legibility.

Alex tried to follow Ellie's interest, but none of the books yielded anything comprehensible. Those that survived time were in Latin or Hebrew or languages long dead. Had they not proved indestructible by normal means, she would not have even dared touch them out of fear the paper would crumble in her hands. She remembered the yellow dailies in her newspaper's archives being sensitive to hold. Tomes from bygone eras were well outside her experience.

"Can you even read?" Alex asked.

"Yes, I can read, dummy. A, B, C..." Ellie started. Alex flipped the girl's waist-long strands of silver hair into her face.

"Smartass."

The two giggled. Even though the weird child could seem distant, even ethereal at times, there was worse company to be stuck with. If she were honest with herself, Alex was thankful to have a companion. The silence in the chamber unnerved her, the only sounds coming from the hiss of flame in her hand and the soft padding of their feet over the stone floor. It felt like death, a true death, a punishment for disturbing something she should not have found. Yet, she did find the library, or at least Ellie brought her there. Which only made the entire situation even more disturbing.

As they navigated the countless aisles, the mysteries of the library nearly overtook their search for an exit. They eventually reached a section where the books were well-preserved. Most of the scrolls and loose parchment had been replaced with heavily bound volumes, their contents dark and unbroken.

"I don't understand how the ink can fade but the paper is protected," Alex wondered aloud as they stopped to pore over a few collections.

"You can probably bring them back," said Ellie. She was engrossed in a page rendered in colorful ink, each fine detail hand-drawn by a master artisan of his day. "Magic is weird like that."

Alex raised a skeptic eyebrow. "You think the sigils are magic?"

"Magic is just the power of the earth, isn't it? The swirly things are the letters to use the power."

"Don't you think more people would know about the runes if they were that simple?" Alex ran her fingers absently over bindings as she glanced down at Ellie on the floor.

"Maybe. If they took the time to remember. People forget about the earth a lot now," Ellie replied. "People in the blue captain's home know some of the words, but they don't remember most of them."

"Do you think people need the sigils to use that magic?"

"No, I don't think so. Sometimes it calls to people but they don't know what they're hearing."

At first, Ellie's vague explanations frustrated Alex. Then, memories of the time just after her parents died flickered back to life. She remembered how she couldn't sleep, couldn't stay indoors out of rage and restlessness. More than a few times, she would find herself drawn out at 2 a.m. to open fields with no people or technology, places that called to her with their silence, their openness, their simplicity.

She could never explain that unique force beckoning her out of the house. Could that have been what Ellie and the others were talking about? That magnetism to simply exist within the world free from the fetters of computers and other distractions? This wasn't the first time someone from Lost Earth referred to the sigils as being an almost primal force. They never went so far as to call it "magic," but there was always an underlying sense that the power of the runes was a holdover from an era where people and the earth had a much greater understanding of one another.

With her mind untying the knots of how her and Ellie's worlds were connected, Alex aimlessly pulled a book off the shelf. It was another volume of sharp, precise letters in a language she could not recognize.

"Well, maybe that magic can help me read some of these books," Alex mused. She sat down to rest her legs after the day's action. Creepy library or not, it was better than returning to the war with Osiris for the time being.

As she flipped through the pages, colorful illustrations popped out at her. Like the book in Ellie's hands, the colors were rendered by hand with brilliant inks and even flecks of gold and silver. The fine details astonished Alex. She imagined craftsmen sitting in a candle-lit monastery, painstakingly rendering even the minute details of leaves over several months. That was their life and their calling, a gift that transcended the ages.

One drawing depicted a Greek scholar, toga and all, addressing a crowd of listeners under a night sky that very well may have been an accurate star chart in all its precision. Another page was fire and ice as gods clashed above the clouds in eternal warfare. The next page...

Alex gasped.

Centered under an archway of ivy and marble, a young girl stared out of the page. Her silver hair flowed over a white dress like smoke in glass. She was no older than seven or eight, with innocent blue eyes that held the universe inside.

She stared at Ellie, rendered in loving portraiture centuries ago.

# VII

Alex stared at the portrait, then at Ellie, then back. The likeness was unmistakable. On one hand, the revelation made perfect sense. That a mysterious girl found at the bottom of the ocean would be mentioned in an ancient text only seemed like the natural progression of Ellie's oddity. However, it seemed so simple, so easy. It was just *there*. Alex held it in her hands!

Aside from the illustration, a few words were woven into the painting but in the same illegible text as the rest of the book. Alex tried to find some context, some clue to their meaning but was forced to give up. It was then she noticed Ellie staring at her from the floor.

"What did you find?" Ellie asked.

Alex bit her lip. She didn't want to risk upsetting the child or triggering some sort of long-lost voodoo. Then again, Alex was sure that keeping secrets around Ellie was a futile effort. The child had a habit of revealing more about those around her than they knew about themselves.

Alex took a seat next to Ellie. "Do you remember anything about where you came from?"

"You mean where you found me?" Ellie tilted her head.

"No, I mean before that. Before you went to sleep."

Ellie stuck her tongue out, mulling over whatever memories she had locked away in her whimsical head. "I remember there were some men in robes. They liked talking about time. And there was a nice lady with a sad smile when she talked," she said.

"So you don't remember how you got to the temple in Bimini? Or why you can do all these things normal people can't do?"

"Nope!" Ellie shouted emphatically. She enjoyed the sudden attention from her friend.

"Do you recognize this?" Alex passed the book to Ellie. The girl stared at it for a moment before bursting out in a fit of giggles.

"That's me!" Ellie shouted. She handed the book back to Alex. "They made me too short, though."

Alex scratched her head. Talking to Ellie was useless at best and headache-inducing at worst. She opened the sphinx clasp on her new bag. It was just the right size to slide the book in. Perhaps Samir would have ideas on how to translate it.

"Don't feel bad. Maybe you'll be in a book one day, too," continued Ellie. Her grin vanished, and she looked up at the stone ceiling above them. "We should go."

Alex shot to her feet. "Are we in trouble?"

Ellie shook her head. "No. We can leave now. It's safe."

Marching off into the darkness, Ellie left Alex chasing behind. They no longer meandered their way through the vast hall. The young girl tore past the stacks with an instinctual focus, like a little bird driven towards its birthplace during migration. Alex couldn't make out where they were going and grabbed Ellie's hand in order to keep pace with her.

Soon, their candle was not the only source of light around them. In the distance, Alex saw the faint orange glow of more sconces bolted to the walls. As they neared, the dot of light split into two candles standing guard beside a rusted iron gate. Beyond it, stairs spiraled upward out of the earth. Alex rushed forward and pulled on the bars before she noticed the blue glow of sigils clustered around the handle underneath her hand. They swirled round a solid metal block where a keyhole would normally reside. She kicked the gate with a defeated grunt.

"Do you know how to undo these?" Alex asked. Ellie shook her head. Of course their magnificent escape earlier would have been a one-time thing. Alex cursed her luck.

Ghaoithe had undone a lock once as they broke into the Osiris base. Pacing before the gate, Alex reached into her memories in the hopes of retracing what the captain drew on that iron door. Nothing stood out.

Ellie tugged at Alex's shirt. "Try the sword," she said.

Without any other ideas, Alex sighed. She grasped Excalibur's hilt and made a wide cut at the gate's handle. The sharp steel clanged against the iron but otherwise bounced off without so much as leaving a knick.

Shaking her head, Ellie said, "Don't cut it. Use it like a key."

"You're not making any sense," Alex snipped. She knew the girl was trying to help, but the riddles wore on her nerves.

Without flinching at Alex's biting words, Ellie grabbed the sword's hilt and lifted Alex's hands. The tip of the sword pointed just beneath the handle of the gate. Slowly and methodically, Ellie pushed the sword forward. It slid into the iron block as if it were a slice of bread. With a click, the sword flashed with brilliant runes of its own along the blade and the gate slid outward.

Alex let out a yelp. She leaned over her blade to study the runes she had no idea existed, but she only found her reflection mirrored in the steel.

"That would have been nice to know about, like, forever ago," Alex said.

Ellie wiped her hands on her dress. "It's ok. You and the tall captain lady are still new at this."

"I'll take your word for it, weirdo," Alex said, tussling Ellie's hair.

Together, they bounded up the stairwell. The gate slammed shut on its own behind them, likely to stay that way for another several eons. Her candle, too, snuffed itself out to leave them in perpetual darkness. Alex was happy to have left the library and her excitement over the book drowned out whatever lurked in the shadows. They edged their way closer to the top, never letting go of the other's hand. Their spiraling exit stretched upward for ages, a much longer journey than their trip down. Eventually, the air became lighter and cooler with the faint hint of a draft.

The outline of a door leaking with the glow of yellow streetlamps met them on an entry platform. Alex pulled the handle to no avail. She tried Excalibur and just as with the gate, the door opened wide to cool desert air. Her new trick was beginning to impress Alex. She kissed the blade and stepped outside with Ellie in tow.

Their surroundings were new to them. They had ended up in a vastly different portion of the city than the one they entered the library through. Gone were the markets and roughshod housing. Instead, they stood in a modern district of bright streets and glass offices. The door they had just left was the only sign of anything ancient, and Alex couldn't even be sure it was visible to the modern world with how the sigils worked.

"I don't suppose you can track down Samir's house from here?" Alex asked Ellie. The girl shook her head. Whatever instinct had taken over among the books had passed.

To their left, Alex could see the pyramids poking up above the buildings, lit with brilliant spotlights worthy of Wonders of the World. She could also make out the line of high-rise offices and skyscrapers that followed the Nile's path. Getting her bearings as best she could, Alex turned down an alleyway to her right and trekked towards what she hoped was the palace district.

Staying among the shadows was harder than she had imagined it would be. Cairo took on new life in the evening. The girls had to dodge people at several turns, mostly younger adults in Armani shirts. They stood outside of bass-rattling clubs, smoking hashish and portable vaporizers. The streets were awash in neon purples and greens as the capitol transformed into a hotspot for forward-thinking youth culture.

The military, too, kept watch. They stopped to share cigarettes with the trendy crowd or stand guard over the louder establishments. On more than a few occasions, Alex and Ellie had to duck under an archway or behind a high wall to avoid being seen by the armed men. Under no circumstance did Alex believe an American girl with a sword on her back would be welcome alone in the streets. With Ghaoithe or Samir's men, maybe, but certainly not alone.

As the night wore on, the electric city gave way to a more traditional Cairo with squat, close buildings and few sounds but the chatter of friends through open windows. Then, no sound but a light wind as a familiar stretch of grand estates rose before the exhausted travelers.

Alex grabbed Ellie and dragged her down the avenue. They rushed past towering gates, searching for the three-headed fountain marking Samir's property. It sparkled under nighttime spotlights, raining jewels as a welcoming gift to the exhausted refugees. Pressing the intercom furiously, they waited for the voice on the other end to inquire who called. Instead, the gate began to rattle open without question. From the mouth of the palace huffed Samir and the *Cloudkicker* party. Ghaoithe pushed past the crowd and squeezed Alex in her arms.

"Are you hurt? What happened?" Ghaoithe asked. Alex hugged the captain back, offering reassurance against the stream of questions.

"I'm fine," Alex said. "Just a little shaken up."

Ghaoithe's eye probed Alex. Then, she stood and turned to Ellie. "We're going to have to have a discussion with you, young lady."

Samir stepped in before the captain could continue any interrogation. "Praise Allah everyone is ok. However, while I agree we must find out what happened, we should do it inside."

It was then that Alex noticed his servants no longer hid their guns inside the folds of the jackets. Now, they carried rifles openly across their arms, standing firm as they gauged their surroundings. She felt the tension bearing down on the garden, a stark contrast to their first arrival.

Nodding at Samir, Ghaoithe motioned for everyone to make their way inside the estate. That the armored explorer pointedly took up the rear did not go unnoticed by Alex. She knew that something had happened in her absence, some important piece of information that desperately needed to be relayed.

As they entered the foyer, Fleet clapped Alex on the back with a jarring thud. "Looks like ya still had time to go perusin' the mall's wares," he laughed.

Confused, Alex scrunched her eyebrows at him until she remembered the emerald handbag at her side, now containing the text from the library.

"Oh, this was a gift," Alex said. Her eyes shot open wide. "Mohammed! Are he and Abdul ok?"

A heavy grunt sounded in response. From the right of the main entrance was a lavish sitting room with its door wide open. There, Mohammed rested on a plush armchair, his left leg perched straight on an ottoman. A bloodied bandage had been wrapped above the knee. Abdul stood beside him, his suit disheveled but otherwise unharmed. Mohammed gave a curt nod in Alex's direction as he stiffly sat up upon Samir's arrival. The host urged Alex and Ellie to take seats of their own on a posh lavender sofa nestled among glass cases filled with Egyptian antiquities. Samir brought himself to the floor, crossing his legs with flexibility beyond his size, while Ghaoithe and the rest leaned against the walls. All eyes were on Alex.

"Please, young ones, what happened after you left Mohammed?" Samir asked.

Alex rubbed her eyes. The adrenaline from her day had started to wear off, leaving her drained.

"I just started running. There were Osiris vans everywhere. I managed to avoid them for a while, but I got trapped in a doorway. Next thing I know, Ellie is behind me," she said.

Roy and Kirk glanced at each other in disbelief. Alex forgot that they had not yet truly met Ellie, let alone become accustomed to her antics, her ethereal nature, her ability to shatter glass walls at just the right time...

"You just poofed," Ghaoithe asked, motioning with her hands, "behind Alex, Ellie?"

Ellie shrugged. "I was reading a book in the garden and then I thought Alex was in trouble and then I was there."

Samir stroked his beard as he mulled over her words. He seemed far less surprised by the girl's act of materialization than his colleagues. "It would seem our little friend does not understand her own powers," he said. "However, a gift is a gift, and we must be thankful for it. What about after her appearance? My agents searched even the forgotten city and found no trace of you. Osiris appeared just as confused in their patterns."

"We were in a huge library of some kind, deep underground. It was definitely part of Lost Earth. The books were protected by sigils," Alex said. She reached into her handbag, pulled out the tome inside, and handed it to Samir. "We found this inside."

Upon taking the book, Samir's eyes went wide. He held its pages reverently in his hands as though scared to touch it. "Alexandria!" he whispered in awe. "It does still exist!"

"Wait, you mean *the* Library of Alexandria?!" Alex shrieked. A ripple coursed throughout the others in the room at the revelation.

Samir nodded vigorously. "Yes. At least, if what you say is true. There have always been rumors, but to think it real... please, humor an old man. What was it like?"

Alex had no trouble recalling the library and its incredible network of shelves. The new understanding that she had been inside granted her a new energy, and even Ghaoithe was silent to hang on every word.

As Alex finished, the group sat quietly to imagine what they had heard. Only Samir, after a long pause, tempted a question. "I know it is folly to ask, but do you remember where you entered from?"

Ellie and Alex shook their heads in unison. "No. I had no idea where I was when I got cornered. It was locked from the inside with runes anyway. I don't think anyone would have gotten in there without Ellie," said Alex.

Samir frowned in childlike disappointment. He ran his fingers over the books binding in longing before his face lit back up to its normal self. "Then we will continue searching. Yet you give me hope, Ms. Stirling. I pray you will one day share its wonders with me," he proclaimed. "This book alone is more than any of us could have dreamed of seeing from its vaults."

"I was hoping you could translate it. Look inside, about halfway back."

Samir gently opened the cover, its binding cracking through the fresh air. Its browned and tattered paper crinkled with each flip of the pages but otherwise showed no signs of crumbling under the strain. The giant man pored over its pages with increasing interest, halting only when he discovered the illustration of Ellie. Those nearby gasped at the revelation, but Samir seemed unfazed. Running his fingers lightly over the portrait, his eyes flashed over the words and details.

Eventually, he sighed and admitted defeat. "It is no luck. This is an ancient language beyond my skills."

"Do you think we can find anyone who can?" asked Ghaoithe. She leaned with her arms folded against the wall, supervising the proceedings with intense interest.

Samir thought for a moment. "If you are heading to Dilmun, you must seek the House of Scribes. If it is a language I do not know, they may be the only hope." He handed the book back to Alex. "Keep this under guard. Few have been honored to see such a treasure."

Alex nodded and eased the book into her bag once more. She was ready for the meeting to be adjourned and for her head to find a pillow, but a figure popped into her mind. "There's one more thing," she said. "Before Ellie appeared, I saw a woman on a rooftop. She had this huge gun and looked like she stepped out of a *Crocodile Dundee* movie. I think she was the one that shot at me in the market."

At the mention of the woman, the *Cloudkicker* group straightened in attention. Roy and Fleet glanced at each other while Ghaoithe's eye burned towards Alex. Only Damian continued to lounge back against a writing table, lost in the meaning of the description.

"Do you remember anything else about the woman?" Ghaoithe asked.

"Not really. She was too far away. I remember she had long black hair."

At Alex's description, Samir stood. He turned to Ghaoithe, his face painted with thin lines that clashed with the personality Alex knew. He said, "It is as we feared. My men will work overtime, myself included. We must return your bird to the skies as soon as possible."

Ghaoithe pointed at the girls on the couch, she said, "You two are not to leave the house without me nearby. Not even to visit the gardens."

Her tone did not leave any wiggle room for debate, but Alex's interest had been piqued. "Why? What's going on?" she asked.

"It appears you are being hunted," Samir warned.

# VIII

There was nothing natural about the *Ascendant*. As Sorin plodded down the cold steel hallways, he hoped for a semblance of familiarity but was left wanting. The computerized mechanisms confused him. The sway of the ship did not feel right under his feet. He found no solace in the clipped, professional manner of the crew that barely acknowledged him as they beelined to their next order of business.

Such was the trade-off for betrayal.

Sorin never expected Ghaoithe to understand. She was a traditionalist, a digger who spent more time looking down at the earth than acknowledging what was ahead. She had no inclination for politics or the realities of life that normal people lived through outside of her own bubble. If she only left her rickety, outdated vessel for more than a moment, perhaps she would understand why Sorin joined Osiris. She would see the good that could be done. Osiris could show her like they had shown him. Sorin believed in Osiris.

So, he paid no attention to the uncomfortable fact that the crew of the airship viewed him as an outsider. He ignored the glances his way as he stomped through the halls and the unheard statements of "What is he doing here?" His clothes were looser and considerably more garish than the slick gray-and-emerald uniforms of the others, but he didn't care. Sorin only cared about one opinion on the ship.

As he shrugged off the glances his way, Sorin grew ever more aware of the *Ascendant's* size. The *Cloudkicker* had often seemed large enough, the sigils embedded into the hall bending physical space just enough to give extra comfort for the crew. Kirk had worked his trade with those runes to give the ship an intimate but not claustrophobic atmosphere. Compared to the *Ascendant*, the Sky Thief's ship was an ant against an army. The Osiris ship may not have had the speed of the gritty clipper, but it dwarfed anything Sorin saw in the skies before. Walking from the quarters to the bridge felt like a marathon in itself. He dared only guess what kind of modern firepower the ship held in its cargo. Even more unnerving to Sorin was the lack of runes. Deacon's own scientists crafted sigils on the hull for flight, but the interior was pure man-made engineering. No tricks of rune-light here; the ship truly was as big as it appeared.

Eventually, after getting lost at least twice in the winding halls, the steel door to the bridge loomed ahead of him. He gripped his ID card and awkwardly held it in front of a tiny black box to the side. A red light on it beeped, turned green, and the door slid open.

The bridge stretched on as a long corridor. A row of terminals on the left side was manned by navigators, system operators, and other crew. They clicked furiously on holographic pads that mixed sigils with new world technology. Maps and graphs popped onto screens at eye level. It was a bright, dead light that glazed over eyes without emotion. Sorin preferred the homey atmosphere of the *Cloudkicker*, but even he had to admit this new bridge presented solutions beyond his understanding. It wasn't just cutting-edge; the machines it contained were the first of their kind. The monitors displayed all of the versatility the *Ascendant* could contain, and Osiris went through great lengths to ensure nothing less than magnificence.

Behind the crew was a raised walkway and then a narrow platform along the right side of the bridge. On it was a long row of benches aimed at a seamless glass window that stretched along the wall and around the nose of the ship. Against the sea of clouds outside, Deacon sat alone on one of these benches, fingers tapping to an unheard rhythm on the polished handle of his cane. Sorin hesitated to approach, but Deacon waved him on without turning.

"Ah, there you are! How are you feeling, my boy?" asked Deacon. He pushed his spectacles down his nose to inspect the statuesque specimen in front of him. Aside from a healing cut on his forehead, Sorin appeared in perfect health.

Sorin sat, unconsciously keeping a body's distance from his grinning boss. "I am fine. Only shaken and adjusting to this life," he said.

"You'll adjust, I assure you. Once you have truly seen the wonders at our doorstep."

Sorin nodded silently, as much out of devoted habit as anything. Deacon did not need to preach about the power of Osiris; Sorin fully accepted and relished it already. He had spent years learning of Osiris' creed, told by Deacon and other leadership. Days flew by on the *Cloudkicker*, each a pesky nuisance between secret meetings where Ghaoithe's meager hauls were revealed to be little more than toys. Osiris promised wonders. They delivered tenfold. Sorin wanted nothing more than to be a part of it, even if it meant starting as an errand boy.

So far, Sorin had not done his job well. He rubbed the back of his head, still sore after being flung against a wall. He dared not look Deacon in the eye for fear that his employer would notice his embarrassment. His failure hung over his head like a ticking pendulum.

"About China…" Sorin began, leaving the words hanging in the air. He struggled with conversations where he could not assume control. With Ghaoithe, it was easy to pretend, to look down upon her. Not so with Deacon.

Deacon dispelled the worry with a chortling laugh. "It is not your fault. In fact, we learned more from that incident than we had in weeks!"

Sorin remained unconvinced. He shook his head. "Still, I should have acted earlier. They should not have escaped."

Deacon rose from his seat. Gripping the balled handle of his cane, he strode up to the windows to observe the expansive earth below. They flew over an endless green canopy, wild and exotic as it vanished over the horizon. The clear view was a brief respite; storms rolled in and out on a whim over the few days they had been parked in the sky.

"Creating a better world is never seamless," Deacon said. "Mistakes are made. Failures happen. I would be remiss to blame anyone struggling to do their part. Did you know that when I started here, I had little more than a bag of clothes to my name? I am no stranger to setbacks."

At Sorin's wide-eyed befuddlement, Deacon smirked. "It is true. I was a pauper in every sense. In fact, I was much like you, a lad with little more than a vision of a brighter future. I worked my way up, and not without failures of my own. I saw a world without starvation and need. I pushed for better practices and technology, utilizing science and fusing it with this wonderful language of Lost Earth. It was not easy, and many times when I thought my work finished, it came collapsing down. People died, and those left became more and more ravaged by the elements and by themselves."

Deacon turned to Sorin, preaching with all of the vigor of a seasoned politician. "But, I did it! I harnessed the power at our doorstep. Now, we have crops that can grow in the harshest of environments, yields that give us more than we need so that we may pass it on to the impoverished. We eliminated illnesses and are close to eradicating more still. Through Osiris, I completed what others said were impossible tasks, not for wealth but for humanity. With those hurdles conquered, I can move on to bigger things to solve the sins of this world."

Adrenaline pumped through Sorin at the words of his savior. He did not understand all that transpired, but he felt the weight of Deacon's accomplishments through the passion in the man's voice. He would learn about Osiris's world of technology and relish the fruits of progress.

"I believe in you, sir. I believe in Osiris," Sorin said. "I promise I shall do better next time."

Deacon let out a mournful sigh and shook his head. "You trust so easily. Osiris is simply a name. In truth, they are as much at fault as any."

"What do you mean?" Sorin said. He had never heard Deacon speak ill of his employers.

Deacon returned his view to the window. "Osiris is as much complicit in the ills of the world as anyone else. There have been times, I am sorry to say, they have favored profits and influence while turning an eye to the problems created."

"But you are here to change that."

Deacon raised a brow at Sorin and grinned in such a way that scared the young man again. "I am, my boy. I am. It is time to consolidate so that we are no longer a mindless amoeba consuming without foresight."

"I will do anything I can to help, sir. Let me make up for China."

"Good! Good!" Deacon encouraged. "You are still young and strong. You have plenty of life ahead to learn from. But I have already made plans for the others in the Osiris circle. That is too base a task for one such as you."

"Then what do I do? What of Pandora's Box now?" Sorin asked, his mind suddenly bursting with eagerness to help.

Deacon bared his teeth. "Come here."

Sorin stood at the command and joined his master by the glass panes. Already, the threat of rain coalesced on the horizon. Soon, they would not be able to see anything but a waterfall cascading down the sides of the *Ascendant*.

"Do you see that spot over there?" Deacon directed a thin finger to a point not far below the gathering clouds. The carpet of green treetops had been leveled to a brown patch of earth. Trails of smoke rose to join the darkening skies above. Sorin could almost imagine the barking of orders as men worked their pickaxes within the pit.

"What are they doing?" asked Sorin.

"Research, my boy."

Sorin didn't understand how the parched ground connected with the artifact they hunted. "What of Pandora's Box? What of the girl?"

"All in due time," Deacon said. He placed an arm around the younger man's broad shoulders. A shiver ran up Sorin, though out of excitement as much as fear. "As for the girl, that is where you come in. I have a... specialist to the north of here I want you to meet."

Sorin held his silence. He watched the smoke pile high before drifting towards the storm.

Jessica Vargas. The Desert Siren. Alex's assailant. Even her name sent Alex's mind into worry as she imagined a real-life equivalent of Belloq or Boba Fett. She would have laughed at the ridiculousness of having her own assassin had a bullet not already come close to taking off her head.

"She's the best sniper anyone's seen. Keeps mostly to herself and only works for hire. She doesn't usually deal with Lost Earth folk, but she won't let a contract go unfulfilled," Kirk had informed Alex.

Alex did not need further convincing; anyone that could worry Ghaoithe and Samir had earned their credibility.

The *Cloudkicker* team trekked swiftly through the desert, accompanied by Samir's armed escorts and reinforced vehicles. The captain moaned in her seat, wracked with nausea from the Land Rover's unfamiliar movements, but she refused to leave Alex's side. They sat pressed together in the back of the last car alongside Damian, the only other adult small enough to squeeze into the seat. Ellie sat between Roy and Fleet in the middle car. Kirk and Samir spearheaded the envoy.

Alex did not mind the tight quarters. She felt protected by Ghaoithe's armor and was more concerned with her friend's motion sickness than an attack on Samir's capable men. She tried to distract Ghaoithe with car games she remembered as a child, but "I Spy" did not hold much sway when the only surroundings were sand and more sand.

At least they had air conditioning this time.

"*45 klicks until arrival,*" a voice blared from the CB radio on the dash.

"We can hoof it from here," Ghaoithe groaned. Her tan face had paled to a become a gnarly shade of yellow.

"Sorry, ma'am. We have to take you right up to the hull," said their driver. He was met with more groans.

"Quit being a baby. I was shot at and you can't even handle a car ride?" teased Alex. Nonetheless, she placed a hand on Ghaoithe's tense forearm. The captain glared in response, but she dared not move more than her eye lest her stomach decide to forfeit its battle. Giant quivering fingers gripped Alex's hand.

Damian, however, had no issue with the ride. He flipped through the pages of their unearthed book. He would chirp periodically about each new mystery discovered within its pages.

"Maybe Ellie is someone's child, accidentally trapped in time by Roman mystics or something," he suggested enthusiastically.

Alex sighed. She had heard all sorts of theories during their ride, from a second Atlantis to aliens disguised as the blue kingfishers in Ellie's portrait. None of them made any more sense than the next. Besides, Alex was the ship's archivist, and she bristled at the thought of someone else attempting her hard-fought job.

"First of all, if she's related to Pandora's Box, she'd be Greek, not Roman. Second, if anyone had mastered stopping time, I'm sure we'd have something about it in Ghaoithe's book," Alex corrected.

"There's a lot in here that our relic encyclopedia has probably missed! Look," Damian help up the illustrated pages so Alex could see as he flipped through, "all of these pictures are from stories we know, but they're all messed up. Arachne, Prometheus… they're all in here. It's like when Hollywood makes a gritty version of Cinderella, and the story's kind of familiar but everything's all cyberpunk and the prince is actually a robot."

"What's cyberpunk?" Ghaoithe murmured.

Alex shrugged her off. She leaned in to snatch the book from Damian's hands.

"You might be good at escaping prison cells, but leave the research to us," Alex said.

Damian rolled his eyes. "I'm just saying there's something odd there. They don't look all fantasy-like like most pictures of mythology."

"So they're cyberpunk now but fantasy is taking it too far?"

"Exactly. A Christopher Nolan version of Greece."

"Who's Christopher Nolan?"

"I think you lost a few brain cells while you were stuck in our cargo bay."

"Aren't you supposed to be open and impartial as a journalist?"

"Who the hell is Christopher Nolan?!"

The Land Rover came to a halt. The jolt sent Ghaoithe out the door. She lurched on all fours to the sand as her stomach emptied. The rest of occupants in their motorcade stepped out while she regained her equilibrium. The sight of the heaving captain brought a guffaw from Samir.

"You never could handle riding in the back seat," he laughed with a shake of his head.

Surrounding them were dunes and empty desert for miles in any direction. From the head of their motorcade, the familiar face of Tory appeared from blank air. Several of the Cloudkicker's sailors followed.

"Ya go on land for a few days and ya already lost your touch, Cap?" Tory cackled.

Ghaoithe stood on trembling legs, too tired to holler back. Tory settled on a weakened hug from her captain before turning to the bearded man that saved them.

"I take it my packages arrived well?" Samir asked.

"Just in the nicka time, too. You're a right savior there, Mister Samir," Tory replied as she clasped hands with the burly gentleman.

They began to load up the extra stores that remained in the trunks of the SUVs. One-by-one, crates of lasting goods were brought through the void in the desert, disappearing through the runes and into the *Cloudkicker*. A few select bags had been marked exclusively for the captain's quarters, though Alex could only guess what they contained. She doubted they were just to replenish the stores of liquor on board.

Ghaoithe, firmly back in her own territory, steadily gained strength once her mind had business to attend to. She immediately ordered Ellie and Alex to board the safety of the ship. With several hands assisting, the captain rushed to take flight and escape the vulnerability of the desert.

As Alex readied to board the ship, she made one last pass by Samir. He reached down and enveloped her in one of his now-familiar bear hugs. Once he put Alex down, he pulled out a small box and handed it to her.

"This is for you. I know how archaic things can be in Lost Earth. My heart feels better knowing you have at least the basics for emergencies," he said.

Alex opened the box. Inside was a cellphone. It was a simple, cheap flip-phone model with no touch screen or camera. Alex examined the gray chunk.

"Is this a…" Alex began.

"A burner phone, yes," Samir said. "No GPS or anything else Osiris can track. The only number you need is already in it. Do not hesitate to call."

Alex smiled and placed the phone back in its box. "Thank you. I'll make sure not to let this one get crushed."

Samir chuckled idly before his expression grew serious. "We are in this together. I can see with how Ghaoithe acts around you that you are one of the good ones, and to me that means you are as much a part of my family as she is. Please, remember what I have told you. Keep her safe."

"I will," Alex said. This time, Alex initiated the hug, squeezed as hard as she could, and boarded the ship with a final wave.

Once the last of the cargo disappeared into the wards, Ghaoithe trotted up to Samir. She embraced him, refusing to let go for several moments. When they finally broke apart, Samir gazed at the captain with red eyes.

"You have never been one for advice, child, but please use caution these next few weeks," he said.

"I'll try," was all Ghaoithe could muster in response. She shifted her weight and scanned the horizon as an awkward silence fell between the two with many things they wished to say but could not.

At last, Samir tilted his head at the invisible ship. "Why the girl? What makes her special?" he asked.

"She holds some secret that Osiris wants. I don't know what it is specifically, but I know we have to keep them from her."

"I did not mean Ellie."

Ghaoithe thought for a moment, her imagination fraught with ideas of Alex narrowly escaping the sniper's shot. "They want to teach me a lesson for showing them up," she concluded.

Samir sighed and rested a palm on Ghaoithe's shoulder. "You are too dense sometimes."

They gazed at the desert as grains swirled and danced among the dunes. "You know, you have never shown me the bird that stole you away," Samir said.

Ghaoithe turned her head towards him and smiled. She reached for his hand and pulled him forward. They crossed the threshold of the wards and the *Cloudkicker* breached their view, its steel hull shining and massive against the sky. Already, the darkened runes sparked with new life as the crew fed its engine a new crystal.

"I understand now, child. She is everything they say."

# IX

Liftoff rumbled through the innards of the ship, knocking trinkets off shelves and rudely awakening those who dared to rest during the day. Even Ghaoithe had trouble recalling the last time the *Cloudkicker* took off directly from the ground. Unused to the hard earth, the ship made its displeasure known to its inhabitants as it reunited with the skies.

In the galley, Alex held her plate tight. Her coffee, however, was a lost cause. It clattered over the edge of the table. Around her, the less fortunate diners cursed and grumbled as eggs fell to the floor and steaming liquids splashed over fingers. Their surroundings lurched for several more minutes before stabilizing into the slow, rhythmic bobbing they were accustomed to.

"Knew ol' Kirk would coax her up," grinned the sailor sitting next to Alex, a missing tooth interrupting his smile.

With fresh supplies in tow, the crew swarmed the kitchen eager for something hotter than stale biscuits. For his part, Richard the chef kept up with demands, knocking only three impatient men upside their heads with his ladle. Once order had been restored, the galley roared with life. Alex's peers carved a spot for her among the seats. No sooner had she stepped aboard had rumors ignited among the crowd.

"Never woulda thought the Desert Siren would have trouble catching such a little minnow!" laughed one woman as she smacked Alex on the back.

Alex blushed at the praise. Having spent so much time around the captain and Fleet, she often worried about how the rest of the crew viewed her. Was she just the captain's plaything to them? The funny-sounding girl from the Midwest the leaders took pity on?

Her fears were unwarranted. Alex had become a welcome addition to the ship, no longer the strange new girl playing pretend pirate. Her companions begged her for the story of her escape into the Library of Alexandria and groaned with disappointment upon learning the fabled turquoise bag had been locked safely away in her room. With Sorin's treachery still fresh, she carefully left out any details of the tome she had found. Such was the interest in Alex that she secretly screamed with relief when Ghaoithe appeared in the doorway and beckoned her. Escaping the numerous pats on her shoulders and offers for drinks, she slipped out of the room with her captain.

"Something wrong?" Alex asked.

Ghaoithe shrugged. "Not really. You just looked like you needed a break. They'll unhinge your jaw if you let 'em."

"I didn't know I was so popular all of a sudden." Alex rubbed life back into her cheeks. She followed her captain as they started through the halls, aiming for nowhere in particular. The wild chatter faded and turned to low conversations in bedrooms and the calming white-noise of sigil-light in the walls.

"You've always been a bit of a wonder on this ship," said Ghaoithe. "Though I'm sure being landlocked for a few days didn't help their enthusiasm for anything new. Give it time and they'll find something else to gossip about."

"Maybe you should discover another mysterious child somewhere."

"Oh, that'd be old news to them within a day. I find relics all the time, but I've never escaped a bullet shot by Jessie Vargas," Ghaoithe chuckled. She knocked on the armor over her chest. "Not without help anyway."

Alex soaked in the languid pace, taking each step through the halls with Ghaoithe to its fullest. Though she now felt at home aboard the ship, Alex rarely had the opportunity to spend time alone with the captain, and Ghaoithe still seemed a mountainous figure to her. The way the captain brushed off her accomplishments as if they were nothing only made them that much more interesting to Alex.

It was not that Alex had not come close to death before. If anything, she'd come much closer to it in her life than most people. Yet, her encounter in Cairo had sparked an alertness that had not existed after animated golems, laser-shooting Osiris drones or a fire in Roanoke. Instead of dreading her fate, she wanted to see what it had in store. She reflected on her time before the *Cloudkicker* and realized that she couldn't remember most of it. Nothing noteworthy remained. She had instead wallowed in her own despair for years, content in allowing life to simply play out. Now that she was through that phase and the reality of her new voyage sunk in, she was resolute in her demand to regain the excitement of living.

Was this the same enthusiasm that had driven Ghaoithe for so long?

Alex shot a sideways glance at her captain. She noticed Ghaoithe smiling at some private thought and could not help but wonder what it was. Despite all they had been through in such a short amount of time, most of their interaction had been largely one-sided. Alex felt no need to hold back her past; she figured the captain had done her research anyway. However, Ghaoithe kept herself locked away in her blue shell. It added to her allure, but Alex wanted in.

"Why yellow?" Alex asked. She leaned a shoulder against the wall and crossed her arms.

The captain halted and arched an eyebrow. "Yellow?"

"Your armor," Alex nodded. She straightened and ran a finger over one of the sigils protecting Ghaoithe's chest. They were not etched as deeply as Alex initially thought and gave off a warm, tingling sensation. She felt Ghaoithe's breath seize for a moment beneath them, uncertain of being willingly touched. "All of the other runes I've seen have been blue," Alex continued. "Why is your armor the only thing to have yellow runes?"

"This was made differently than anything else I know of," Ghaoithe said. She grasped Alex's hand before gently pushing it away. "It'd ruin the fun if I said anything else."

Not one to give up so easily, Alex gave Ghaoithe a playful punch to the shoulder. "Aw come on. Give me something to work with here," she said.

Ghaoithe laughed and shielded her face with her arms, taking a few quick jabs at the air around Alex. "You'll have to knock my secrets out of me, Miss Stirling!"

"Fine! I yield!" Alex giggled as she held her hands up in defeat. "I just don't get you. What are you hiding in that head of yours?"

"Nothing up here but maps and a wicked hot cider recipe," Ghaoithe said, poking her temple with a finger. She put her arm around Alex as they continued down the hall. "Maybe one day I'll let you hear my stories—*all* of my stories—but I'm not ready yet. Those things are in the past. They can't be changed. No use dwelling on them."

"I'll figure you out yet," Alex argued. "You let Fleet and Samir in. There's a whole person inside you somewhere."

Ghaoithe ruffled a hand through Alex's curls. "Let's not go that far. There are things even they don't know. Still, I suppose I may be able to tell those secrets to someone. Someday."

"I'll keep pestering you until you do."

"I would expect nothing less," Ghaoithe said. They stopped as they reached Alex's room. "We have a couple of days before Dilmun. You should enjoy some free time. If you don't mind, I'd like to borrow Excalibur while you do."

"Does this mean I get out of lessons for a bit?" Alex joked.

"You'll have it back by this afternoon," Ghaoithe replied with a wink. "If it lit up in the library like you said, we may need a new approach to how you wield it."

"Suits me. Just don't keep me in the dark about what you find. It's my butt it's protecting," Alex said. She disappeared into her room and reappeared a moment later with the blade snug in its scabbard.

"You'll have a full report," Ghaoithe promised. "And Alex…?"

"Yeah?"

"Thanks for the walk. We should take them more often."

"Any time, Captain."


Knocks rapped Alex's door. She jumped in her seat, her concentration taken away from her studies of the ship's artifact log. Opening the door, Alex was greeted by Damian, Excalibur wrapped in his arms.

"Hey, you get lost in there or something? We've been looking for you." Damian stepped into the door without invitation.

Alex pursed her lips and grabbed her sword from him. "What do you mean? I've been in here reading."

"It's been, like, eight hours since we took off. You missed dinner," Damian said with no small amount of shock. He considered meals an unalterable force in the day.

"I just lost track of time," Alex covered. Her book consumed much of her interest, renewed with what she had learned in Cairo. She absorbed what she could, taking notes with paper and ink Ghaoithe scrounged up for her. Unfortunately, she no longer had a way of keeping track of time since her smartphone was destroyed by golems in Bimini Road. Reminded of this sad truth, she felt as if eons had passed since her run-in with those stone giants.

"Clocks do exist in this world, you know," Damian said. He plopped onto Alex's bed, a sign that he had no intention of leaving quite yet.

For a brief moment, Alex considered throwing him out, but she held her snippy retort. It's not that she didn't like Damian. On the contrary, she found it nice to have someone else from her world to talk to about movies, TV, and other "normal" things. However, he was a ball of energy, and his ideas of boundaries had been skewed after years on the streets of Los Angeles and Lost Earth. She worried about starting conversations with him if she was not in the right mindset lest she end up trapped by an endless stream of words.

"Make yourself at home, then," she eventually relented.

"Ghaoithe didn't find anything, in case you were wondering," Damian said. "On the sword, I mean. She and Kirk gave the thing a pretty solid poking, but whatever you did to light it up wasn't happening."

Alex looked at the sword, perplexed. She figured the captain and Kirk would have the runes known backwards and forwards by the time they were finished.

"Maybe it's just something with those locks?" Alex offered.

Damian shrugged in response. "Could be. I'm not the one to ask. Whatever you did, just be happy it worked."

*You mean whatever Ellie did*, Alex thought to herself. Some part of her knew that the girl played more than a little role in unlocking Excalibur's secret, though she couldn't for the life of her explain how. Resting the scabbard against the side of her desk, a change of subject popped into Alex's head.

"What do you know about the captain, anyway?" Alex asked casually.

Damian straightened and waved his hands. "Whoah! Not touching that one. You do your own dirty work."

Alex rolled her eyes. "I'm not asking for any dirt. I just want to know more about her. Getting her to talk about anything other than the *Cloudkicker* is like opening a soup can with your teeth."

"Why do you want to know about her so badly?"

"I just do, okay?"

Damian eyed Alex warily, but he could not trace any ill intent. Shrugging, he ran a hand through his hair as he sifted through his memory.

"It's not like I know much about her, either. From what I understand, she just kind of appeared with the *Cloudkicker* out of nowhere way before I came around. Just some kid piloting an airship in some fancy armor of hers. No one paid her any mind until she started asking around for a crew. From what I heard, a couple of people had it in their minds to take advantage of her and steal away her ship. She laid 'em out right in front of everyone the moment they tried. No one knew anything about her getup back then, and she could already handle herself in a fight as it was."

"Wait. You mean her bullet-proof armor? I thought that was just another thing with the runes. How would they not have known?" Alex interjected.

Damian said, "That's more of a question for Kirk. I'm hardly a wizard like he is. All I know is that there's still a lot of things sigils can do that people are still learning about. You've seen it, though. It's not like kevlar that just blunts the impact. Any kind of projectile straight-up just bounces right off. Bullets, arrows, even rain. Only way to take her down is to get up close or use something else. Might not mean much in a fistfight or a fire, but it's handy for taking care of old traps in a cave or whatever."

Alex rubbed her forehead. Anyone could tell the captain wasn't normal, even by Lost Earth standards, but learning about Ghaoithe raised more questions than answers.

Damian continued, "Anyway, once she'd strutted her stuff and gained the respect of her sailors, they disappeared for a good few months. Just off the radar, forgotten as anything. Next time they show up on the map, they've discovered Atlantis and gotten the city running again. A little girl finding a city lost to even these Lost Earth people. Rest is history. Now everyone knows that if there's some kind of artifact of legend out there, Ghaoithe's the one that can find it."

"That's it? She just appears out of nowhere and starts finding things?" Alex asked.

Damian thought for a moment, trying to simplify his thoughts for Alex. "Not many know where she comes from, no. Maybe Fleet. But, she's done a lot of good since then so people don't tend to ask. That's why I came to her after Roanoke got burned. Ghaoithe can be tough, but she's fair and does a lot to help people out. She finds these relics and puts them in good places where they can be shared with the community. Museums, philanthropists and whatnot. She thinks people should love the world they live in. Someone once told me she even found the Fountain of Youth, but it didn't make people younger; it just never stopped flowing. So, she had it installed in this tiny village that struggled to find clean drinking water. That's just how she is."

"If she's so popular, why isn't everyone else doing the same thing?"

"Look, Lost Earth isn't that different from the one we left. People get up, go to work, try to make a living in their own way," Damian explained. "Yeah, these legends exist and everyone knows it. Not everyone wants to go to the backwaters of the world for months to dig around in dangerous places looking for them. It's almost like what she does is counter-intuitive to their lives. We live in a reality where people go to great lengths to hide their homes, yet she wants to go out and uncover all of these secrets. Plus, everyone knows her and Osiris got issues. Not too many wanna get caught in that. People want simple around here."

Alex considered Damian's explanation for a moment. She had never really considered Lost Earth in that way before, a light gray not too many shades away from her home in Missouri. When she had been taken aboard the ship, she assumed the entire world was filled with people like Ghaoithe searching for adventure aboard high-flying steel vessels.

Having seen Cairo and Roanoke, landing in foreign locales the world over after the fire, Alex now saw that the Sky Thief was the anomaly. People welcomed her and their world existed in a state where relic hunting was possible, but for the most part, they were just a culture like any other. Sure, runes and some level of ancient magic seemed to exist to make those lives different from her own, but people were ultimately living the only lives they knew.

The revelation left Alex dissatisfied. Nothing in Damian's explanation gave insight into the captain. If anything, it made her mysterious shadow even longer. Alex craved to know about Ghaoithe's armor, where she came from, why Pandora's Box was the tipping point. To the former reporter, unsolved puzzles were mosquitoes buzzing around her head, picking at her until every last one was killed. The closer she got to Ghaoithe, the more buzzing she heard.

Letting out a frustrating groan, Alex said, "Fine! I give up! I'll just wait until she tells me herself. We should just focus on Dilmun for now. You know anything about it?"

Wide-eyed at Alex's outburst, Damian said, "Can't be any worse than when I lived in Compton for three months."

Downing the last tepid sips from her mug, Jessie raised a hand toward her bartender. As he nodded in acknowledgment, she leaned back to enjoy the languid afternoon heat. Closing her eyes, she could almost imagine that she was sitting on a beach in Malibu. A faint breeze tickled her cheeks, and she smiled.

She knew he would be coming. Whether it was in a minute or a day, another dunderheaded goon from Osiris would waltz into her life and send her packing with more orders. She promised herself that no matter how long or short her respite ended up being, she would enjoy the vacation. Deacon no doubt planned to put more pressure on her, but if he truly wished her dead, she would already be entrenched in some hole in the sand, fighting off hordes of men and women in tailored suits.

Instead, she thanked the barkeep as he returned with another chilled mug. She dove into it, relishing the faint taste of honey perfected over centuries. If there was one thing she enjoyed about Egypt, it was their contribution to humanity in the gift of beer. Such charity allowed her to forget, if only momentarily, that she fired the first strike in what would certainly become a drawn out and bloody war.

It was some solace to her that she only started the war rather than end it with one shot. The moment where she missed had replayed continuously in her mind since the end of their chase. Some part of her knew she should be frustrated, but the other parts gleefully accepted her role in upsetting Osiris. It would only be a temporary happiness—Osiris would not allow it to happen again—but she learned to accept her wins where she could.

Whether it was the buzz of alcohol or the schadenfreude towards her masters, her mood remained untempered when a shadow passed through the bright Egyptian sun and sat beside her.

"You were expecting me," Sorin said.

His thick Eastern bloc accent startled Jessie, who was used to the proper, clipped speech of most Osiris soldiers. Jessie turned only enough to register his frame. Sorin picked at his button-up shirt as if unused to the feeling. Dark tattoos crept out from below the neckline. Jessie had expected a suit yet this man acted as if wearing one would kill him. Interesting.

Jessie shrugged. "They had to send someone sometime. Just wish you'd held off another day. Been awhile since I've had some of Cairo's specialty."

Sorin said nothing for a moment. He waved a finger at the bartender, who returned swiftly with another fresh mug. The Osiris operative took a deep swig and wiped his mouth with his arm.

"You do not seem afraid for someone close to having a price on her head," he said.

At this, Jessie barked out a laugh. "Hon, I've known Deacon's reputation long enough to understand that if I was marked, he wouldn't leave me alive long enough to sell for much."

Sorin nodded as he hunched over his beer. "Then you know what I must do here."

"Don't worry. I'm not planning on putting up much of a fight."

"He would have believed you more if you had not missed."

The warning hung in the air for a moment, neither side willing to give. Jessie finally turned and looked at the newest lackey sent to be her watchdog. He certainly checked off the lunker stereotype she expected, but there was something more just beneath his surface. It lurked in his over-tense shoulders, his eyes that fixated on things as though they were draining the forces out of his prey. He was a pretty boy soldier, but Jessie could not let her guard down.

Sorin ignored Jessie's observations. Emptying his mug, he threw a few coins onto the table.

"So why did you miss?" he asked. The question felt oddly genuine. Unused to curiosity among Deacon's guard, Jessie was taken aback.

"Your guess is as good as mine," Jessie said after a moment of thought. "Maybe it was the girl dropping her purse. Maybe it was a brief moment of conscience of my part. I'm just as new to this kind of situation as your company."

Sorin gave a haughty snort. "I imagine it must feel strange for the Desert Siren to miss."

Jessie rolled her eyes and grunted in disgust. "Don't call me that. It's a dumb nickname."

Sorin stared at her for a moment, soaked up every sweaty inch of her, and returned to his glass. As a new round of drinks arrived, Sorin said. "Still, you should not have missed. It was a dangerous thing, whatever made you do it."

Jessie leaned back and stretched her long legs. The humidity within the tavern bore down upon them, and she unbuttoned an extra button of her blouse. She took great care to watch Sorin, and frowned when his eyes did not so much as flicker at her. This was not a man with vices to easily exploit. At least not with looks alone.

"You've been going at that captain for a long while now. She must have you really bugged out," Jessie said.

Sorin shook his head. "It is not her we are worried about. Ghaoithe is predictable and hard-headed. Her armor poses a problem, but we can move past that. It is the blonde girl, Alex, we need gone," he said.

"Deacon made that quite clear," Jessie said. She narrowed her eyes at the hound beside her. "What is it with her that's so important?"

If Sorin was under orders to keep quiet, he either didn't know about them or didn't care. "She is an outlier. Very smart girl, but in over her head. She makes Ghaoithe excited, unpredictable. The captain would not continue without her. We want Ghaoithe to crawl back to her old life out of our hair. We will, I think it is said, to 'put out the fire.'"

The news troubled Jessie. She could hardly call herself a moral person, not after all she had done, but she at least attempted to find some meaning in her work. If the blonde girl were some logistical mastermind or an arms dealer supplying the Sky Thief, Jessie could do her work cleanly. But just a normal girl, a pawn in some grand chess match between Deacon and Ghaoithe? Jessie threw back her drink in one gulp and wiped her mouth with her sleeve.

"You are not comfortable with this," Sorin noted.

"This business is never comfortable."

Sorin stared at Jessie again for a moment, analyzing her with more gears running upstairs than she wanted to admit he had. Finally, he turned back to his glass.

"That I can drink to," he said. "Do not rush for now. We will leave in the morning."

# XI

In Alex's tome of artifacts and legends, Dilmun's page was surprisingly sparse. In discussing this problem with Ghaoithe, the captain apparently decided that the ancient city was already common knowledge in Lost Earth and thus had no need for a detailed entry. What history Alex managed to pick up described Dilmun as both a paradise along a desert coast and a toxic haven for illicit rogues. At one point, it was believed to be the birthplace of humanity, the real Garden of Eden.

Having already discovered the Garden of Eden below the Caribbean Sea, Alex remained skeptical of Dilmun's promises.

Like other cities of Lost Earth, Dilmun hid from view. As the airship slowed to coasting speed, the captain ordered an approach towards two rocky outcrops that jut above the beachside bluffs. They circled the pillars counterclockwise twice before charging between them from the oceanside. As they passed the threshold, the wings of the *Cloudkicker* reacted in a brilliant display of light, and the desert before them turned into an expansive city as if turned on by a switch. It spanned for miles away into the desert, a collection of low buildings, palm trees, and people moving like blood cells through the grid of streets below.

As the *Cloudkicker* glided into visible range of Dilmun's airship docking spire, Ghaoithe waved off any attempts at stealth. The *Cloudkicker* hitched defiantly in plain view, sun glinting off its silver hull. Though other ramshackle ships clung to the tower's side, Ghaoithe's dwarfed them in style and presence.

"You aren't worried about Osiris knowing we're here?" Alex asked. Despite being among friends, she couldn't help but glance into darker corners of the bridge as if the corporation watched them from afar.

Fleet grunted and said, "They know we're here, and they ain't gettin' closer without a larger force. Dilmun's full of rotten dealers, but those dealers are protective of the status quo. They won't let the city slip into the hands of Deacon and his goons."

Until that point, Fleet refused to offer Dilmun any praise. Alex did not want to underestimate a city that even Osiris dared not trifle with, but Fleet's warnings left Alex more curious than afraid. As the crew prepared to disembark, Alex stood with her nose almost pressed against the glass windows of the bridge in an attempt to peek at their newest adventure.

"It doesn't seem that terrible. It looks like Cairo, but greener," Alex said.

"Ya almost got shot in Cairo," Fleet reminded her. Alex quieted. She solemnly grabbed her bag and tightened Excalibur's straps around her chest.

As they exited the tower, Alex braced herself for blistering desert heat only to be met with cool, salted breeze from the ocean. The docking station opened to a wide avenue. Palms stretched up into the heavens at various places along its length. Dockworkers strolled about in a parade of tattoos and cigarette smoke. The *Cloudkicker* landed near the southern edge of the city, a fair distance away from the downtown trading district, but even here a few scattered vendors welcomed them to Dilmun with scents of cinnamon and cardamom under brightly colored banners.

"It's so pretty!" gasped Ellie as she tugged on Damian's hand.

Damian grinned at her. "It is! It reminds me of back home. Feels like Santa Monica without the spray tans."

"And Venice and Malibu and Laguna…" continued Ellie in a sing-song. Alex raised an eyebrow at Damian, who returned a confused shrug.

As they made their way down the avenue, more bits of life sprung up around them. The squat warehouses turned into blocky homesteads with clothes drying on wires tied between balconies. Shop windows smelling of coffee and breads appeared at street level. Most of them had cracked windows, their walls chipped at the corners, but they were nonetheless filled with morning patrons going about their business. A few awestruck eyes turned to Ghaoithe as she passed.

The captain halted at one vendor without warning. She rushed over and left her crew behind for a few moments. They watched curiously as she haggled back and forth with the owner. A moment later, she returned with a box of round, flattish fruits.

"Dates," she said through a full mouth. She handed the box to Alex.

"They're… chewy," Alex said. The fruit rolled about in her mouth, slightly sweet with the faintest touch of honey.

"Just watch fer the seed," Fleet said as he popped one in his mouth and passed the box along. Ellie picked one up and warily bit at an edge. Her eyes went wide, and soon the date was gone.

As the group continued on, Alex noticed the diversity of the city. More people darted about the streets the further they walked, and everyone was slightly different. Dilmun truly was a trading post, with merchants and visitors speaking in every manner of language. She heard English, Italian, French, Arabic, and several others far older than any of those. Their wares, too, ran the gamut of style and substance, from handmade earthen plates to lavish jewelry. The only common thread among the people were the sigils that lit their booths, heated their pots, and brought water to the desert. In almost every building, the touch of sigil-light radiated in some fashion.

"Probably counterfeits," Fleet muttered when Alex chanced upon a set of golden necklaces at one stand.

Alex scoffed back at him. "This place isn't as bad as you said it was. It's no worse than Cairo or even St. Louis," she said.

"We're in a busy area. Just watch yer back as we go on," Fleet said.

Alex huffed in response but declined an argument. For her, the only trouble she could think of was finding the House of Scribes they searched for. Dilmun was lively, but it was certainly old and most of the buildings would have blended together if not for the establishments within. No doubt it could hold an ancient sect of writers, but knowing where was a question entirely up to Ghaoithe.

The captain led them through the streets as if by instinct, a bloodhound in search of good hospitality. They turned off of the main alley as the airship's tower drew farther and farther into the distance. Here, the streets narrowed, and the sun had a harder time squeezing between buildings to reach the ground. There were still storefronts, but they were not as clean-cut as those on the avenue. The cracks on windows were not offset with vigilant dustings by their owners, and an aura of dirt covered their glass. What few other travelers the group saw in the streets kept their heads down in passing. The only eyes that touched the group did not do so with innocence. Now and then, the crew passed even narrower alleys, dark even as the sun rose to its peak.

Alex was sure the change in atmosphere was her own imagination taking over. Part of her was excited to see the real city of Dilmun away from the market shops and wide avenues. She had trained for this kind of excursion, so long ago, as a journalist. To dig deep into the grime of civilization and find the real stories beyond touristy vistas and trinkets made for the illusion of experiencing a place.

None of the others seemed all that bothered, either. Ghaoithe continued at a leisurely pace. Even Ellie continued to chirp at Damian. Only Fleet glanced about every few moments, and he had done so since they landed anyway so he didn't count.

Out of one doorstep came a sharp whistle. "Oy, you's a perky one ain't ya?" said a voice.

Alex did not acknowledge the catcall. It was a small thing, nothing she had not heard before, but it raised the hairs on the back of her neck in electric warning all the same. Maybe Fleet did have at least a little bit of a point, after all.

"What exactly are we looking for?" Damian asked. Ellie now sat on his shoulders. If her weight was any strain, he showed no sign of it, grinning as she played with his shoulder-length hair.

Ghaoithe said, "A hotel. Roy went on ahead to pull some strings with an old acquaintance."

Alex scanned the neighborhood. A few eyes glinted at her from inside darkened shops. This was not a neighborhood for a swanky resort.

The hackles on the back of Alex's neck did not calm as they walked. She found herself looking into every doorframe, every window for another voice to call out. A presence burned into her from behind, a laser pinprick of heat that would not turn off. The shadows around the group were silent as they passed, yet they were not alone.

"It's the Table. Pay them no mind," Ghaoithe said. She continued to pop dates into her mouth like they were Easter chocolates.

"The Table?" Alex asked, at once both confused and relieved by the distraction of conversation.

Ghaoithe nodded. Her eye darted to an alley to her right as they passed. For a second, Alex thought she saw a fleeting something within, but she blinked and it was gone.

"The Table is, well, not quite a government. Not in any way you know of," Ghaoithe explained. "It's a group of three. They're trade brokers that keep this city running. Nothing comes in or out without them noticing. You get used to being watched after a while."

Alex did not think she would get used to it. She rubbed her neck and tried to shrink beside Ghaoithe's frame. "Sounds an awful lot like Osiris to me," she observed.

Ghaoithe chuckled. "Don't worry. The Table are no friends of Osiris. They're just pragmatic. Lost Earth has needs, too, and the Table sees to it that they are fulfilled."

"You'll excuse me if I don't quite trust a shadow government right now," Alex scoffed.

Fleet's voice rumbled behind her. "I don't trust 'em either, but we can use friends where we can right now. It's everyone else in Dilmun ya have to worry about."

While far from praise, any admittance from Fleet about the Table's worth served to ease Alex's mind for the moment. She still leered at empty alleyways and rubbed the back of her neck from time-to-time, but she did her best to ignore it as her captain advised.

Their journey through the back streets of the city ended with another wide avenue. Alex let out a breath at the return of crowds and bright sunlight. She scanned the skyline to get her bearings, but the buildings and people obscured any sign of the landing tower behind them. The only place of note waited across the avenue. There stood a large structure with sigils that looped above a wide entryway set with blue and white tiles. Stone columns lined an outdoor patio. A few visitors sat there, their clothes echoes of their respective homelands. Men in crisp white jackets and trilbies read newspapers beside cups of espresso. A few women chatted amongst themselves, some behind burqas and others swathed in low-cut designer tunics. No one paid the approaching group any mind beyond quick glances of inspection.

A man leaned against the doorway, a rolled up paper tucked beneath his arm and long cigarette billowing from the midst of his thick beard. Upon seeing the captain's armor, he tossed his cigarette to the ground and rubbed it with his heel. He extended a hand.

"You must be Captain... ah, you'll excuse me. I am not so good with an Irish tongue," he said.

"*Gwee-heh Lynn-she*," the captain pronounced with a rehearsed cadence. She accepted the man's handshake.

"I will not remember that. I will call you Captain," said the man.

He turned with a wave of his arm. "Come. Welcome to my inn."

The interior of the inn was no less subdued. It was well-adorned, with wrought bronze lattices along the walls and a clean tile floor. But gone were the raucous discussions Alex had become used to in such establishments of Lost Earth. Those who sat in the concourse rose their voices above no more than a low murmur. The diners in the cafe to the right were no louder, content in their news and coffee. In a darkened corner, a small group sat around a tall hookah that filled the air with a heady, sweetly fragrant smoke.

The man, whom Alex assumed was the innkeeper, brought her group to the small reception desk. He took a long quill pen out of its holder, scribbled a note on a piece of paper, and stuck the paper into a worn red binder. Then, he opened a drawer that jingled with the rustling of keys and handed one to Ghaoithe.

"I have made your arrangements with Roy. You have the fifth floor. He is waiting for you there," said the man unceremoniously.

Alex gawked at him. "We have the entire floor?"

The innkeeper gave her a bemused, pitiful look. "There are certain arrangements among innkeepers' circles. Roy and I are no strangers." He said nothing more and dismissed them with a flicker of a match as he lit another cigarette before returning to his post outside.

The innkeeper was right that Roy awaited their arrival. As they opened the thick door to the fifth floor, his deep bass called from within, "'Bout time! I was just about to leave a note for you."

He stood in a bright sitting room. On either side, two doorways presumably contained the bedrooms. Sheer pink curtains fluttered gently by an open walk-out window that led to a small balcony, the noises of the streets adding ambiance from below. The suite was cheerful and airy, a complete contrast from the shadiness of the lobby areas. The creme walls were well worn, but not uncared for, and Alex could almost daydream that she had arrived in the hillsides of Tuscany had it not been for the outside air that the single ceiling fan did little to abate. It spun lazily, runes glittering across each blade, to no avail.

"If I'd known you had these kind of connections, I would have called you for a vacation years ago," Alex said.

Roy crossed his arms. "So, you're saying my tavern wasn't to your liking?" he said with false exasperation.

"Don't be too impressed with it quite yet," Ghaoithe interjected. "We aren't staying long for now. Where were you headed, Roy?"

"Back to the ship to help Kirk and put out feelers. We'll be back late after you're all done with the Scribes."

Ghaoithe nodded. She looked at the others. "Let's not waste any time, then. Drop what you don't need and we'll head to the House."

Damian grunted. Ellie clung to his back, her eyes fluttering heavily. She let out a long yawn. "I think that probably counts us out, then," Damian said.

"I'd rather not go without Ellie there. This whole thing concerns her," Ghaoithe said.

"Let the child sleep, Lynn. Damian and I can keep after her. Whatever the Scribes tell ya ain't gonna change whether she's there or not," Fleet said. He patted her hard on the back before launching himself into a thick armchair next to the patio window. "Besides, the old and the young tire easily. We get privileges."

Ghaoithe narrowed her eye in judgment but stopped short of reprimanding him. She shook her head and looked to Alex for support. "You aren't going to take part in this mutiny, are you?"

For a moment, Alex considered it. The room was exceptionally pleasant after such a long walk. The thoughts of what beds awaited around the corners of those doors called to her with soft sirens' songs. However, the weight of the book in her handbag balanced the scales in the other direction, and curiosity won out.

"I don't think I'd forgive myself if I missed the House of Scribes," Alex said.

Ghaoithe roared with appreciation. "There's a right adventurer!" she said. The captain put her fists on her hips and faced the others. "Don't think you lazy oafs can claim the good beds while we're out."

As Alex and Ghaoithe made their way to leave, Fleet and Damian cast short waves goodbye, their eyes already half closed and lulled to rest by the heat of the sands.

# XII

From the outside, the House of Scribes left little mark on its neighborhood. If anything, the location worried Alex as Ghaoithe led her down a tight alleyway barely wider than her shoulders. The stone walls they passed cracked with age. None of the warped doors set in them gave a clue to their inhabitants. If Osiris truly was in the city already, Alex and Ghaoithe would have no chance of escaping should they attack, doomed to make a final stand in the shambles of a forgotten avenue.

"You're sure we're in the right spot? How long has it been since you were here? Hardly seems like the place for a school," Alex asked if for no other reason than to calm her own nerves.

Ghaoithe looked over her shoulder at Alex with a reassuring grin. "Don't tell me you're getting yellow over a few librarians," she said.

"It's not that. What if Deacon beat us to them and are just waiting? What if the Scribes can't read the book at all? We're hinging a lot of bets on one dark alleyway, and you aren't nervous about that at all?" said Alex.

"I am nervous, but not about Osiris or the Scribes," Ghaoithe said.

The admission fell flat on Alex. Ghaoithe walked with the same confident demeanor as always. However, the unabashed persona that once drew Alex towards the Sky Thief grew increasingly frustrating as the stakes of their mission grew higher.

"Then what?" tempted Alex. When the captain did not stop walking, Alex raised her voice, "Ghaoithe, can you even try to be real with me for once?"

Ghaoithe did stop. After a pause, she turned to Alex, her eye cast downward. She cleared her throat.

"I'm sorry, Alex," said Ghaoithe. "I've been so lost in trying to figure out our next steps that I forgot this is still new to you. I'm not ignoring you. I promise."

Alex sighed and crossed her arms. She stared at Ghaoithe until the captain met her eyes. She sighed again and walked over to Ghaoithe. "I know you're not ignoring me, but you are damn hard to read. You go from giddy one moment to saying you're nervous the next. You can be open with me. I just wish you'd take advantage of that sometimes," Alex said.

Ghaoithe smiled. She ruffled Alex's blonde curls and leaned back against the stone alley. "You're right. Look, I get like this near the end of a find is all. I'm sure Fleet can tell you all about it. When your whole life is relic hunting, actually finding an artifact feels kind of like the day after your birthday. You spend all this time looking for something and then you find it and it's over. You go right back where you started."

"You're not worried we'll get there and find out the book is a bust?"

Ghaoithe shook her head. "I don't go to the Scribes unless I have to. They don't always agree to help, but they have never been wrong. Regardless of what the secret to all of this is, the only thing left to do after leaving that building is beat Deacon to the finish line. That's what makes me nervous."

Alex joined Ghaoithe against the wall and rested her head against the captain's arm. "Well, if it makes you feel any better, I'm looking forward to that adventure. Thank you for telling me."

They stood there a moment, looking up at the line of blue slipping through the rooftops above them. Finally, the captain leaned forward and thumbed down the alley. "Let's get that leg of the road started then," she said, beaming once again.

When they at last came to the entrance of the House of Scribes, Alex could not tell the difference between it or any of the other doors on the street. Ghaoithe raised a hand and knocked gently on the faded emerald paint. From the other side, muffled movement answered their greeting. The door cracked open, and a long, pointed face glared out at them. Upon seeing Ghaoithe's armor, he nodded and opened the door fully.

"It has been some time, Sky Thief," the man said plainly. "Come in. I expect you'll be wanting to see Scholar Orland."

"Always such a warm welcome, Burt. Nice to see you again, too," Ghaoithe said.

As they crossed the threshold into the House of Scribes, Alex's body went numb. It was a similar feeling to her legs falling asleep, but it rippled through her entirety for only a moment before it passed and left her rubbing her arms in the inner chamber. Alex gasped at the reason for the strange sensation. So large was the interior of the building, she thought she had stepped into another dimension of sorts. Sigils covered every inch of the walls that rose far above them, lighting the House with their glow. Chamber after chamber stretched beyond the entryway. Scholars passed through the halls, entering and exiting countless doorways along their length, hands occupied by tomes of every size and shape. Alex half-expected them to be monk-like, thin and garbed in brownish robes, but most were dressed no differently than she was with heavy bags full of texts at their sides. Wherever the walls lacked doors, shelves piled with books stood in their place.

"How? Where?" Alex stammered. Their greeter, Burt, peered down at her.

"I don't suppose I would have been so lucky for Ms. Loinsigh to have explained our work?" Burt said with a grimace.

Alex shook her head. Though Burt was lanky and hardly built for strength, Alex felt every bit of her small stature beneath his gaze.

"I see. In that case, the House of Scribes is the utmost center of ancient knowledge. That includes the language of the sigils. Creating such a place is quite simple for the scholars. We have learned everything the runes can offer society," said Burt. He turned to Ghaoithe, his eyes lingering on her before moving towards the hall of doors. "Well, almost everything."

Ghaoithe cackled and clasped Alex on the back. "Don't worry about ol' Burt here. He's always got his nose in the air, but he's right about the sigils. You know, this is where Kirk trained when he was getting started."

"Kirk? Here? I'm sure that went over well," said Alex. She attempted to catch the words in the book of a passing scholar but she only glimpsed a colorful drawing before it disappeared among the crowd.

"Yes. Scholar Kirk was a prime example of wasted potential," said Burt with a sneer. Ghaoithe snorted in an attempt to stifle her laughter.

They turned down another long corridor lined with polished grey stone. As they traveled farther in, the sigil lights faded. The stone walls turned increasingly worn and rugged as oil lamps appeared along the path to replace the dimmed runes. Alex almost believed she traversed the halls of a medieval castle, and she was not far from the truth.

At the end of the hall, a spiral path wound downward, flickers of light casting shadows towards what lie beneath. Burt stopped, bowed curtly, and left the women on their own.

"Lively fellow, isn't he?" Alex said once he was out of earshot.

"Ah, don't pay him any mind. He puts up with a lot acting as caretaker here. He's actually got a heart of gold. Well, maybe bronze," Ghaoithe said.

They descended the staircase. At the bottom, they arrived at a small chamber, bright and warm under the lantern lights. Like the rest of the House, books covered every inch of the walls and floors. Only a single piece of furniture sat in the middle of the room, a long flat table occupied by a turtle-like man hunched over a scroll. At the sound of footsteps, he raised his head and looked at Ghaoithe and Alex with milky, glassy eyes. Alex gasped before she could stop herself. Ghaoithe nudged her with an elbow. The Scholar pursed his lips.

"I guess I should not have expected better manners from Ghaoithe Loinsigh," said Orland.

"You'd be disappointed if I actually had any, and you know it," said Ghaoithe. At this, Scholar Orland's stern expression turned into as much of a wry smile as the folds of his skin would allow. He turned to Alex, his blind eyes boring into her with curiosity.

"You brought a friend, I see. A Miss... Alexandra Alexis Stirling? Of New Delta, Missouri?" he said.

Alex's jaw dropped. "How did you...?" she stammered.

"Your captain enjoys using me to play tricks on her companions," Orland said with a wave of the hand. Alex heard Ghaoithe chortling softly next to her. "I am blind, yes, but in the realm of ancient texts, there is more than one way too see. Knowledge is an aura, and those of us who have spent our lives among it have learned to sense it in other ways. Now, what do you have buried in that purse of yours, child?"

Still dazed, Alex took several seconds to register Orland's request. She hesitantly pulled the book from the Library of Alexandria out of her satchel. Flipping it to the painting of Ellie, she gave it to Orland's outstretched hand, half expecting him to stare at it without recognition.

"Where did you find such a magnificent manuscript? It has been quite some time since this language has seen the light of day," he said as he drew the book across the table. His hands, thin and pale from beneath overlarge sleeves, explored the pages with precise determination.

"The Library of Alexandria. We were hoping you could translate it for us," said Alex.

"The Library of... oh my. What the House would give to pick at your mind, but I sense you do not have the time for such luxuries," said Orland with an earnest tone of awe. As he worked on the pages before him, Alex worried he would be unable to read before him, but he took only a second before he continued, "Ah, you bring me the story of Hope."

From beside Alex, Ghaoithe unleashed a string of curses. Alex wondered if the captain had lost her mind.

"Of course! I should have known! How could I be so blind... no offense, Scholar," Ghaoithe uttered once she calmed down. The Scholar shrugged off the phrase and leaned onto his desk to stare at Ghaoithe with bemusement.

Alex looked between them. She slowly raised her hand as if to draw her teacher's attention in grade school. "I don't get it. What am I missing?" she asked.

Ghaoithe paced back and forth, rubbing her chin between her fingers. "Hope. It makes complete sense now. Ellie is Hope. Elpis."

"It's been a long time since I've taken Greek Mythology. What's that mean?"

Scholar Orland cleared his throat. "The gods left Pandora the source of all the world's evils, which she then opened and unleashed. That much is commonly known. However, left behind in the urn was a single sprite, Elpis, the embodiment of Hope. I assume this is the 'Ellie' your captain refers to."

After a moment, Alex's eyes widened. She turned to Ghaoithe, practically screaming, "And we missed this? How could we miss something so obvious?!"

"How could we not, Alex? I have never, in all of my expeditions, discovered an artifact that was a living, breathing person," said Ghaoithe. "There are signs of the gods all around us, hidden in these relics and lost places, but I've never actually *met* one of them!"

By now, Alex joined Ghaoithe's pace, lost as the wheels turned in her own head. "It fits, though. Her powers, her understanding of things she shouldn't. Any time we were in trouble—truly in trouble— she activated her powers or whatever. When we were hopeless and had no other way out. In China, in the alley in Cairo. It all makes sense. She came to us in times of need to give us herself," she said.

"If it was that simple, why did she not stop Vargas from shooting you in the first place or keep the *Cloudkicker* from crashing? Is it because we were still able to get out of those situations on our own?" continued Ghaoithe. "And why help us? How come Osiris wasn't able to control her?"

As the two theorized on Ellie's powers, Scholar Orland paid them little attention. Gnarled fingers grazed over the book's pages with an experienced, feathered touch. Through whatever means he read the pages, he grew somber with each word.

"There's more," he said in a commanding tone practiced over the ages. Ghaoithe and Alex stopped their musings and looked at him.

"More? Does it mention the location of the urn?" Ghaoithe said. Her voice trembled with anticipation. Alex had never seen her so excitable.

However, Orland shook his head. "This text is not as I thought. It is more than just the story of Pandora's Box and Elpis. You claim to have Hope, this Ellie, with you right now?"

Ghaoithe nodded.

"Then you must keep her safe at all costs," continued Scholar Orland.

At his warning, Ghaoithe's ecstasy vanished, replaced with a grim, even disappointed, businesswoman. "Tell us the bad news," she said.

Scholar Orland cleared his throat. "This book does not come from traditional writers. It appears to have been written by a sect who believed in the literal truths of the gods. Predecessors of our own society, so to speak. Here, they go into length about the preservation of Elpis, her location and the means to find her carefully guarded and passed down through generations of the chosen."

Alex tugged at a forlorn curl as she thought. "A sect? Like a secret society?"

"Not much we can do to save them now. What I want to know is why they went through such lengths to hide Ellie in the first place," said Ghaoithe.

"The reason for their stewardship is written here, though the specifics are not given," explained Orland. "According to the keepers of the child, the evils of Pandora's Box were unleashed upon the world by a mortal, but Elpis holds the power to force them to return to their original state. The keepers, understanding what mortals had become since the unboxing, vowed to prevent this from happening.

"However, not all among them agreed. Dissenters rose as their empire began to fall through lavish excess and foreign invaders. This rebel faction blamed society's hubris on the sins unlocked by Pandora. In their eyes, these sins distracted humanity and caused man to stray further away from the Pantheon of Creation. Knowing of the power of Elpis, an internal strife ensued as the keepers were split between those who wished to protect her and those who wished to use her power to return humanity to its traditional, pristine state. It seems as though the protectors lost and were forced to move Ellie and their own whereabouts as they were hunted throughout the ages."

"That explains the coordinates in my old movie poster. They must have been hunted by Osiris for centuries. With their numbers almost gone, they hid their information as best as they could before the last of their numbers were found. To think they survived until just recently...," Alex said.

The two women froze. Though they did not say it, they knew the other thought of the same thing: the city beneath Bimini, devoid of all of the wonders of man. Deacon's praise of that Eden, with its lack of sins and temptations, came crashing back into their minds.

"Scholar, you said the keepers believed Elpis has the power to return the world's evils back to Pandora's Box? How much truth do you think is in that book?" Ghaoithe asked, her voice wavering.

The scholar sat silently for a moment. Finally, he softly responded, "If all you have said about the girl is true, it is more a likelihood than not."

Ghaoithe's hand fell on Alex's shoulder as she tried to steady herself, though Alex was in no better shape upon hearing the admission. Orland did not share their experiences since finding Ellie, but the gravity of their silence conveyed all it needed to. He lowered his over-sized head into his hands.

"I do not know if what you think is true," he continued. "Osiris is very old. It is possible they absorbed the radical idealists as they have so many others through time. It is also possible this Deacon alone has the lineage of the rebellious faction. Whether their current leader is a member of the old sect or not does not matter. He knows of Ellie's power and must not be allowed to use it at any cost."

From the stairwell, shouts echoed into their chamber, followed by clapping footsteps almost falling over themselves to reach the bottom. Alex and Ghaoithe turned and gripped their weapons.

From the entry way, Damian tumbled headfirst onto the floor. Alex called to him and rushed to his side. His face was cut and bruised, blood matted in his hair. He grabbed Alex's shirt and stood. "Osiris. They found us. Fleet and I fought but... they took Ellie."

Ghaoithe rushed to the door. She halted just long enough to turn and ask, "Where are they headed?"

"To the eastern gate. Word's already starting to get out that they're in the city. You might catch them. You *have* to catch them!"

Ghaoithe only heard "eastern gate" and she was gone.

# XIII

Ghaoithe clawed her way through the crowd. She silently cursed her size. Others may have marveled at her ability to navigate ancient passages despite her stature, but tombs were easy because they were stationary, predictable. Humans were fluid, and even an ox can drown in a flood. With Ellie on the line, though, she had no choice but to be brutish towards the poor merchants in her path, no easy task at the peak of Dilmun's trading hours.

*East gate. It's the closest to the inn,* Ghaoithe thought as she moved among the throngs. With that knowledge, she held one advantage over the kidnappers: The House of Scribes planted her firmly between the inn and the gate. She prayed her starting point could overcome the crowds and Osiris's head start.

As she reached the main thoroughfare to the gate, Ghaoithe scanned the crowd for a clue. A flash of white hair, modern clothes... anything out of place in the trader's mecca. No such luck.

*Come on, Ellie. Make some noise.*

From just out of sight of the main street, she heard it. It wasn't the calls of a young girl, but it was just as foreign to Lost Earth: the revving of a diesel engine behind a row of squat buildings to her left.

Ghaoithe charged.

She entered a narrow alleyway that rounded into a dead-end loading area for several of the buildings. There, a squat cargo van with an olive canvas over the bed idled. No sooner did Ghaoithe plow into the area did the truck roar to life. Shouts from inside ordered the truck to leave. A burst of automatic gunfire exploded just as Ellie's wide stare met her own from beneath the flaps of the canvas.

Between the captain and the truck, two Osiris hitmen stayed behind. Over their robed disguises, they brandished modern assault rifles.

Ghaoithe scowled and drew her rapier. "I don't have time for this. Move," she threatened.

The two hitmen looked at each other through their masks and shrugged. They opened fire.

Ghaoithe ran towards them. The bullets bounced off her armor as the sigils within it flashed with each strike. She darted for the right gunman first and was upon him before he even realized his bullets were useless. She aimed for his hands with a quick strike of her rapier. The gunman cried out in pain and doubled over.

From behind Ghaoithe, the second man dropped his gun the moment she entered brawling range. He jumped onto her back and threw his arms around her neck in an attempt at a choke hold. It worked for about two seconds before Ghaoithe did the only thing she could think of: she fell.

As she landed on top of her assailant, she heard a crack and moan. She rolled off the mercenary, who clutched his lower leg as he rocked back and forth on the ground. From around the corner, surprised shrieks echoed through the alleyway as Osiris's truck made its way through a crowd unused to motorized vehicles. Ghaoithe returned her rapier to her sash and started to pursue Ellie when a blow to her back knocked her to the ground.

The first man, his hand punctured and bleeding, stood with the barrel of his gun toward her.

"I dunno what magic yer using, ye blue witch, but yer not gettin' th' girl," he said as he flipped the gun around to point the barrel at the captain just a few feet away. He pulled the trigger. As the bullets bounced away, Ghaoithe's fist filled his vision. He hit the ground cold.

In the main thoroughfare, the truck's presence still lingered. The crowd chattered amongst each other and pointed towards the entry gate. Above their heads, Ghaoithe saw a trail of sand kicked up as Ellie's kidnappers made their way into the dunes beyond the city. They moved slowly, but their head start kept Ghaoithe from chasing them on foot. She looked around, desperate for any hope of catching Osiris while they were still within sight.

Her answer came in the form of hooves. Just inside the city walls, a makeshift corral had been constructed for an equestrian auction. Several horses jaunted about in the open space while trainers moved them one at a time to a crude stable area. All of the horses were impeccable, their taut muscles hindered by the surrounding fence. One of them, a Godolphin with slick nut-brown fur, whinnied at Ghaoithe as she approached it. She slowed as she approached and allowed it to stare her down with curious eyes. This was the one. A round of shouts came from the stables as she unlatched the gate and climbed onto the horse's back.

*Sorry. Gotta save the world*, she thought as she charged out of the city gate in a blur of brown and blue.

Ghaoithe blazed forward on the steed as though it somehow understood that this was its destiny. In the distance, she spotted the Osiris cargo van as it rushed into the desert, barely more than a speck in a shimmering horizon. The high dunes surrounding Dilmun offered some resistance to the modern vehicle, but if they managed to pass just a few short miles more, Ellie would disappear into the flat expanses beyond.

The cargo van gained form as Ghaoithe closed the gap on thundering hooves. The olive truck roared as it tried to escape over the loose sand surrounding the city, its canopy top flapping violently.

From within its bed, Ghaoithe spotted armored figures moving about, unsure of how to take on the Sky Thief's armor directly. Ellie's head popped up over the truck's gate in a flash of white. She reached out a hand as two guards struggled to pull her away.

"Ghaoithe! They're hurting me!" she cried. Her pale face was reddened and glistened under the harsh desert sun. She was close enough that Ghaoithe could smell the truck's exhaust.

"Keep fighting! I've got you!" Ghaoithe called. She inched closer and reached out for Ellie's hand.

The van lurched forward as it topped another dune. Ellie bounced within the bed and vanished behind the gate. As it hit the downslope of sand, the truck pulled away from Ghaoithe's horse. She looked up. A flat expanse of salted earth filled the horizon. Only a a few minute dunes blocked the expanse. Bearing down, Ghaoithe willed her steed to gain as much ground as it could, its breaths chugging like the steam of a locomotive. For a moment, she believed she was about to catch up. Until she heard the sound behind her.

It started small, a rhythmic bass that blended in with the plodding of the horse's gallop. As the sound gained form, it pounded Ghaoithe's body with tremors that rumbled with each beat. She turned around. A sleek, ebony helicopter pursued her, trapped her in a vice between the truck and Dilmun.

Jessica Vargas peered through her scope. Ghaoithe was almost back on top of the truck, but the salt flats offered permanent escape if they could hold her off for just a few more moments.

"Bring it around! I can't get a good shot from this angle!" Jessie called into her headset. The force of the turn tightened the straps that held her to her seat, and she fought off another wave of nausea. Once it ended, the helicopter's open side made for a clear window to her target directly below.

As she leaned into the scope again, Jessie slowed her breaths as best she could. Jitters about flying would work against her if she let them. She thought only about what she saw ahead, the feel of cool gunmetal against her heated skin, her finger waiting for just the right moment to strike. She would not miss a second time.

Below, Ghaoithe drew her sword as she came within jumping distance of the truck. Another flash of white hair from inside. For the briefest of moments, Jessie wondered what would happen to the girl, what horrors she would inflict upon an innocent child by acting as an accomplice to Osiris. She cursed herself for allowing herself to think of such things at a critical moment, but she also cursed her own future.

Ghaoithe raised herself out of the saddle, nearly ready to leap into the truck for a fight. She was immune to whatever Jessie shot at her, and she knew it. As long as she donned her armor, bullets remained a useless tactic to kill her.

The horse, however...

Jessie's shot echoed through the sands. She held firm against the recoil that wracked her shoulder. She did not open her eyes.

Ghaoithe body flew from the saddle as the horse collapsed underneath her. She hit the sand, tumbled, and laid motionless. When she had the bearings to lift herself up, the truck was already out of reach. From within its canopy, Ellie screamed for help to no avail. As her voice faded into the flats, it was Ghaoithe's turn to scream.

Their mission accomplished, Jessie and the helicopter turned and headed back the way it came, leaving Ghaoithe to stumble back on foot to Dilmun.

# XIV

Ghaoithe trudged down the main thoroughfare into Dilmun. For the first time in her life she hated the sun that shot pain through her eye. The crowds made her dizzy. Osiris's helicopter mobilized the city and sent its citizens into a coordinated panic. A normal person may not have seen it, but Ghaoithe did: the faster hustle of traders, the looks that darted her way, the hastily written notes passed from hand to hand in urgent relay. It made her head spin, as though the vertigo that wracked her every step wasn't enough of an insult after Ellie disappeared into the desert flats. The only solace she had was the wide berth given to her every step. Just as news of the helicopter ignited the city, so had news of the Sky Thief's pursuit.

She could already hear Alex's optimistic chirp telling her to slow down, that they would find a way to get the girl back. Ghaoithe wanted nothing more than to drown herself in the biggest lager she could find. If the captain was capable of taking emergencies with Alex's simplistic view, perhaps her life would have been a lot easier and she would not need to wear the armor that kept her bound to her past mistakes. She didn't take her errors in stride, despite whatever face she put up for Alex and the rest of the crew. Her mind swirled along with the crowds in an attempt to find a pathway she may have previously missed. There would be no lager or rum tonight or for many nights to come, only coffee.

Osiris forced the the first twist of the Rubik's Cube in her head, and it would not stop until all the colors were aligned.

Right on cue, Alex's voice pierced through Ghaoithe the moment she stepped into their room, at once both grating and entirely welcome.

"Oh my god! Ghaoithe, you're hurt! Are you ok?!" followed by a much more solemn "They got Ellie, didn't they?"

Ghaoithe closed her eye and nodded. She returned Alex's embrace, her curls soft against the captain's chest. It helped center Ghaoithe, kept the world from tilting about, and she became acutely aware of the warmth that covered the side of her face.

"I need stitches," said Ghaoithe. Even to her own ears, she sounded as dry as the sands she had just crawled from.

At the rattling of a plastic box, she opened her eye. Fleet strung threads through a needle from an aid kit already in use across the room. Next to it, Damian nursed his hand with a pack of ice. His fingers had nearly doubled in size since he came crashing into the House of Scribes.

"You should have seen the other guy," Damian said meekly at Ghaoithe's judgment.

Alex shot him a look that suggested it was not the time for jokes. She nudged Ghaoithe towards the bed.

"You need to sit down. Just tell us what happened? Oh god, Ghaoithe, you're really banged up," Alex said in rapid succession. She hurried to the nearby bedstand and poured a couple fingers of vodka into a chipped mug. Ghaoithe waved it off, which only caused Alex's brow to furrow in even more worry. She looked rather like a disappointed bulldog. Relenting under the pressure, Ghaoithe took the glass and sipped in weak reassurance.

"Vargas. She was in the helicopter. Took out my horse from under me. I was so close to having them… goddammit!" Ghaoithe cursed as Fleet dabbed the cut on her forehead.

"Story can wait, Lynn. I ain't even got to the needles yet," Fleet said. He took the cloth in his hand, dipped it into the cup of vodka, and made another pass at the captain's wound to another round of swears.

"Usually this goes the other way around. You don't even seem scratched," Ghaoithe noted as Fleet sewed the gash shut. She kept talking, as much a distraction than anything. Her clenched fists, knuckles white beneath bronzed skin, did not go unnoticed by Alex. She recalled the captain's dislike of needles and placed a comforting hand on Ghaoithe's forearm.

Fleet's eyes did not move from his work as he spoke. "They clocked me good before I could do much. Probably shouldn't even be doin' this."

Four stitches later, he tied the thread and made one more pass to clean the remaining blood from his partner's face. As soon as he clasped the aid kit shut, Ghaoithe made an attempt to stand, but he placed a firm hand on her shoulder to force her back down onto the bed. Ghaoithe flashed a defiant look at him.

"I'm not sitting around, Fleet. Not with Osiris gaining ground on us," she said. Her nostrils flared as she huffed.

Fleet raised a stern finger at her. "They already got her, Lynn. Rushin' out ain't gonna change that anytime soon. I know how that armor of yers works, and I'm guessin' what ya need is a hot bath and some rest."

Alex looked between them, not quite understanding the exchange. She did know, however, that Fleet was right. Despite her normal bravado, Ghaoithe's behemoth shape had been hunched over from the moment she stumbled into the inn. Sensing a standoff, Alex stood and tugged gently on Ghaoithe's arm.

"I'll draw some water. It'll be good for you," she said.

Outnumbered, Ghaoithe sighed and nodded. Alex retreated into the next room to prep a bath. Their room's tub was a claw-footed antique that didn't look like much, but was large and deep enough to contain Ghaoithe. No doubt Roy worked his knowledge with the inn's owner just for such a need. The only way to distinguish it from its Victorian-era copies were the sigils that wrapped along the faucet. By the time Alex managed to toy with them enough to figure out a proper water temperature, Ghaoithe hobbled inside and shut the door behind her.

"You can stay," Ghaoithe said with a pointed tone. Alex's cheeks flushed as Ghaoithe sat on the toilet cover and removed her boots. Her reason for keeping Alex became apparent when she struggled to unbuckle the straps that held her armor in place. She looked at Alex with a hint of embarrassment. "I could use some help. Don't you dare tell Fleet or I will put you on latrine duty the moment we get back to the *Cloudkicker.*"

Alex gave a mock salute as she moved to help her captain remove the armor. She'd rarely managed to touch it before, keenly aware that Ghaoithe was not likely to grant that privilege to many. She ran her hands over the smooth leather, taken aback by the slight warmth that tingled at her fingertips. It felt almost alive, an extension of the captain's own skin. Even through the crash, it was unscathed and clean. Once unfastened, it split and fell from its owner like a flexible turtle shell. Alex gasped.

"Jesus, Ghaoithe! Are you sure your ribs aren't broken? We should get Fleet," she said. Through the scars and various markings on Ghaoithe's torso, her skin had turned a nasty shade of purple that stretched just beneath her left breast and curved down to her backside.

Ghaoithe turned to Alex, wincing as she did so. "No. I know what that feels like. This isn't much better, but I'll be fine."

Sliding off her pants and ruby sash, Ghaoithe's legs and hip were battered with similar bruises. She closed in on the tub. With Alex's help, she lowered herself in. The room filled with steam, and Ghaoithe let out a contented sigh. Despite her worry, Alex smiled in amusement; Ghaoithe was still slightly too large for the tub and her legs hung over the edge. Alex sat on the floor and rested her arms on the tub's rim, cradling her chin with her elbows. She looked at Ghaoithe as if the captain might inadvertently drown without her watchful eyes. Ghaoithe made no remarks to complain.

"I know you did your best. I don't blame you," Alex said. She felt that if she stayed silent, Ghaoithe would stew over her failure to rescue Ellie.

"You weren't there," Ghaoithe snapped. "I almost caught them. Just a few more inches, and we'd be on our way out of here right now."

Alex shrunk. "I know. You're right, I wasn't there. But I know you shouldn't blame yourself, either."

"I... just drop it for now."

"Okay."

Alex let stillness take the room. Through the quiet water, she sneaked glances at the captain, at the fresh bruises and old wounds. She had only seen Ghaoithe without her armor once before, and the sight was no less unnerving the second time. The captain's skin accumulated a network of scars over the years as it had been torn, burnt, and mutilated in her search for answers. Many had been smoothed by time. The thought of a young Ghaoithe, little more than a child before her armor was crafted, enduring such hardship tugged at Alex and squeezed her breath.

Yet, it was not just distress that tightened Alex's chest as she considered Ghaoithe's body. Had she never spoken to Samir she may never have seen the captain's vulnerability, but here she understood. She saw the bronzed skin that retained the faint glow of youth. Ghaoithe's carefully tussled hair, interwoven with short braids like the shieldmaidens of the ancient north, framed high cheekbones and smooth skin. Behind the distraction of an eyepatch and canvas of scars, Ghaoithe was a normal, beautiful woman in her prime, a woman only a few years older than Alex but one who had lived twice the life. This revelation both attracted Alex and terrified her with a spark that jolted her very core.

As she followed the lines of Ghaoithe's long, lithe legs, she felt a wet hand touch her own. She turned and found Ghaoithe's peering eye inches from her own.

"What is it, Stirling?" Ghaoithe asked.

Alex turned guiltily away to stare at the swirling patterns of steam that rose from the bath. Once she straightened her thoughts, she turned back to face her captain. "Ghaoithe, are you ok?" she asked.

Ghaoithe raised an eyebrow. "Are you worried I'm dying or something? It will take more than falling off a horse to kill me."

Alex shook her head. "I don't mean just that. I mean do you want someone to talk to? You've already been through so much. How can you just keep doing this over and over and act like everything's perfectly fine?"

Her own honesty left Alex shaken. Surely she had crossed some kind of line, but she couldn't help herself once she started talking. She waited for Ghaoithe to snap back and tell her to leave. Instead, the captain shook her head with a sad smile.

"I won't lie and say things are always great. I've had a lot taken from me, but those things also remind me of the kind of person I need to be," Ghaoithe said. "They gave me direction."

Alex raised her head off her elbows. "Taken from you?"

"You remember when we first landed in Roanoke, I told you I wasn't sure if everything worked right?"

"That wasn't just a joke, was it?"

Alex expected Ghaoithe to close up, as she often did when asked questions about her past. However, the captain said, "No, it wasn't. Do you want to hear the story?"

Alex nodded. Ghaoithe, with some effort, propped herself up. She pointed to a mark, just above her right pelvic bone. A circular, discolored blotch about the size of a cigarette burn marred her skin. Compared to her other scars, it seemed insignificant and could have easily been confused with a bad childhood case of the chicken pox. She lowered herself back into the bath.

"Frog dart," she said without flair.

Alex's eyes widened. "You got hit with a poison frog dart? And lived?!"

"Just barely," Ghaoithe continued. She traced the marks on her chest with an absentminded finger. "Out of all of these mistakes, that one was the only one that had a genuine chance of killing me. It damn well hurt like it, too. I was green back then, barely more than maybe ten or eleven, searching for the City of Gold in South America. Which I'm still searching for, by the way," she added as Alex opened her mouth to speak.

"Anyway, I came across some other ruins and thought 'Hey, why not?' I'd never been to South America, though, and wasn't as privy to the traps of their ancestors like I am now. I eventually tracked down a temple, hidden deep in Peru, that might have held a clue. I made it through the outer chambers just fine and was about to take hold of this lovely ritual headdress inside the main tomb. Ended up triggering an air trap. Little holes, you see, and if the flow of air out of them is blocked, the pressure shoots out something elsewhere. In this case, it shot poison darts."

"How did you survive? I thought those were super toxic," Alex asked. She leaned forward, enthralled by Ghaoithe's adventure.

Ghaoithe shrugged. "Poison was old, maybe? Lame source frog? I have no idea. Shriveled up my insides real quick, though, so maybe it was just luck they hit my ovaries instead anything higher. They probably would have killed a normal-sized person, but I was already taller than most men. This was before the *Cloudkicker*, but even my hired hands weren't going to leave a young girl to die. Bastards did make off with the headdress afterward, though.

"I spent a good week in and out of consciousness, learning firsthand why some tribes used small doses as a psychotropic. When I came out of it, I was in Roanoke for the first time. My healer said I should have died, but I didn't go without irreparable damage. At my age and development, she said my thoughts would never be right, that I might never feel the same way about certain things as other women. Guess she was talking about my hormones but there's plenty of other stuff since then she could have meant. Anyway, it took another solid two weeks before I was comfortable walking on my own again, let alone before I could even consider the whole 'never having kids' thing."

A sob caught in Alex's throat. She couldn't even pretend to know what it was like having such a major part of life swept out from under her without a choice, to have the decision made for her before she was even a teenager. She rubbed her eyes with the back of her arm. Ghaoithe tilted her head and looked at Alex with a confused expression.

"Don't you wonder, though? Do you regret not being able to have kids?" Alex asked once she composed herself.

Ghaoithe rubbed her chin and stared at the ceiling. "No, I can't say I do. The only thing I've learned in doing this whole relic hunting thing for so long is that the more I explore, the more I find there is to learn about the world. I could criss-cross this planet for five lifetimes, and it still wouldn't be enough. I don't want to spend the one I have being sidelined by anything. There's too much I still have to do," she said. She turned back to Alex.

Alex met Ghaoithe's unwavering eye, envious of her complete resolution. It was contagious. She thought of her time back in Missouri and the endless stream of family photos that were becoming the norm when she scrolled through her friends' online profiles. They once seemed so normal, but Ghaoithe's conviction scrubbed away those accepted truths and replaced them with something else.

"I never thought of it that way," Alex said. "In New Delta, that was just sort of the endgame if you stayed there. You grew up, got married, and had a family. No need to find anything else or push beyond your boundaries. You'd maybe take a trip to Disneyland or Hawaii or something, but for most people that was the extent of curiosity about the world. Vacations were just ways to check places off a box, not to actually learn about them. Until you brought me aboard, I just figured that would be my lot in life, too."

"That's not so different from Lost Earth, though. Not really," Ghaoithe said. "And can you really say those people aren't happy?"

Alex shook her head.

"I think they are," Ghaoithe continued. "Maybe even happier than we are sometimes. Being a relic hunter takes a certain breed of person. We do it because there is no endgame, because we will always have this drive to find out what's just outside of what we know. I think you make a great explorer, but I wouldn't blame you if you wanted to put this behind and return to something simpler. My choice was made for me, but you still have yours."

"That will never happen."

"That's good. If I can't have kids, then you, Fleet, and Ellie have given me more than a handful to watch over," Ghaoithe said. She winked with her good eye.

Alex splashed Ghaoithe with a playful hand of water. Ghaoithe retaliated in kind. The two giggled, their water war far more important for the moment than anything else in the world. In the end, Alex's clothes were as drenched as Ghaoithe and her dampened hair clung to her like a golden dress.

Ghaoithe sank back into the water and stared up at the ceiling. "Hey, Alex?" she said in a near whisper.

"Hm?"

"Thanks for being here for me."

Alex blushed and nodded. She crossed her arms on the edge of the tub and laid her head back down. The two sat in silence, taking in each other and holding off the shared thought they both knew was inevitable.

"What are we going to do about Ellie?" Alex asked. She hated saying it as the words came out. She wanted to stay there peacefully forever, but she knew it had to be done.

A crease formed between Ghaoithe's eyebrows as she looked darkly at Alex. She said, "It's time we stopped trying to fight a war by ourselves."

# XV

Roy and Damian walked through the streets of Dilmun with strict instructions in hand.

"I can never tell what's up with this city," Damian said. "You'd have no clue if all this furor was over Osiris or just normal business hours."

Roy grunted a noncommittal response.

Damian continued, "I mean, they have to know what's about to go down. There's no way Osiris would just blitz into the city without the Table making some kind of statement about it. Say, I wonder if there's an actual table, like one of those big Supreme Court affairs…"

"That's a bench, not a table." Roy did not look at Damian, his attention turned solely on their route through the maze of Dilmun. Their destination was not the easiest to locate.

In truth, finding the Table made Roy nervous. Dilmun did not run on the barter values and communal partnerships that still existed in most of Lost Earth. The Table called the shots and allowed the city to operate as a trade hub that rode the fine line between Lost Earth and modern worlds. Though several factions clamored for power throughout the years, the Table's word trumped them all and kept an uneasy balance to prevent the city from tearing itself apart. Some considered a seat at the Table a high honor, but the responsibility was said to be granted only to those with thin enough moral fiber to do what was necessary. They weren't above assassination attempts of their own, if word on the street held any truth.

"I could so go for a Cosmopolitan right now. You think they serve people in these secret meetings?" Damian continued.

"You know, you talk a lot for a pickpocket," Roy said.

Damian laughed. "Deception is the best way to work. The easiest people to steal from are the ones too preoccupied to notice. How do you know I haven't stolen your wallet three times over by now?"

"Because I'd break your fingers in your sleep if you did," Roy said. A flash of white broke through dark lips. "Besides, we ain't worth nothing these days."

As they bantered, they entered a narrow alley lined with low, broad storehouses. Most were closed or in the process of shuttering as the sun sank beyond the horizon. No one looked their way, too busy securing stockpiles of grains, pottery, and other wares for the next day's markets. Among the sandstone walls, five men in black robes clustered near one of the warehouse's side entrances with no indication of stirring in the waning hours. Though they spoke amongst themselves, their eyes darted out every few moments into the crowd from behind dark shawls. The rest of their faces were covered.

Damian stopped. He asked, "How do I look?"

"Like you fought a train and lost," said Roy.

"This is stupid. Why would Ghaoithe send me instead of coming herself. Or at least send Alex," Damian said. He licked the palm of his hand and used it to slick back his unruly mane to little effect. Roy folded his arms.

"Give yourself some credit. Ghaoithe kept you around for a reason. You've handled yourself on the streets long enough to know how these things work better than any of us. Besides, the captain's in no position to move anywhere right now, and Alex isn't leaving her side."

"And if we don't convince them?"

"We have to convince them. There's no other option," said Roy. He started towards the masked guards. Damian hustled after him.

As they approached, the group ended their conversation to glare at the two newcomers. One of the men held up a hand. His other grasped the hilt of a particularly cruel-looking cutlass. Roy halted and raised his own arms in deference.

"We're with the Sky Thief," Roy said. The guard's eyes narrowed in judgment of the two. He held out his hand, palm up. Slowly, Roy reached into the folds of his vest and pulled out a white paper no larger than a business card. Words scrawled in crimson covered one side, an invitation procured by Roy. No one had dared to ask how. After giving the note a once-over, the guard nodded and turned to shout at the other men in Arabic. Damian let out a relieved breath he didn't know he was holding. The masked ensemble unlocked the tiny warehouse door, and the two were escorted into its dim interior. The door closed behind them, leaving them in the dark with the man who inspected the invitation.

"This way," said the guard. As Damian and Roy's eyes adjusted, they could hear their handler's footsteps echoing down a corridor. They followed. They did not have to travel far before the footsteps were replaced by the sound of more locks being turned. Another door opened, and they could see once again.

Inside was the warehouse interior, stacked with storage crates and metal shelving of all sizes. Tobacco smoke filled the air and created an eerie mist below high-set industrial lights that cast deep shadows in the gaps between shelves. As they made their way through the maze of trade goods, their heels clicked along smooth concrete flooring. After the Lost Earth aesthetics of the rest of Dilmun, the modernity of the Table's meeting place shocked Damian. Even Roy glanced about nervously, taken aback by the sharp contrast. They could have been walking through the Port of Long Beach for all they could tell.

Finally, they turned a corner and reached the center of the

warehouse. Lit by a cone of light, three figures sat in metal fold-up chairs around a circular table covered with green felt. Each had a cigar in their mouth, a dark bottle at their sides, and a spread of cards in their hands. Damian gasped.

The Table was a poker table.

"Roy Mason and Damian Locke representing the Sky Thief," said their guard. The man on the right of The Table grunted and waved a hand. The escort disappeared back into the mess of crates.

"Sit down," said the one on the right. He wore a fine Italian suit, unbuttoned in the stale air. He motioned with a thick hand to two extra chairs that waited beside him. Damian and Roy sat down as commanded and looked around, uncertain how to begin. The Italian laughed. He reached down to a neon-green cooler at his feet and pulled out two dark bottles. He said, "Don't be so nervous. We are here to chat, right?"

"Maybe if the Sky Thief could have appeared herself, we could actually get something done," said a feminine voice across from the Italian. She was a dark, large woman almost as tall as Ghaoithe, with a boxer's build and short, neatly trimmed hair.

"Do not mind our Brazilian friend here. She's just a fangirl disappointed she could not meet your captain," said the third figure. He, too, wore a finely tailored suit. Unlike the pale Italian, however, the third figure seemed molded by the sands of the desert, with thick brows and coarse stubble covering a young, handsome face.

Poker aside, the Table looked very much as Damian and Roy expected: rich, powerful, intelligent, and extremely out-of-place among a society that did not have so much as digital wristwatches.

At their jests, Roy relaxed in his seat and accepted the bottle from the Italian. Twisting off the cap and taking a swig, he settled into his role as negotiator. "Captain Loinsigh sends her regards. Unfortunately, she's not able to move much at the moment," he said.

"Oh, we know all about it. People can't whisper in this city without us hearing it, let alone end up in a high-speed chase with a helicopter," said the Arabian. He scratched his chin, focused on the cards in his hand. "As you can imagine, the whole thing has put us in a rather awkward position."

The Brazilian folded her hand and leaned back to take a long drag from her cigar. In the full force of the light overhead, an old scar was visible on her left cheek that ran down to her neck. She said, "The people here look to us for safety, to keep them free from Osiris and modern influence. The girl you brought has put that trust in jeopardy."

Roy pursed his lips as he thought about Ghaoithe's fall outside the city. "Do the people of Dilmun really expect you to take out a helicopter if it came to that?" he asked.

The Italian chuckled. Ashing the last of his cigar into a tray on the table, he promptly reached into a jacket pocket, pulled out a fresh one, and lit it. "You don't think these crates are just full of spices, do you? Give us some credit. Not everyone in Lost Earth is so secluded."

The humor was lost on Roy. He leaned back in his chair and folded his arms. "What's done is done. We have bigger problems to worry about now," he said.

"You have issues, certainly, but there are some that would see your crew removed from Dilmun for the time being. The people love the fabled Sky Thief, but they enjoy a life free of Osiris troubles more," said the Arabian. As chips for a new hand were doled out, he licked his thumb and began shuffling the faded deck of cards. He gave it more attention than he did his guests.

Damian squirmed in his seat. The conversation sounded far too serious for him, as though he were a janitor overhearing some important investor's meeting. He did know one thing, however: the *Cloudkicker* needed the people in the room or else more than Dilmun would find their cities under Osiris control.

"You're already involved, like it or not," Damian blurted out. He thought for a moment that another voice had said it, but the glares from the Italian and Brazilian informed him that the voice was his own. He squirmed in his seat under their weight. Only the Arabian smirked with some amusement as he dealt hands to the Table.

"Why would that be, Mr. Locke? We have avoided the conflicts Osiris has with others in the past. I see no reason that should change," he said.

Damian sought help from Roy. The older man nodded, a silent approval to tell the Table what they knew. Damian wasted no time in going into detail about the *Cloudkicker*'s give-and-take battles with Osiris. At first, the Table appeared unconcerned, with the Brazilian scoffing and mumbling "Idiots" at several points during their retelling of sneaking into one of Osiris's complexes. As the story continued, the three keepers of the city began to take more interest. By the time Damian reached the House of Scribes and its ominous prophecy, the Table were enthralled, their card game forgotten.

"You're certain that Ellie is the girl mentioned in the book?" said the Brazilian. Her cropped hair splayed in every direction after she ran a distressed hand through it.

"It makes sense," said Damian. "The way she talks and acts, it's like she's in tune with something out there we aren't supposed to know about. She *knows* things no eight-year-old would understand. I haven't even seen the crazier stuff like the captain and Alex."

Roy nodded in agreement. "The boy would know. He's closer to the girl than any of us. I honestly think Ghaoithe's scared of her."

The Italian snuffed out what remained of the stub of his cigar. The others followed suit. He did not pull out a new one. "We are not to doubt the House of Scribes, but if what you say is true, why does she not just escape on her own? She seems to have that power," he asked.

Damian stood up and paced behind his chair. "It's not something she can just do on her own. It's like a... a safety measure of some sort," he said. "From what Alex was saying, it only works when there's no hope left. I guess as long as we're still standing, then there's still a chance to stop Osiris."

The Table looked to each other in silent contemplation. The Italian's fingers twitched across the felt. The other two responded in kind as

Damian and Roy waited. As they finished their coded discussion, the Brazilian turned to them.

"Why come to us? Defending the city is one thing, but we cannot win an all-out war with Osiris," she said.

"Leave the fighting to us," said Roy. "What we need is your network. Information, leads, anything to give us an edge up on where Osiris is focused."

Damian nodded. He leaned onto the back of his chair with both hands. "We don't have to tell you guys how these things play out. Sow the seeds of distrust, start the propaganda engine, all that jazz. Get people to finally turn against Osiris for good. Maybe we can slow them down. Dilmun is the best trade hub in the world to get that started," he said.

"And if that's not enough?" asked the Arabian.

"Then I hope you like eternal toga parties without the wine or sex," said Damian.

The sound of buzzing lights filled the room as the group contemplated the future Deacon sought. After a moment, the Italian nodded, then the Brazilian, and finally the Arabian.

"Tell your captain it is done," said the Arabian. "We'll start spreading word out immediately and send supplies to your ship. Osiris will know what we're doing, and we may not be able to help much more in the coming days. I'd suggest not returning here for some time."

With that, the Table stood. They exchanged handshakes with Roy and Damian, and wished them luck. A few moments later, the escort arrived to lead Ghaoithe's men back through the array of shelves and back into the hot Dilmun sun.

"So, that's it? It was that easy?" asked Damian as they started the long trudge back through the streets. Though the conversation with the Table went far more smoothly than he anticipated, he could not help but think their mission just got much more difficult.

Roy sighed. "If it were anyone else piloting our ship, no, but the captain's proved enough myths to be believed. Besides, Osiris probably hurt their own cause flying over the city like that, too."

"What happens now?"

"The hard part. We just poked a dragon out of its slumber," said Roy. However their conversation with Dilmun's leaders went, it wasn't apparent in the dread in his words. They continued back to the hotel without saying anything, each coming to terms with the fact that *Cloudkicker* was no longer a single relic hunting ship but the forward spear for an army.

# XVI

Becky knew. On some level, she knew once Alex failed to return home from the hospital. Still, Becky listened to Ethan's explanation with open ears, believed his story about Alex getting an assignment to research river travel from the paper, and went about her business. She moved to Chicago without so much as a text from her supposed best friend. Eventually, she gave up trying to reach Alex, landed her dream job, and moved on with her life. Until China, everything was honky-dory.

When Becky saw the *Cloudkicker* fly into the distance from the glass walls of her temporary office, she wasn't sure what to be more upset over: that the friend she looked after for the better part of a decade left her behind for a flying ship, or that her dream job was nothing more than a chess piece in a much larger game. The barrage of events left Becky somewhere between laughing at the surrealism of it all and wondering if she could shatter the windows of her suite to make one final jump. She chose sleep.

They had spent nearly their whole lives together. Becky was there when Alex needed a kickball partner. She was there to hold Alex's hair back over the toilet after crashing frat parties they were far too young to be at. She was there to pull Alex out of the muck when a fire turned a once-vibrant girl into a broken husk. Becky loved Alex as much as any sister.

It was Becky's turn this time.

No, she didn't require thanks or commendation for watching Alex over the years. She genuinely cared for her friend. But she had needs, too. She never told Alex that the trip to Chicago was as much to get away from her as it was to start a fresh career. Over the years, Alex became a full-time job in her own right, and Becky longed for breathing room. She wanted her own apartment with her own furniture where she could work on her own career. No more turning down dates to watch movies with a near-catatonic roommate. No more constant struggle to raise Alex's self-esteem. Sure, Becky intended to check-in with a phone call now-and-then, but she got to say goodbye at the end of the night and prowl for one of those cute law students at Northwestern. Was a little time for personal growth so much to ask for?

Apparently so.

Becky watched from her chic high-rise apartment as Alex left China aboard a winged ship of Hermes's design and knew, in that moment, that the life she thought she had earned was never hers at all. Worst of all, her best friend neglected to offer any explanation, any solace amid the confusion. Did Alex even *try* to find Becky before flying off on her escapades?

Alone and confused, Becky sobbed and cursed and planned her own escape. She refused to be pulled into Alex's weird personal issues, even if they did involve an airship and a giant, glowing woman. The next morning, just as Becky moved to confront Ethan about the ordeal, she met Deacon and her life spun on its heels for the second time in as many days. She knew very little about the man, only that he was Ethan's business partner. She expected the kind of rotund, lecherous businessman that lurked around the upper echelons of her hometown, not the sharp, bespectacled gentleman that brought canes back into fashion. He even brewed her a cup of tea.

"You must think so terribly of us, but please allow me to make a proper apology. A few explanations are in order. You deserve as much" Deacon said. Becky obliged.

Deacon did explain everything. About Osiris. About Lost Earth. All of it. Under different circumstances, Becky would have scoffed at such a fairy tale, but her disbelief was tempered by the glass walls among the mountains of Huangshan. She had no right to call into question Deacon's story. Not anymore.

Alex had joined Osiris's direct competitors, an amateur band of grave robbers that disagreed with the company's methods to bring the world into a brighter future. Deacon tried to reason with Alex, but she refused to listen, caught up in the adventure and rush of drastic action. This, at least, made sense to Becky. She knew of Alex's inherent flair for instability better than anyone. According to Deacon, Ethan had been telling the *Cloudkicker* inside information that allowed these anarchists to push into the offices. Osiris hoped Becky's presence would deter such action but were unfortunately mistaken. Alex was too far gone, caught up in the heady winds of the drama she craved.

Contrary to what Alex believed, Osiris wasn't a bad company. They created a lot of good. Deacon toured Becky though the compound, showed her the numerous projects they worked tirelessly to finish in downtrodden areas of the world. Yes, they were a corporation with shrewd tactics, but their endgame was so much more beneficial than Becky had ever seen from the so-called philanthropists that normally made headlines. Osiris actually achieved their goals. They were more than an empty promise. She could see it there, firsthand.

Yet the more Deacon talked about the company, the more Becky's presence stuck out like a dandelion among roses.

"What does all this have to do with me, though?" Becky asked. "With Alex gone, why am I still here? You only gave me this job to get to her."

Deacon sighed and placed a reassuring hand on her shoulder. "You are allowed to think so little of us, but don't think so little of yourself, my dear. I have no intention of dismissing a woman of your talents if you wish to stay," Deacon said.

"My talents?" Becky asked. She raised a skeptical eyebrow, wary that perhaps he was as lecherous as she initially thought.

Deacon leaned on his cane and eyed her with utmost seriousness. "We vet everyone we bring into the fold, and you have the qualities we need. You see yourself as another mid-rate designer of clothes, but you show so much more! You're an organizer, a planner. Why, if given the chance, I have no doubt you could run one of our subsidiaries with barely a wave of the hand. That may be some time away yet, but I would like to put you in a position that leads you there. Of course, if you choose to stick with your fashion work, I have an eye for finery and so few decent designers these days." And his suit was very fine, indeed.

Becky mulled his offer over, rolled it about her conscience, examined what little she knew of Deacon's character. Then, she thought of Alex's progress.

Before long, Becky stood aboard her own vessel, the Osiris flagship *Ascendant*, a craft much larger and more capable than the aging skiff Alex sailed upon. Her hands trembled, and she occupied herself by jotting a few notes on her clipboard. She double- and triple-checked her arrangements even after Deacon assured her they were exemplary. He waited beside her, still as a rock and clothed in a long-tailed rose sportcoat of her own design. She smiled as she glanced at it and attempted to mimic his rigid stance through her nerves. Behind them, the walls of the airship droned with holographic displays of the Osiris logo—a blooming tree inside a green circle—and newscasts of their endeavors around the world.

Any moment, the polished bay door in front of them would open and their guest would arrive. Deacon mentioned little about her, only that the child's genetics held the key to curing many of humanity's illnesses, perhaps even the secret to prevent true aging. She was going to change the world as they knew it, he promised. Becky's mind clamored with the dozens of arrangements she made for such a selfless volunteer. She personally ensured the bedroom was pleasant and comfortable, just as Deacon asked. Then there were the orders to the kitchen, new clothes, Deacon's personal calendar, medical supplies (most of which she couldn't pronounce, let alone understand), the list of specialty tutors…

A clang signaled the arrival of their company. The door slid upward and flooded the entryway with light. Desert heat blasted Becky before the door closed behind the three entrants. Sorin's unmistakable muscle stood next to a vibrant woman in tan safari clothing drenched with sweat. The wicked rifle slung across her back matched her expression. Between them stood a child with porcelain skin and comet hair.

"One child wasn't enough for you, Deacon? Had to wrangle one of the angels over here, too?" said Jessie with a wave of a finger in Becky's direction.

Deacon chuckled. "This is my new assistant, Ms. Rebecca Nolan. Ms. Nolan, I believe you read the dossier on Jessica Vargas?"

Becky's cheeks burned as she reached out a hand in greeting. "Pleasure to meet you."

The other woman sneered and brushed past Becky without a second glance. "Whatever. I'll be in my room with several cold ones if you need me to do any more of your dirty work before I'm gone," said Jessie as she disappeared into the hallways of the *Ascendant.*

Becky's arm remained frozen for a moment before she became keenly aware of the young girl staring at her with unblinking eyes. Outwardly, the girl was no different than any other girl of eight or nine, but something about her gaze made Becky's skin crawl with goosebumps. She composed herself and knelt down to Ellie's eye level.

"You must be little Ellie! It's so wonderful to have you with us. I made sure your room is really comfortable while you're here," Becky said in her best sing-song voice. Children were never her forte, but she was determined to try her best. "If you need anything, you just ask Aunt Becky, okay?"

Ellie slowly blinked. She met Becky's eyes then passed over to Deacon. "It's ok. I know you won't hurt me this time," she said. Her voice barely rose above a whisper, but it was steady and commanding. Becky swore the air bristled with a slight chill, but she shook it off as her imagination.

If Deacon noticed anything out of the ordinary, he gave no sign of it. He smiled a response at Ellie and turned to Sorin. "See her to her room. We have a long trip ahead of us," he said.

Sorin nodded. He took Ellie's hand and walked her down the bright steel corridors of the *Ascendant*. The girl's hair shimmered and bounced under the bright LEDs before she turned a corner and left Becky wondering what, exactly, she just saw.

"She scares me," Becky said. She fiddled with her clipboard once she realized she had said her thoughts aloud.

Deacon leaned forward with both hands on his cane as he watched Sorin and Ellie depart.

"The future only scares those who are unprepared for it, Ms. Nolan."


"If you don't take that armor off, I'm going to strip you in your sleep and beat you with it."

"You really think you can stay awake longer than I can?"

From across the room, Kirk groaned as he lit another cigarette. "You two are worse than a coupla caged honey badgers," he said.

Ghaoithe and Alex ignored him, locked in their own battle of wills. Ghaoithe sat on her bed and refused to budge. Alex stood over her, arms crossed. From the window beside them, shouts from the nearby market signaled the beginning of what promised to be another long day.

After a few more moments of tension, Fleet lowered his notes onto the piled desk before him. "Just do it, Lynn. If I have to grapple ya, it might make things worse and we've already lost enough time," he growled. Alex turned to him and mouthed a silent thank you. Fleet shook his head and returned to his work.

Ghaoithe let out an exaggerated sigh and unclasped the fastens of her armor. Alex immediately lifted Ghaoithe's undershirt and checked her injuries with studious precision.

"I'll be fine to go outside for fresh air, you know. That's the whole point of the armor," Ghaoithe complained.

"We're not worried about you getting shot. We're worried about what moving will do to your ribs right now," Alex snipped back. "With how tight you wear that thing, it's a wonder you didn't hurt yourself even more this morning."

"I can't stay cooped up in here much longer. I've survived... stop that!" Ghaoithe swatted Alex's hand away as she prod at a particularly sore spot at Ghaoithe's side. She regretted doing so if for no other reason than the smugness that dripped from Alex's voice.

"See?! You are still recovering!"

Ghaoithe grunted. She turned to stare out the window as her check-up resumed. It faced the morning sunrise, warm enough to beckon her outside but angled just right to avoid the binding glare of white stone and sand. In places like Dilmun, residences often covered their windows with thick, red curtains to hide what went on behind. Not Ghaoithe. In the few days she hobbled around the room, she never closed the curtains once.

Alex was right, though. Ghaoithe barely moved for the better part of a week and not for lack of trying. Her crew kept a close eye on her, even pampered her as much as the circumstances allowed. It was nice for about a day before she grew eager to return to the streets. A week was near torture. She occupied herself with her notes to figure out where Osiris might hide Ellie. The crew updated her each day on the rumors among Dilmun's information brokers, but even that silently upset her. She believed in living the world. Anyone could read about a place or listen to their friends talk about a vacation, but nothing could replace the actual experience. Today was the first day she could stand and bend over without her sides crippling her with unbearable fire. Ghaoithe sneaked her armor on the moment the room emptied for morning rounds. The effort took longer than she anticipated, and her partners returned with fresh muffins before she could escape. Ghaoithe's search for Ellie would have to wait another day.

Not that the rest of the crew were any happier about that, though they did their best to keep the tone light during their research. Yet each of them worried, in their own ways, if the world would inexplicably change at any moment by the power of Pandora's Box reuniting with Elpis.

Alex noticed Ghaoithe's silence. She lightened her fingertips on Ghaoithe's skin, careful not to poke the ugly bruises too roughly. Most of the captain's side no longer resembled her exotic tan, replaced with sickly greens and yellows as it healed. A few darker blotches of inky purple marked the worst of her injury. Alex lowered Ghaoithe's shirt once she was satisfied.

"It's healing ok. I think you're right about nothing being broken, but I'm no doctor. How's your head?" Alex asked.

Ghaoithe traced the stitches on her forehead with a fingertip. "I've had worse," she said with a sly smile.

Alex blushed at the subtle reminder of their conversation in the bathroom. She liked knowing something about her captain that others did not, something real and human about a woman most in Lost Earth seemed to know only by reputation.

"Just hold out for another couple of days to put your armor on again," Alex said. She recalled as much as she could from her softball days where she amassed her own collection of marks and hoped it would suffice here. "You won't be taking on helicopters again for awhile, but you should be fine to get out and about then."

"The next time, we'll have the *Cloudkicker*. Your modern machines won't worry me as much then," Ghaoithe said. She returned to her window.

The rest of the morning passed quietly. Overhead, the steady rhythm of the wooden ceiling fan made a vain attempt to stir the thick air around them. Fleet and Alex compiled their notes. Kirk tinkered with a disk no larger than his palm, etching sigils across its surface as he saw fit. For what purpose was anyone's guess. Ghaoithe stared out the window while she ran scenarios through her head. The weight of Ellie's capture crept into each of their thoughts. Outside, the hum of tradesmen and market barkers provided a white noise backdrop that belied the conflict waged just out of sight.

A distant bell tolled with a single chime. At its call, Alex groaned with frustration and put her papers down. Their words blended into a soup. After a week of reading, her ideas fizzled out.

"This is hopeless. We're no closer to figuring out where Osiris took Ellie than we were when we started looking," said Alex.

"Maybe you should go knock on their door. I'm sure they'll be happy to share with you," Kirk said from his perch behind his desk. He squatted on his chair like a vulture surveying scraps, skeletal knees almost touching his chin.

"Oh, like you've been so helpful," Alex snapped back. "You've been tinkering with that thing all day and won't even tell us what you're doing."

"You'll know if it works," Kirk replied without looking up. He continued to scrawl runes over the disk. When nothing happened, he scratched more notes onto his papers, seemingly oblivious to the others in the room if not for his snide comments.

Restless and unable to deal with the acrid smell from Kirk's growing pile of cigarette stubs, Alex threw her defeated hands in the air. "Fine. I'm hungry. I'm going out for a bit," she declared. She was out of the room before anyone could object.

The somber thoughts inside the inn evaporated under the sun. It was just what Alex needed. Of course she wanted to find Ellie, and the setback with Ghaoithe was more apparent with each passing moment. Osiris could reset the world at any second. Yet, that impending doom also helped Alex remember what exactly she wanted to protect in the first place. She had tried as best she could to tame her relentless assault on problems she could not solve, and in doing so started to wonder what exactly she was even doing.

As she strolled down one of Dilmun's boulevards, she looked at the vendors, the rune-powered stalls, the clothing that had not changed in centuries. For so long, she had been trapped in a small bubble in one tiny corner of the world, completely unaware that such a society existed. In the chaos of chasing Osiris, she forgot to stand back and appreciate where she stood. Whatever happened, she never wanted this incredible world to become routine. In several respects, she completely sympathized with Ghaoithe, who could never accept moping about in hotels at every setback as a hazard of their daily life.

So, Alex walked in the captain's place. The ancient buildings granted her respite as they had for so many others before. None of the storefronts screamed at her with harsh neon signs. Nowhere did she hear the omnipresent, inoffensive crooning of 90's Top 40 hits. The constant stream of social media no longer assaulted her every moment. The people of Lost Earth did not need cable news or 24-hour supermarkets to survive. Though she could not pinpoint when it happened, Alex concluded she could live without those things, too.

She passed between sun-bleached buildings and resolved to enjoy the moment free from the claustrophobic hotel room, free from Ghaoithe's stubbornness, and free from whatever impending doom awaited them all.

A few blocks from her hotel, she came upon a market court buzzing with the second wind of energy that came with the early afternoon. A circular fountain sparkled among a crowd in need of the same respite Alex sought. Children laughed as they played tag while their parents sprawled lazily on top of the fountain's smooth granite edge. Alex made a mental note to ask Ghaoithe at some point how school was handled on Lost Earth.

Many of the buildings around the court contained eateries of some kind. Alex craved coffee. In a crossroads like Dilmun, she did not have to search for long. A corner shop barely larger than a walk-in closet beckoned her with the scent of arabica. Alex ordered a strong cup. Behind the counter, the barista touched a sigil along the wall.

Runes sparked to life as they brought a tower of water to boil, which the barista expertly measured along with fresh grounds to concoct a beautiful-smelling coffee. Alex handed the server a few plain copper coins from a bag Ghaoithe gave her. She still did not understand payment in Lost Earth, and Ghaoithe was no help.

"Eh, currency's only good for small things like food. Just ask them how many coins they want and if it seems like too many, don't pay it. It all gets smelted down at some point anyway," the captain had told her.

"So do you use gold and silver for more expensive things?" Alex asked.

"What use is gold? It just sits there and looks pretty. No, copper and iron are much more practical to have on hand. Anyone that needs more than that is probably looking to trade wares or information. We look after each other here. Mostly."

Alex stopped her questions and went with it.

Content with her brew, Alex left the shop in search of a comfortable resting spot in the square. She found a wall nestled in the shade of a canvas awning that was surprisingly unoccupied in the heat. For the first time in what felt like years, she was able to just sit and relax and not think about anything and everything at once. Her old thinking tree stump in Missouri was now a rock wall on other side of the world. No résumé needed for a career of travel, after all. There, among ancient peoples and languages she did not speak, Alex understood that she was the same as them. Lost Earth never stopped growing, as she once believed. People adapted, learned new ideas, reached for goals of their own. Lost Earth did not exist because they were stranded in times forgotten; it existed because its people chose to stay there and evolve in their own way. They made the same choice Alex did her first day on the *Cloudkicker*.

A man walked among the crowd near the fountain, unremarkable in every way but his yellow robes. They flashed against a backdrop of whites, blues, and grays, drawing the attention of Alex and others nearby. She watched as the man stood on the edge of the fountain and turned to face the crowd. He clasped a book in his right hand.

*A street preacher? That's new,* thought Alex.

The topic of religion in Lost Earth was usually handwaved by Ghaoithe and the crew. Reflecting back, Alex could not remember seeing any places of worship in their stops. She supposed the idea of there being a singular belief among people became muddled when artifacts and myths from all faiths were brought to light by relic hunters such as Ghaoithe. As a young girl from a small town who dutifully spent her childhood in church with her parents every Sunday, such a prospect was both terrifying and incredibly exciting.

Curious about the preacher, Alex stood and joined the edge of the gathering. The man's eyes darted about. He cleared his throat several times as his hands toyed with the book. From so far back, Alex could not get a clear view of it beyond a black binding and glimpses of a silver emblem on its cover.

After a length of silence, the crowd murmured in impatience. As it seemed about to disperse, the man finally called out in a nasally, wavering voice, "Citizens of Dilmun! You are being deceived!"

A few people near Alex chuckled. She did not find it funny. Red flags waved in her head.

"Our way of life has changed," continued the preacher, "and we are at a crossroads! Some among you would have us believe that we can hide behind our traditions. That time is over! We must cast aside such foolishness and seek help if we wish to survive the coming tides!"

"You look like you couldn't survive a strong wind!" heckled a man near the front. Another round of laughs erupted.

"Look to the future, my friends! I have been granted the gift of foresight from those who can bring us our destiny," continued the preacher.

Alex continued to move forward. She stood on her toes to get a closer look through the sea of shoulders. Finally, she saw the book in the preacher's arms with clarity. The silver emblem shone only for a brief moment as the preacher traced it with his fingers, but the image was clear: a blossoming tree in a painted circle.

"We must seek help from those called Osiris if we wish to survive," said the preacher. "They can help us achieve our potential!"

"You mean help exploit us!" shouted another man in the crowd. This time, there was no laughter to follow. At the mention of Deacon's company, the air crackled with tension. Ripples of conversation went through the throng like water struck with lightning.

"Now let's hear him out! We all know what that company could do if they wanted. We should play it safe, be on the right side of things," argued another voice.

"You'd sell us out to profiteers with no respect for our ways," yelled a woman.

Suddenly understanding how far she had moved up, Alex looked behind her. *I have to get out of here*, she thought. She slipped through bodies that packed tighter and tighter with each word.

"Our ways aren't worth dying over!" continued another dissenter.

Muffled arguments broke out near the front of the crowd. Someone threw a punch at his neighbor. The fuse was lit, and chaos erupted. A man tried to pull the Osiris doomsayer from his perch. A cutlass was drawn. Arguments turned to swears and everyone surged at once.

Caught in the middle, Alex struggled to escape. Bodies pushed her in every direction, most of which out-sized her by considerable amounts. She shoved her entire self against the tide of flesh to no avail. The air dried up around her. Her right hand went for Excalibur only to grasp at nothing, the sword left behind in her haste to leave the inn. She cried out for people to move, but the furor had grown too large. No one heard her. Stars crossed her vision as she gasped for oxygen and the stampede closed in from all sides.

An arm wrapped around Alex's waist. She was half-pulled, half-lifted through the crowd. Behind her, the ruckus fell into the background. As she took in the aroma of ocean-fresh air, she looked to her savior with an embarrassed acquiescence.

"I'm ok now, Ghaoithe. You can put me down," Alex said meekly.

The captain complied and stared down at Alex with crossed arms. "This is, what, the second or third time I've bailed you out of trouble, Stirling? Seems you have a knack for finding it when I'm not around," Ghaoithe said.

"You're not supposed to be out and about yet."

"Your suggestion has been registered with the captain and respectfully declined," said Ghaoithe. She rigidly brought herself to her full height with a grunt. "Now, let's get out of here and back in the clouds where we belong."

# XVII

"It felt like a Metallica concert but much, much worse," Alex groaned. She clutched a glass of water in her hands and leaned back on the bed to stretch her legs. The rest of the Dilmun expedition sat in the inn around her. Their support comforted her. She knew, however, that they also needed to discuss far more pressing topics in the wake of the scuffle.

Rooted near the window, Roy crossed his arms and leaned against the wall. He had returned to the inn immediately once word of the fight started to spread. "It's starting faster than I thought. The Table didn't waste any time gettin' their propaganda out," he said.

"Yeah, but neither did Osiris," countered Alex.

Roy shook his head. "Dilmun's a trade hub with a lot of people and it sounds like there's plenty of pushback against Osiris here already. If an open city like this won't accept Osiris outright, they ain't got a shot in the smaller traditional towns that make up most of Lost Earth," he said. His baritone drawl offered the reassurance Alex needed at the moment. After the street brawl, she lacked his confidence.

"We still have a problem," said Ghaoithe. She hovered over the table of notes. She moved stiffly, but Alex gave up on getting her to take off the armor. "We're still no closer to finding Ellie."

At the mention of the girl, Damian sighed and sunk into his seat. Dark bags hung under his eyes. Alex had not seen him look so tired since he was first found stowing away on the *Cloudkicker*. He'd spent most of the past week poring over records in the House of Scribes.

"I got nothing. The Scribes couldn't find anything else in that book. No clues, no coordinates. We're back to square one, dudes," he said.

"What about chasing Osiris operations?" Ghaoithe asked. Though not used to technological living by any means, Ghaoithe still had a knack for research, which sometimes included modern newspapers and paper trails to follow.

"They're ghosts, man. The whole network's been tied up with false leads. Our only choice there would be to chase down their operations one-by-one and hope we find the needle in the haystack."

Ghaoithe cursed and shuffled through the papers on the desk. Dissatisfied, she picked up the book with Ellie's history and flipped through its pages. Alex worried Ghaoithe would rip through its pages in her frustration. The mood carried over to the rest of the crew. The only one unbothered by the captain was Kirk, who continued to toy with the plates at his desk with methodical attention. Alex wanted to jump up and slap him, force him to show something other than his laissez-faire attitude to their predicament, but she instead sat and smoldered along with everyone else.

When she reached the end of the book, Ghaoithe slammed it down on the table and fell into her chair. She drew air through her teeth as her still-sore body complained about its treatment. She glared at the book in blame.

The ancient leather binding stared back, taunting Ghaoithe in mockery, and she knew what to do.

She shot out of her seat with a whoop that shocked the others in the room. Even Kirk stopped his experiment to look at her curiously. Ghaoithe's side protested the movement, but she ignored it as she grabbed the book and waved it high in the air as though she had just won a trophy.

"This book might not have a clue for Pandora's Box, but I know where we can find one that does," Ghaoithe said.

Fleet, who sat across from her at the table, scratched his beard. "And how're ya proposin' we do that? It took us years just to track down Alex's poster," he said.

Ghaoithe grinned and the light in her eye took a mischievous turn. Alex had already learned to associate that glint with trouble. "We're not looking for hidden coordinates this time. We're going to find a book that tells us directly," Ghaoithe said. "We're going to find the Library of Alexandria again."

The crew thought about the suggestion for a moment and their heads slowly nodded. Everyone's but Alex's. They others turned to look at her as if she were already the resident expert on the subject. She shook her head.

"I already told you don't know how I got there. We'd have to turn all of Cairo upside down, and that's if it wasn't hidden by sigils I triggered by accident," Alex said. She didn't outright oppose the idea. The clock ticked by on Ellie with every second, however, and she wanted an idea they could actually follow through on. A wild goose chase was the last thing they needed.

Ghaoithe must have sensed Alex's uncertainty. She walked over to the bed and stood in front of Alex.

"Places in Lost Earth act as sort of holy sites to people in the modern world, right?" Ghaoithe said. "People go to places because they are called there by forces they may not understand. They go in search of hidden things they may never find. It's not because those things don't exist; they just don't have all the information about how to get to them. In our case, we can follow the maps and the signs. If we don't have those, though, we can use the next best thing: a dousing rod."

"A dousing rod? You don't mean…" Alex followed. She reached back on the bed and grabbed the hilt of Excalibur behind her.

Ghaoithe nodded, and Alex felt the fizzles of excitement in her chest. "I suppose it's worth a shot. I don't know how to control the runes on it, though."

"You'll need to learn fast, then. We're heading back to Cairo tonight," Ghaoithe said.

For the first time in a week, she laughed.


Jessie hated herself. Beside her, snoring deeply enough to wake the heavens, Sorin slept. He actually looked forgivable in such a vulnerable state, like a handsome, muscular cherub. She turned back to the ceiling. None of the options in her mind sounded great, but it was one of those momentous times in a person's life where the road before her stretched forward with no blocks or warning signs.

Her only option was to continue walking.

In her head, Jessie went through everything she had learned one step at a time. With Ellie captured, she had no reason to stay aboard the *Ascendant*. The ship represented everything she despised about the company. Its lights were too bright, the rooms too spacious. The galley waiters scoffed at her when she ordered beer with her meals instead of wine. Why did a ship's mess hall even need waiters? Or tablecloths? Everything about the ship was a lesson in excess. It felt like a Las Vegas casino more than an aircraft. And, just like a casino, odds favored the house.

Extravagance no longer sat well with Jessie Vargas.

Yet, she stayed. On this night she ended up, as she did most nights, in search of a drink. Though midnight came and went long ago, the holographic screens droned on about a new Osiris wind farm that brought energy to a remote village in Kazakhstan.

*A devil's bargain*, thought Jessie as she passed them. She saw no one else but the occasional patrol. Her boots thumped through the metal corridors on a lonesome journey.

She came to the only place she liked on the ship: a claustrophobic affair nestled away by the crew's quarters. Even though the decor echoed a swanky Manhattan club more than the dive joints she now preferred, it was the closest she found to comfort. The bartender didn't deride her choices here.

As she entered, she paused as she spotted Sorin near the bar. He glanced at her briefly then returned to his pint. She frowned and sat next to him, their faces painted in a rainbow of low-wattage neon. Sorin said nothing. He did not even look at her as they sat in silence beside one another. Only after a drink did she notice his eyes and shoulders drooped. She also noticed the several empty pints next to him. Jessie waited for an an explanation she knew would come in time.

It's not like she wanted the companionship. By all accounts, she would have been fine leaving Sorin to his own struggles. Yet some small part of her also needed the conversation, the distraction from her own thoughts. Deacon's laptop could be used for that, surely. It was not like she had not used countless other men for her own pleasure before.

"It is the day I left my family to join Lost Earth. I drink to them," Sorin said eventually.

Jessie rubbed her temples and signaled for the bartender. "Why don't you tell me about them? I know what it's like to leave people behind, too," she said.

"What do you know?" Sorin snapped. "You left for you. You do not know the meaning of family. Even now you stay on the ship out of fear, worried only for your own safety. You are a vile woman. A coward."

Jessie held up her hands in protest, but she did not say anything. He was right about the ship, if nothing else. She was afraid to depart, to let Osiris slip into secrecy away from her view once again. They offered to shuttle her down to the surface anytime she wanted.

However, Sorin was wrong on other fronts. Once he calmed down, Jessie drank from her own mug and leaned in to him. "Is that what you think? That I left my family for my own sake?" she asked.

"It is what I know. I have read your report. I watched your old films, though I do not understand them. I see no loyalty in you. I see a woman who could not handle pressure and chose to leave," Sorin said.

Jessie leaned back in her chair and arched an eyebrow. "So, you also know about the cartels, the government bribes, the paparazzi that would not even let my children attend school safely? I did what I had to do so they could live a normal, decent life away from my shadow. I exiled myself and let Osiris purge everything about me so that my family could live. Does that sound like a woman who cannot handle pressure to you?"

When she finished, Sorin glared at her. She positioned herself for an easy escape if she needed. Instead, the man laughed. He raised his mug and gave hers a gentle tap with it.

"Perhaps I was wrong. You sound as my mother did. Such is a fire that cannot be faked," Sorin said.

It was there that Jessie Vargas first saw Sorin as more than just a pawn to Osiris. That such a brute could care about family never crossed her mind. A tinge of empathy pulled at her insides despite her better judgment. She may have even smiled at him. They talked about their families, of her wild life in South America and his simple one in Romania. By the third mug, she found him attractive. By the fifth, they were on their way to his room.

She forgot how much she needed it.

If they had stopped there, there was a chance that she would have stayed aboard the *Ascendant*. The heady glow that came post-lovemaking did not last, however, and she opened her mouth to speak. Jessie knew it was the addiction to stirring the pot, her insistence on being miserable rather than finding some sense of normalcy, that made her do it. Yet, the question had bugged her since she first received the docket from Osiris, and she needed to know.

"Why the girl? The white one?" Jessie asked. She snuggled up to Sorin, embraced by mountain-made arms. Their talk of family and loyalties brought with it curiosity about her target. She never wished to learn more than was necessary about her jobs, but the silver-haired child kept appearing in her thoughts.

Sorin held onto her and did not answer. Jessie worried he would clam up and change back into the man she knew before the bar, but he said with a loud yawn, "Deacon will use her to open Pandora's Box. He will rid the world of evils by putting them all back in."

Jessie turned to him, her mouth agape. "Put the… Sorin, what does that mean?"

"It is as I said. We shall return the earth to Eden. Everyone will be free of sin for good."

With a final hug, the alcohol took over and Sorin rolled to his side to sleep. Jessie, however, was jolted awake.

She processed the implications of Deacon's plan. At first, she didn't understand it, but she knew too much of Lost Earth to dismiss it. Little by little, the puzzle pieces fell into place. Sorin told the truth. She saw the world Sorin spoke of, a world free of sin, of evils and, ultimately, of choice. No discussion, no creativity, no individuality… all of it gone with the opening of a lid.

She looked again at the man beside her, and she wanted to cry. Not for herself or her decisions, but because she knew what would happen next, and it scared the hell out of her.

It was time to leave the *Ascendant*.

She wasted no time as she ran to her own room and packed her things. She fled in the night so many times in her life it was practically muscle memory to her. Somewhere in the ship, a young girl bravely defied her captors, and yet Jessie fled. She disgusted herself. But, it needed to be done. There was nothing Jessie could do now under the eyes of Osiris.

Minutes later, Jessie's shuttle touched the ground. She ran.

# XVIII

Despite the grim task ahead, the *Cloudkicker* was eager to return to the skies. Fed with a fresh crystal supply, it rose smoothly above the cloud layer without complaint. Once there, it made haste toward Cairo, charged by its blue sigils below and kissed by moonlight above. The ship was so steady in flight, Alex almost forgot they were sailing at all. Only the occasional glance at the billowy clouds below reminded her that they were on the move again. She sat at her usual perch above the bridge with Ghaoithe and Fleet, happy for the company. Try as she might, sleep would not come. The same could not be said for the rest of the crew, and Ghaoithe kept the lights low on the bridge. The full moon and cotton ocean provided more than enough ambiance for the evening.

On Alex's lap rested Excalibur. She ran an oiled cloth over its steel. "Do you really think this will find it for us?" she asked.

"I have absolutely no idea. It sounds like there are a lot of things about the sword I didn't know," Ghaoithe said. She rubbed her chin and leaned in to study the blade. She only saw her reflection. The runes Alex described had not reappeared since her first time in the library.

"Coulda been a reaction, or maybe somethin' triggered it. Or maybe it was an accident. No way fer us to know until we get there," said Fleet. He paid no mind to Excalibur. Instead, he retraced their previous trip to Cairo on a map unfurled across their poker table.

"Do you really think anything involving Ellie is an accident by now?" said Alex.

"No, I guess not. That don't mean we're any closer to understandin' a thing about how she works."

Ghaoithe agreed. "I'm not much of a believer in destiny, but artifacts work in mysterious ways sometimes. For all we know, it was you the sword was responding to."

"Well, I always fancied I could give Arthur a run for his money," Alex joked. She gave the sword a small flourish in the air. A displeased grunt sounded from below as one of the sleeping navigators rolled over. Alex took it as a cue to sheathe the sword. The three leaned in to look over the map with hushed voices.

"Did you send word to Samir?" Alex asked Ghaoithe. She secretly hoped they would meet with the captain's old mentor again.

To Alex's disappointment, Ghaoithe shook her head. "Not enough time. We're going in and then getting right out. Just us three. The less anyone outside this ship knows, the better. I'd prefer it not even leave this room."

On the map, Fleet marked two locations with X's and circled one. He said, "This one with the circle is the market where Vargas shot at ya. The other is Samir's. Figure'd we could at least narrow the search a bit. Now go over what all ya remember about the Library again."

For the rest of the evening, they listened to Alex as she recalled what she could about the chase through the market: the shipping area of trucks, the gigantic wooden door, the stairwell that plunged deep into the ground. Sometimes, Ghaoithe stopped her to ask for more details. Time ticked away with each moment Ellie was gone, but the captain promised to no longer rush their search. This change in the Ghaoithe's method pleased Alex, though she knew better than to gloat aloud. By the time the crew began to stir with daybreak through the windows, Alex was exhausted. Once the other two were certain that she could not remember any other hidden details, they dismissed her for a deserved nap. She passed out shortly after her face touched her pillow.

As they approached Cairo, they took a low approach with the *Cloudkicker* skimming the tops of the surrounding dunes. They landed less than half a day's walk away, a distance Ghaoithe hoped would keep them away from prying eyes once they applied the invisibility runes around the ship. She forwent their usual expedition gear. Instead of heavy packs of climbing rigs, extra clothing for various terrain, and fire kits, they carried only light meals, enough water to last the trip, and study materials for the Library.

Dusk crept over the horizon, and the team departed. Ghaoithe wrapped herself in thick, black robes to conceal the glowing sigils underneath. She carried Excalibur, as well. Alex offered little resistance to the idea. Any kind of entrance was better than their last sojourn.

Even so, the walk was not an easy one. Fleet and Ghaoithe relied heavily on Alex to navigate the network of modern society. The two weren't quite as closed off as the rest of Lost Earth, but they were still uncomfortable around thoroughfares of heavy traffic, too-bright convenience stores, and billboards advertising tourist traps. Alex struggled at times, too, for Cairo stretched for miles and was not an easy city to navigate under the cover of night. She wished she had modern money to hail a cab. Had she still been a fresh-faced farm girl rather than a tested explorer, she likely would not have even finished the tiring journey.

With the Great Pyramids as constant beacons over the skyline, they managed to lurk their way through the shadows. As they entered the city proper, Alex did her best to lighten the mood and keep everyone's thoughts from straying to the serious matters ahead. Ghaoithe, in turn, chat up a storm of her own to discuss Egypt and its history with Alex.

"We're not total savages. We know what football is," Ghaoithe said with a laugh as Alex started to explain the sport with the cheers from a nearby stadium echoing down the streets.

"How am I supposed to know? So far, the main forms of entertainment I've seen in Lost Earth are getting drunk and cards," Alex retorted.

"At least it's not baseball…"

"You realize I grew up near St. Louis, right? Don't you dare…"

"…so incredibly boring. Nothing happening for three hours…"

Alex refused to talk to Ghaoithe for the next mile.

Eventually, with the help of Fleet's map, the souk came into view. Without the clamor of haggling or the ethereal half-light of the sun coming through the canvases above, the shopping center transformed entirely. Small creatures darted between stalls. Low voices carried around stone corners. The canvases above flapped ominously in the chill desert breeze.

Alex, with Fleet and Ghaoithe as protective buffers, could not have been happier. She enjoyed the energy of the open market, but she absolutely loved the seedy Aladdin-esque underbelly.

The three of them looped through the complex in short order, an easy task with its linear, narrow pathways. Once convinced that no one followed them, Ghaoithe stopped and pulled off her black layers. Free from its constraints, her armor acted as a giant night light, bathing her companions and the nearby stalls with a pleasant glow. She unstrapped Excalibur's sheath and handed it to Alex.

"Now's the fun part, lass. Think ya can retrace yer steps?" Fleet asked.

Alex ran a finger over Excalibur's cool edge. "I think so. Maybe? I'm not sure what I need to do with this though," she said.

"You'll know when it happens," Fleet said. He knelt down to Alex's level and placed a hand on her shoulder. "Just concentrate. Don't get too worked up over it. We don't even know if the sword'll do anything, so rely on those wits of yers fer now."

Alex nodded, though her confidence remained dim. The pressure closed in on her, reminded her of what was at stake if she could not locate the entrance to the Library. She stretched her arms and legs, swung the sword in a wide arc, and held it aloft like she was reenacting the cover of an 80's fantasy novel. The blade reflected the moonlight and Ghaoithe's sparkling armor but gave no light of its own.

She tried again. All of her thoughts focused on the memory of the runes that burned within the sword.

Still nothing.

"I wonder if Bilbo had this many issues with Sting," Alex muttered. She brought her arm back down.

"At least you don't have hairy feet," said Ghaoithe. She raised an eyebrow. "Do you?"

"No. More importantly, since when do you know about *The Hobbit*?"

Ghaoithe shrugged. "I read."

Alex sighed and shook her head. Her concentration over the sword gone, she turned instead to the alleys that made up the souk. She closed her eyes and imagined them as the lively market from her last visit. Without any further provocation, her legs moved.

Fleet and Ghaoithe exchanged glances and followed suit. Soon, they stood in front of a small shop with little to mark its identity. Through the security gate at its entrance, they saw an array of handbags of all colors and sizes. Alex closed her fingers around the rungs of the gate and peered in. On the wall beside her, just above her hair, a chunk of plaster had been blown out of the wall.

"Well, this is where we start," Alex said with little fanfare. Already, the scraps of memory in her head sharpened into solid visions. At first, everything was fuzzy and consisted of little more than a color of a shirt or a panicked voice in the crowd. A shot. An explosion above her head. Pieces of plaster covered her vision. She ran left.

"This way," Alex said and took off. Little by little, the independent images merged into a single memory. The smell of coffee became a full cafe to her right. The hum of motors in idle led into a loading area. One of the trucks sported a shiny new lock on its back gate.

Ghaoithe and Fleet trailed her with some amusement.

"She's like a bloody hound," Fleet whispered to his captain.

"I know. Isn't it great?" Ghaoithe said.

"At this rate she may end up being a better relic hunter than you."

Ghaoithe shoved a playful elbow at Fleet's side. "Let's not go that far."

They watched as Alex darted about. Though she would never say it, Ghaoithe silently agreed with Fleet. Over the years, she had trained a few relic hunters eager to escape their daily routines. The *Cloudkicker* gained notoriety as a safe haven of sorts for those willing to put in the work to sail. Many still sailed with her. Yet the moment the fiery young journalist came into Ghaoithe's quarters, it was like a door unlocked inside her. She had lived for so long with it closed that she had forgotten it existed. Having Alex around shifted Ghaoithe's priorities in a way she did not expect, and she believed herself incapable of dealing with such a drastic change in her life.

In the recesses of her past, Ghaoithe was still a child. She recalled the hiss of pressurized air. She woke up in a thatched house filled with incense and yellowed bones. A woman she did not recognize sat beside her. She wore an array of herbs and vials across loose leather bindings at her waist. Ghaoithe would come to know her dark, ferocious face over many years of friendship, but the woman frightened her then. She was too weak to move from the foreign bed in the hut.

"You're lucky you're so tall, girl. If you were a normal woman, this would have gone through your lung instead of your waist," said the healer. She held up a thin, wooden spike sightly longer than her thumb. "Frog oil, recluse venom, and a couple other nasty toxins. Most don't make it a couple steps after taking one of these."

Ghaoithe tested a finger against the bandage around her hips. Burning pain shot through her, but she could admit it was not as all-consuming as when the trap first went off. Under the wrappings, she felt two very distinct points beside her hipbones where the splinters dug themselves into her.

"The poison is made to decay anything it touches," said the woman. "You'll have some nasty dots on the outside for the rest of your life, but what's inside you bore the brunt of it. You understand what I'm saying, girl?"

Ghaoithe did not understand. To say her childhood was unconventional touched only a fraction of the truth. Her life tossed aside traditional milestones and conversations given to young girls in favor of bar fights, jungle treasure, and untamed wilds. Besides, most of her vision spun around to the point where she could barely breathe for fear of upsetting her stomach.

"Just tell me what you're trying to say," she said to the medicine woman beside her. She closed her eyes to hold off the dizziness.

The woman rubbed her forehead with long, knobbed fingers as she carefully formed her words. "You're too young to understand what all this means right now, and maybe that's for the best. Women that take injuries like this at your age... they develop differently. A lot of what you know and think about what it means to be a woman may never come to you. Now, it isn't the end of the world, but there may come some days when you're older where you need to accept the lot you've been given."

As it turned out, the darts were not the end of the world, and what Ghaoithe had never experienced could not harm her. Without a frame of reference of what it meant to be a "real" woman, she did not just accept her fate, but embraced it. For nearly twenty years, that was the only truth she knew. With nothing to hold her back, she tore through the barriers of the sky to pilot her life the way she saw fit. She devoted herself wholly to a freedom she knew few others could enjoy, all while she ignored the chasm that slowly deepened just out of sight of the horizon.

She never once considered that it may be possible for her to bridge both worlds.

"We're here," called Alex.

Ghaoithe snapped back to Cairo and cursed herself for daydreaming. She tried to trace where they had walked. Fleet placed a hand on her right shoulder. He gave her a knowing squeeze.

"Don't worry, Lynn. I kept track," he said. Ghaoithe nodded back, appreciative but flustered.

Alex waved for them from the middle of a narrow alley. Unadorned walls squeezed in from both sides. A few doors broke up the monotony along the right side, but they lacked nameplates to indicate whatever took ownership inside.

The moment Ghaoithe stepped into the alley, the memory of her scars vanished in a pulse of adrenaline. Her excitement carried her to Alex's side in only a few strides. There, she found the alcove that protected Alex during their last visit along with a solid oaken door. Its color had been warped by time, and the wrought iron handle had long since been covered in a layer of rust. A quick tug from Ghaoithe told her it would not give for anything.

"I wasn't sure this was the right one. Something just seemed familiar about it," Alex said. She fidgeted about, a student awaiting praise from her instructor.

Ghaoithe encompassed Alex with a suffocating hug and lifted her companion off the ground with a victorious yelp. "You found it, Alex! By god, you found it!" Ghaoithe cheered.

Even Fleet seemed unusually awestruck. He studied the alley while his mouth hung open. "I don't see any sigils, but I ain't ever felt so much of 'em in one place before," he said. "Feels like a bloody thunderstorm's about to start."

Fleet was right. The alley did feel like a thunderstorm on the way. It had that same charge to it, when the air is thick and billowy and arm hairs tingle as though they are about to fly right off the skin. The last time Alex felt anything close to that magnetic pull, the *Cloudkicker* was under a water tunnel at Bimini Road.

"So how do we open it?" Alex asked once her feet touched the ground again. "Three foreigners standing around in a creepy alley isn't exactly inconspicuous."

"We can take our time. If people aren't looking for us, they won't even see this alley," Ghaoithe said.

"You mean we're hidden here? How were we able to find it again?" Alex asked.

Ghaoithe rubbed her chin. "Excalibur, maybe? My armor? I would guess anything with the sigils might act as a key. Maybe it's just because you knew where it was and were looking for it. The point is, we're here," she said.

"Or maybe it wanted ya to find it," Fleet added. Alex was about to laugh, but the anticipation in his eyes told her he was not joking. After all that happened with Ellie, Alex decided to accept the opportunity regardless of where it originated.

They turned back to the door. Nothing Ghaoithe tried made it budge. The sigils that held it in place were stalwart in their purpose.

"Whatever's scrawled on this is airtight. Now's a really good time to figure out that sword of yours," Ghaoithe said.

"I thought you were the great Sky Thief," Alex joked as she stepped forward. She grabbed Excalibur's hilt and pulled it from its bindings. Its blade moved like a dark whisper through the air. Alex held the tip of the sword against the door handle and willed the runes to appear. The door remained locked.

Next, she tried to imagine her energy flowing into the sword, as though it craved her life essence to work. She recalled her training with Ghaoithe. She straightened her back and planted her feet as though she were about to duel the barrier. When that didn't work, she tried etching the sigils from memory with her finger. Finally, she muttered a gibberish incantation of non-words that nonetheless flowed impressively to Fleet and Ghaoithe's amused ears.

*What would Ellie tell me to do here?* Alex asked herself. She closed her eyes, held the sword towards the door, and churned her mind for an answer.

*You're thinking too much. Just relax and do it,* said Ellie's voice in Alex's head. It came to her so clearly she could not be sure whether it was an imaginary conversation with Ellie or the real child reaching out to her.

Either way, Ellie's voice exuded calm patience, and Alex let it take over. She closed her eyes, took a breath, and cleared her mind as best as she was able. She tried to block out her thoughts and live in the moment. The only things that mattered to her were the leather bindings that rubbed into her hands, the Mediterranean breeze that lightly tossed her curls, and the rise and fall of her chest one count at a time. With a smooth motion, she thrust Excalibur forward as casually as her house keys after a long work day and turned it. This time, there was no resistance, only the booming thud of several deadbolts winding within the door.

Ghaoithe clapped Alex on the back. "Something tells me you're getting the hang of this," she said with a raspy laugh.

Alex blushed and put the sword back into its sheath. Before them, the entry chamber of the Library awaited them, lined with the network of complex runes that Alex glimpsed during her previous fall. Far below, a pinpoint of light called to them from the bottom of the stairwell. Last time, Ellie planted Alex safely at the bottom. The stairwell was considerably more frightening from the top.

"Do you really think we'll find a book that can help us?" Alex asked. She recalled the endless aisles of scrolls in the library, but she could not shake the thought of losing precious time to save Ellie because of a wild goose chase.

"Won't know if we don't go down to find out," Fleet said. He stepped into the doorway.

Alex braced herself and did the same.

# XIX

When the *Cloudkicker* discovered Eden hidden under the Bimini Road, Ghaoithe carried a quiet intensity, a workmanlike professionalism to her approach of discovering a new find. Where Alex stared about wide-eyed and new, the captain cautiously approached their discovery with distrust.

That was clearly a different time and captain.

"Will you slow down?" Alex yelled.

Ghaoithe stared at her from several stories below. Even from such a height, the glint in her eye bordered on lust. She turned away from Alex and continued to bound down the stairwell three at a time.

Fleet stayed back to escort Alex the rest of the way. "Don't pay her no mind, lass. I don't think ya realize how much this means to her," he said.

Alex learned of the Library's significance once they caught up to the captain at the bottom of the stairwell. Ghaoithe waited, mouth agape, as she took in the chambers beyond. They were just as Alex remembered, a cavernous network of shelves and piles of paper that receded into the horizon. The candle sconces along the walls bathed the edges of the chamber with a heavenly glow reminiscent of all such great libraries from Oxford to Congress. Alex's previous footsteps were still visible on the ground. They wound beyond sight into the network of bookcases.

"This really is the Library of Alexandria," Ghaoithe said in a hushed tone as if the shelves would vanish once she spoke the words aloud.

Alex netted her fingers and stretched with a satisfying crackle in her knuckles. "Oh, yeah. It's got the inscription above us and everything," she said. She wanted to relish having something over Ghaoithe for once, her first real ancient discovery all of her own. *With Ellie's help of course,* she kept to herself.

Ghaoithe bent down and embraced Alex in a soft hug. "Thank you," said the captain.

Caught off guard, Alex hesitantly returned the gesture. "Are... are you crying?" she asked as she heard Ghaoithe sniffle into her shoulder.

When she pulled away, Ghaoithe's eye was indeed tinged with red. She nodded, embarrassed. "This was the first place I ever set out to find. It's why I became a relic hunter. I never came close. I owe you. A lot," she admitted.

Her bravado shaken, Alex blushed and twirled her foot in the dust on the ground. She said, "It's nothing, really. I'm just glad you could be here."

"We'll have plenty of time for ya two lovebirds to come back once we find Ellie," Fleet huffed from the entrance. He ran his fingers across the stone near the doorway. After a few tries, the wall lit up with sigils that arced into the darkness above. The ceiling twinkled with hundreds of spots like stars in a Midwestern sky and cast a pale glow over the chamber. It wasn't much, but now they could at least see the halls stretch into the distance.

"Well, that would have been nice to know last time," Alex said.

Fleet plucked a candle from one of the sconces. "Just in case."

With the revelation of discovery passed, Ghaoithe turned to the task at hand. She was back in her element, ready to discover and explore and learn. The Library of Alexandria was not just another ancient site. Within its halls rested nearly all of the information Ghaoithe desired to help find other lost relics. Any site or artifact still missing from her own leather journal almost certainly had a clue written in some wayward scroll at the Library. It acted as an integral key to so many mysteries. There was only one problem...

"Where do we start?" Alex asked.

"I kind of figured you'd lead the charge on this one," Ghaoithe said.

Alex shook her head. "To be honest, Ellie led the way for most of the last time. Going in one direction took long enough as it was," she said.

They surveyed the Library as best as they could from their standpoint. With proper lighting above them, they peered down the aisles well enough, but the high shelving made the central parts of the room almost impossible to see. Throughout the chamber, marble columns reached for the ceiling. There were more columns than the group could possibly count, a forest of stone.

"Best thing we can do is take a direction and stick to it fer now. Gotta be a central hub somewhere," said Fleet.

"Assuming we can read anything in it," said Ghaoithe as she inspected a nearby scroll.

After a quick discussion, they decided to head along the left wall, away from Alex's previously explored route. The underground chamber appeared to be a rough square. The bookcases lined up in a grid. As the adventurers walked, they easily searched down the rows for anything out of place. Even at a reasonable pace, however, traversing just one side of the room would take hours.

They did not move at a reasonable pace. Ghaoithe's excitement over the Library resulted in frequent stops so she could pick at the nearest shelves. She paid little attention to the growing frustration of her companions.

"Can you even read any of those?" Alex asked as Ghaoithe flipped through a worn red manuscript. The captain closed the book and reshelved it to try another.

"Some of them. The scrolls were useless, but it's getting easier as we go on. A lot of these are in Latin," said Ghaoithe.

Fleet tempted one of the books on a nearby shelf but gave up after a few pages. He never learned to read ancient languages in the same way Ghaoithe did. "Anything interestin'?" he asked.

"This section's mostly apothecary ledgers, alchemical recipes... that sort of thing. The wards on all these books are basic parchment protection, but what's inside is strange. It's like nothing I've seen before, but it's familiar at the same time," Ghaoithe said.

"Maybe ya found a wayward book from here at one point or another."

Ghaoithe paused. Her eye glazed over at the page in her hand as she tried to recall something just on the edge of her experience. Finally, she shook her head. For once, her voice was soft, almost reverent of the knowledge around them. She said, "This Library could hold every clue we've ever needed, but it would take lifetimes to comb through it all."

Alex ran her hands over one of the books. Its soft leather had been worn by use, but its significance transcended anything tactile even to a layman like her. "I wonder how it all got here from Alexandria," she wondered aloud.

"Who knows? Maybe they knew Julius Caesar was coming and moved what they could to another location? Or this was always a secondary location? Either way, this can only be a portion of what they had originally. The first Library... it's just unfathomable," Ghaoithe said. She reached for a number of books and began to stuff them into her bag.

"What in the world are you doing?" asked Alex.

"If something happens and I die tomorrow, I want to die smarter than I was today. These books are going to help with that."

Fleet cleared his throat. The girls snapped out of their awe.

"We'll make it back here one day, but we still got a job to do. Best be gettin' to it," he said. Alex noted his lack of enthusiasm in the statement; Fleet the quartermaster put aside Fleet the explorer to keep the group moving onward.

They continued onward. Cursory checks on the books revealed everything from business ledgers to cooking recipes to bestiaries of long-gone creatures. Each huddled in their own unique sections of which there seemed to be no end of content. Ghaoithe could not, however, find any trace of Pandora's Box. As she searched, she worried that perhaps she should have followed Alex's original path to the book that led them there in the first place.

As the captain readied to make the call to backtrack, Fleet motioned to them from a few aisles ahead.

"Found somethin'," was all he said as the women joined him. He pointed down the row of books. Sure enough, the aisle did not continue down to the inevitable darkness of the opposite chamber wall as the others did. Though it was some trek away, a solid structure of white stone blocked the path. Above it, the sigils circled and warped around each other to shine a pale beam of light toward the object.

Alex looked down the walls on both sides of the group. "We're about halfway down this side, but I can't tell how far it is to the other end. Think that's the center of the room?"

Ghaoithe shrugged. "It's not a bookcase or a pillar, so it's probably worth checking out. Unless either of you have a better idea?"

With no objections, they started toward their new destination. Subtle changes marked their walk. At first, the aisle was like all of the others with cold stone under their feet and little adornment on the shelves. As they neared the object, the lights overhead brightened ever-so-slightly. Stone flooring gave way to tiled mosaics, dusty but still colorful after years of isolation. Most were simple images of wildlife, robed scholars, or plants, but a few fables popped up, too. Alex recognized Daedalus and his melting wings as well as the plagues of Egypt. She even noticed a portrayal of Excalibur, waves crashing against it as the Lady of the Lake handed the blade to King Arthur. She laughed as she remembered the true origins of the blade told to her by Ghaoithe on her first day on the ship.

Excalibur's painting did not go unnoticed by the captain, either.

"That shouldn't be here," she said. "That's a modern story compared to when this Library was created."

"So the collection hasn't been missing as long as we thought. Ya think someone else knows about it nowadays?" Fleet asked. He furrowed his brows as his eyes darted about in search of danger.

Ghaoithe shook her head. "No. We would have heard about it. It does lead you to wonder just what else we don't know about this place, though. Be on your guard."

The captain tried to sound cautious and professional, but Alex noted the giddy tinge of anticipation in her voice. The news only further added to the pile of dreams Ghaoithe had built up in her head regarding the Library. Had Alex not been so awestruck by everything equally since joining the *Cloudkicker*, she supposed she would have reacted the same over finishing a lifelong project. This was Ghaoithe's Disney World.

By the time they reached their goal, the Library had completely changed. The sigil lights cast a bright glow that may as well have been sunlight through a high window. Colorful murals covered every shelf, and the nearby books were pristine even beyond the runic protection. Only the dust stirred up with every step indicated the true passage of time.

The stone object waited in the center of a clearing. It was a white stone basin almost four feet across and chest high even to the giantess captain. Nothing flowed within it. Spouts on four sides matched the directions of the Library's walls. Carved around its polished exterior, lifeless sigils looped their way across the surface, down an ornate support shaft, and into the floor below.

"I definitely did not expect it to be a birdbath. Or is it a giant decorative goblet? I can't tell," Alex said. She stepped up to it, her head just able to see over the rim. The inside was bone dry but free of any cracks expected of ancient stone. The sigils along the outside of the bowl stopped near the spouts.

Ghaoithe circled the basin. She stooped down to check the underside of the bowl, its support, and the floor below. Then, she stood up and made her way around the open area to inspect each bookcase. When she finished, she returned to the basin with a wide grin on her face.

"I need a rag and some chalk," she directed at Fleet.

"Oh, here we go," Fleet said with feigned annoyance. He knelt down and sifted through the few contents of his bag. He pulled out a handful of rags and a lone stick of white chalk and passed them to Ghaoithe.

The captain bent down and swept the dust from the floor with flicks of the rag. As she circled the room, she uncovered a massive mosaic of a blue and gold star that encompassed the entire area around the basin. The tiles had been preserved impeccably well, the color almost as rich as if they were new. From the steps leading up to the basin, the darkened sigils sprawled across the floor in a whirling display, tendrils flowing in every direction and into the book halls beyond.

"There's so much down here," Alex said. She tiptoed around the floor as though stepping on the runes would break them. Even the *Cloudkicker*'s hull did not display such a network of writing.

"What's it say, Lynn?" Fleet asked.

"Don't know. I don't recognize most of the patterns. It's not for preservation or concealment, near as I can tell. A few sections are missing, though," Ghaoithe said. She swept away another patch of dust with giddy fervor. Once she finished, she stood and admired her cleaning job.

As Alex looked at the intricate runework, she started to notice the patterns Ghaoithe referred to. Sure enough, a few small portions of the layout disappeared altogether as the sigils approached the perimeter of the floor. Her curiosity mingled with the encouraging fact that she was getting better at reading the layout of Lost Earth's ancient writing.

Chalk in hand, Ghaoithe looked to the other two as if to ask for silent permission. They nodded. She set to work. As she moved around the room, she connected the lines where the runework had all but vanished. Bit by bit, she completed the patterns on the floor as best she knew how. The moment her chalk brought the final two lines together, the area sparkled. A dim pulse briefly lit the runes on the floor before they went dark again. Alex waited for something else to happen.

"Did you miss one somewhere?" she asked after a moment.

"Not that I know of. I connected them all with the rest of the Lib—oh here we go!" Ghaoithe said. She pointed to one of the aisles.

From far across the Library chamber, near the wall, a lone string of blue light wove its way toward them. As it approached the first bookcase, it expanded like a network of streams to cover the shelves. The main branch charged forward, each case and aisle exploding in a holiday display of light as it traveled. Through the thick dust and grime of the years, the sigils brought the Library of Alexandria to life with energy that laid dormant for centuries. By the time the light started to swarm the floor below Alex, she could see almost every book, every mosaic tile in brilliant clarity as far as she could see in any direction.

Once the flow of light reached the strange basin, it swirled across the steps, up the pedestal, and around the bowl. The sigils stopped just short of the lip. A soft hum emanated from within the structure. From the four spigots, a gentle flow of bright liquid light filled the basin before going dormant once again.

Alex, Ghaoithe, and Fleet cautiously approached the fountain. The pool inside reflected nothing. It only cast its blue glow over their faces.

"Is that water?" Alex asked.

"Dunno. It's like the runes turned into wine or somethin'," Fleet said.

Ghaoithe waved caution aside and reached forward. When her finger touched the pool, a surge rippled through it. A low male voice boomed from the air around them in a language of gibberish. They each jumped back.

"That anything ya know, Lynn? Doesn't sound Latin," asked Fleet.

Ghaoithe shook her head. She composed herself and placed her hand on the bowl again. "Uh, English?" she tested.

Another hum from the fountain. The voice returned with more gibberish. It clipped every few seconds, the language noticeably changing with each attempt. Soon, it reached familiar territory, going through German, French, and finally...

*"Anglo-Saxon derivative. English. Welcome to the Library of Alexandria Index, scholars. Please state your search request,"* said the index.

Together, the explorers shouted in celebration. Fleet high-fived Ghaoithe and embraced a stunned Alex in a bear hug.

"Hey, Index, where are the books for Latin-era alchemy?" asked Ghaoithe.

*"Block 12. Supplemental material also found in Herbology, Block 523,"* answered the Index. From near the edge of the room, where the team walked earlier, a pillar of light showcased the bookshelf Ghaoithe had flipped through a short time ago. Another light came down in a far corner of the Library.

"Well, ain't that somethin'," Fleet gawked. He turned to the pool. "Hey, Index. Can ya look up information inside individual books? We don't know the titles we're lookin' fer or anything."

*"Yes. All titles and text information are conveyed via the runework on each entry to the Library. So long as a request is on a shelf, all relevant contents shall be relayed here."*

"Well, that explains the runes I was trying to figure out earlier," Ghaoithe said. She placed her hands on the rim of the Index and leaned in. "Do you have any books that mention the location of Pandora's Box?"

*"The Library contains many books on mythology. However, books relating to the exact location of Pandora's Box are restricted. Requesting access without authorization will trigger containment systems. Please say the registered password or make a different request."*

Fleet frowned and stroked his beard. "Password, eh? That'll be troublesome. We ain't got time to run around searchin' the whole place if it won't tell us," he said.

"It's the only shot we've got. If worse comes to worse, we find out which bookcase gets locked up by this security thing and figure out a way to break it open," Ghaoithe said.

"If ya say so," Fleet replied. His hand closed around the hilt of his rapier in preparation.

Ghaoithe circled the Index. She looked down at her feet as she walked, her chin between her finger and thumb. Sometimes, she muttered a word, shook her head, and continued to pace.

"Index, the passcode is 'Osiris,'" she finally said with sure confidence. The three of them waited as the index processed Ghaoithe's suggestion.

"*That… is incorrect,*" it said.

Around the room, clear barriers shot up from the floor to cut off access to the rest of the Library. Each wall rose into the upper reaches of the chamber to an impossible height to scale. The Index went dark.

The three explorers ran together to one of the walls. Ghaoithe pounded on it with her fist, but it gave little more than a shudder.

"Glass," she said.

"I thought you said the books would be locked up, not us!" Alex said.

"It made sense at the time!" Ghaoithe yelled back. She reared back and gave the glass a solid kick with the heel of her boot, wincing from the pain that shot up her bruised side. The glass shuddered slightly but remained unscathed.

A rumble shook the three off their balance. As they looked on in shock, the floor near the altar gave way to a deep nothingness below. The pit did not widen quickly, but with only a few feet between the Index and the crew, it was only a short matter of time before they fell into whatever prison the Library creators planned for unwanted guests. Alex drew Excalibur and thrust it at the wall. Her sword slid upward on the glass seamlessly as though the steel had turned to butter. She tried again and again with the same result. She turned around. The pit was halfway to her.

"Can we jump to the index?" she asked. The basin and its steps acted as an island in the center of their cage.

"And do what? Just casually hang on for a while?" said Ghaoithe.

"Arguin' ain't helpin'!" Fleet interjected.

From behind the glass, a boom echoed through the ancient halls. Alex recognized the sound immediately. She watched as the glass in front of her cracked from the impact of a long, golden tip now embedded into it. The crack spread rapidly like thin ice over a frozen lake. Another boom went out. An impact on the corner of the wall finished it. Shards rained down as the three threw themselves forward into the safety of the Library shelves.

"Everyone ok?" Fleet asked once they were certain the ground below was not going to cave in like the pit just a few feet away.

Alex and Ghaoithe groaned in acknowledgment as they picked themselves off the ground. Tiny glass beads fell out of Alex's hair. She felt more than a few cuts along her limbs, too.

"That glass might have stopped everything in its day, but the Greeks never had to deal with 50-cal BMGs," said a woman nearby. They looked up.

Jessie Vargas stood in the center of the aisle, rifle in hand.

Ghaoithe leapt to her feet and moved between Vargas and Alex. She drew her rapier as her right hand clutched her bruised side. Vargas, however, lowered her own weapon.

"I would have let you drop if I meant to kill you," Vargas said.

"It wouldn't be the first time Osiris has tried to take us alive. What do you want, Vargas?" Ghaoithe growled.

Jessie pulled the brim of her hat low over her eyes. She rubbed her arm as she struggled to gather the courage to speak. "I'm here to help stop Osiris. Let me take you to them," she said.

# XX

Most of the *Cloudkicker*'s inner circle stood outside the cell. Ghaoithe, Fleet, Alex, Roy, and Damian each silently ran through scenarios and questions in their own minds. Only Kirk abstained from the meeting; he maintained the ship's crystal charge in the hull below. Inside the cell, Jessica Vargas awaited their interrogation with an annoyed patience.

"You know, it's kind of nice being on this side for once," joked Damian. He spent much of his own time within the ship's brig after first arriving.

"You didn't shoot at one of my crew," said Ghaoithe. Damian shrunk under the acidic tone that could have melted the bars in front of them.

Vargas lifted her chin in defiance. "And I missed. Your Alex is alive beside you. None of you are rotting at the bottom of a pit. I will not apologize for doing what had to be done to protect my family."

Her honeyed, sultry accent fascinated Alex. It sounded like rich coffee and a ballroom dance in a rainforest villa. She never expected her shooter to be so refined or to carry beauty with an aged grace after so many years in the desert. If they met on the street, Alex would have guessed Jessie to be a movie star or a trade baroness, not the Desert Siren.

Jessie's gun sat out of reach along the wall outside the brig. Earlier, Alex tried to lift it and immediately felt winded. Ghaoithe was the only other one to go near it, the rest of the crew too uncertain of the modern technology's presence. Alex understood what the gun meant. That Vargas could swing it around like a child's toy? With that aim?

Modern tech or not, Vargas was just as much an incomprehensible product of Lost Earth as Ghaoithe's team.

The captain narrowed her eye as she judged her captive. "You did save us in the Library. I can't deny that. What I want to know is why."

The question shadowed the entire trek back to the *Cloudkicker*. After breaking the trap that almost killed the crew, Vargas put up little resistance to a shaken and angry Ghaoithe. The sharpshooter only said she had information to help them find Osiris. They wasted no more time in the Library of Alexandria and made their way back to the airship with haste. The books were not going anywhere, and the captain could not pass up a shortcut to Ellie's location.

"It's not a trap. If I wanted something, I would have let the hole take you and dug it off your corpse later," said Vargas with a tint of amusement.

"That doesn't mean we can trust you," said Ghaoithe.

"Of course not, but you do need me. I know where Osiris digs."

"They handed the information over to a mercenary? Just let you roam into the wind?"

"I… learned about it by accident. From an old friend of yours."

Ghaoithe frowned for a moment before her eye widened. "Oh. I see. That's how it is."

From inside her cell, Vargas pouted and turned to glare at the wall beside her bed. "Yes. That's how it is. Even I'm not immune to a bit of warmth and comfort."

"Was it worth it? Selling your soul for a moment's rest?"

Vargas shot a death glare at the captain, but she could not hide the slight tremble of her chin. She returned to the wall. "No. Not after all he told me. To hear it from him... I knew what I had to do."

Ghaoithe crossed her arms, her leather armor creaking under the strain. Though her ribs no doubt hurt underneath, she was doing all she could to show every inch of her intimidating figure. "What exactly did Sorin tell you?"

"Everything," said Vargas. She turned to the captain. Even in the low light, Alex noticed the lines appear at the corners of the assassin's mouth. "He told me everything. What they were after. What they planned to do with that little girl. I could not sit on that ship after I knew."

The sharp edge in her voice cracked at the mention of Ellie. On the other side of the hall, Damian lowered his head. Roy placed a hand on the young man's shoulder. Only Ghaoithe remained unabashed. She stared into the cage without a word as she weighed the decisions Vargas placed at her feet. The captain admitted, if only to herself, that she was out of options and nearly out of time to figure out how to approach Osiris. If that meant triggering a trap, she would just have to figure out exactly what kind of trap awaited her.

"How can we know anything you tell us is true? Thinking of other peoples' interests is not exactly part of your reputation," Ghaoithe said.

Vargas stood up from her bed and approached the bars. She was tall and lean, not quite as tall as the captain but enough to defy the other's challenge.

"I could have ran, you know. Osiris offered to let me leave the ship at any time and never look back. That was our deal. I got them the girl, and I never had to do another job again. I could be secluded and comfortable and forgotten right now," said Vargas.

"So why didn't you?"

Vargas shook her head. "I am tired of running, but I still have a little more to go. For once in my life, I plan to run toward the problem.

I won't leave that child in Deacon's hands. Peace wouldn't mean much if the world ended due to my own cowardice."

After a long silence, Ghaoithe abruptly left the brig and strode down the hallway. She motioned for the others to follow. Once they were out of audible range of Vargas, she huddled with them.

"What do you think?" she asked.

"I think she tried to shoot me before," Alex said without missing a beat. She found a new respect for Jessica Vargas after meeting her in person but in the same way she respected a wild tiger. She preferred to stay on her own side of the cage.

Her shoulders dropped when Damian spoke out in dissent. "I don't think she's lying. What she means about Ellie… I know how she feels. I think we all do."

"What about you two?" Ghaoithe asked Roy and Fleet.

Roy looked back at the bars at the end of the hall. "I'm with Damian. She can act tough all she wants, but I think she's scared. Stepping onto this ship was her execution sentence if Deacon ever gets a hold of her again," he said.

"So we're just ignoring when she tried to execute me? And Ghaoithe?!" Alex cried. All she could think of was the shot whistling over her head and the massive bruise that still hampered the captain.

"Sorry, lass," Fleet said with a sympathetic look.

Alex, wounded, huffed and stomped towards the stairwell. As she passed the brig, she stopped and pointed at Vargas.

"The captain might forgive you for how much you put us through, but I won't," Alex warned. She vanished off to her room. Not far behind her was the rest of the group. Vargas straightened expectantly from her seat on the edge of her bed.

"Let's get one thing straight," Ghaoithe began, "I don't like you, my crew doesn't like you, and Alex especially doesn't like you. You are here because we have no choice. Your gun will be taken. You will be escorted around the ship at all times and only because discussing strategy is uncomfortable in a cell. You will sleep here every night and eat when we let you. If I sense anything—and I mean *anything*—that makes me believe you are still working for Deacon, I will find the hottest, most barren tract of the Outback that has ever existed and leave you there naked. Got it?"

Through the bars, Ghaoithe was the only one to meet Jessie's eyes. The rest looked down out of respect or contemplation on the captain. Through all of their troubles, the ship acted as their haven, their peace-of-mind. None of Ghaoithe's friends knew her to make a serious threat while on board the *Cloudkicker*. They trod on new ground.

To their surprise, Vargas laughed. Her eyes welled up as she leaned back onto her pillow and covered her face with her arm.

"The first time I made a deal with Osiris, it was to live a free life of my choosing, and now I make a deal to become a prisoner. I suppose this is the price for leaving them. It's fitting," she said.

"If you're expecting sympathy, you're talking to the wrong woman," said Ghaoithe.

Vargas rubbed her eyes with the crook of her elbow. She shook her head. "I do not expect your sympathy. Right now, I just want some sleep and your protection."

Ghaoithe nodded at the others. They turned and made their way to their own quarters to prepare for the coming day. The captain started to follow but stopped.

"Why didn't you take the shot?" Ghaoithe asked.

Vargas lowered her arm to stare at Ghaoithe and then the ceiling. After she mulled the question, she sighed and said, "You may be bulletproof, but you're still human. Deacon knows what losing that girl would do to you. I didn't want to give him that satisfaction so easily. You might not believe it now, but even I've admired stories about the great Sky Thief on occasion."

It was a half-truth, but it satisfied the captain. With a 'hmph,' she turned heel and left Vargas alone in the brig.

Jessie turned on her right side to face the wall. The bed was little more than a stone slab with a scant few sheets strewn on top of it, but she was asleep before she counted to ten. Despite being held captive aboard the *Cloudkicker*, the ship was one of the first places in a very long time she felt truly safe to rest.

Alex huffed as she paced about her room. It wasn't often she missed having her phone since joining the relic hunters, but she did then. She needed to vent, to tell her friends about her day, to scrawl angrily over her journals at the betrayal she felt from the rest of the *Cloudkicker*'s inner circle. They willingly took in a pit viper without more than a cursory vote. A viper that, by the way, already tried to bite both Alex and the captain.

As anger coursed through her, Alex tried to find an escape in her incredibly bare room. She had never been genuinely angry on the ship before and thus never took any note of things to actually do in her quarters. She had been frightened, anxious, and nervous, yes, but never throw-things-at-her-pillows angry. She decided she needed to hang some art on her walls.

When her pacing failed to tire her, Alex dropped to the ground and started doing push-ups at the foot of her bed. She could not remember the last time she did push-ups. Eighth grade gym class maybe? She certainly did not remember them being so easy.

Someone knocked at her door. Alex spit out a quick, "Come in."

Ghaoithe stepped inside. She looked down as Alex continued for a few more pushes before she turned onto her back and began sit-ups.

"Not satisfied with my fighting lessons? Or am I the only one who remembers what you looked like before you became a freeloader on my ship?" Ghaoithe chuckled.

"It's not like... I have anything else... I can do," Alex said between reps. She focused solely on her knees. From the floor, the captain's presence loomed even larger than normal, and Alex knew she would not stay mad at the captain if she looked up at that tanned, troubled grin.

"You could listen for a second," Ghaoithe argued.

"You think... you have... an answer for... everything, don't you?"

"No, I really don't. Especially not right now. That's why I want to talk."

Alex looked up just briefly enough to see the cracks at the edge of Ghaoithe's eye that always appeared when the captain was stressed. They made the captain real and whole, which was the furthest thing Alex wanted to consider then. She shook the image out of her head and continued her sit-ups.

Ghaoithe frowned and sidestepped Alex's angry crunches to sit on the bed. "Do what you need to. I'll wait. You'll tire yourself out sooner than later at that rate," she said.

Sure enough, Alex's rush of adrenaline wore off shortly after. She wheezed and gasped for air as blonde sweat-soaked strands clung to her face.

"Don't even say it," Alex said.

"I wasn't going to say anything," Ghaoithe answered. She stood up, strode over Alex and into the bathroom, and sifted through the cupboards for a glass. Through the banging doors, she called out, "You should really decorate your room. It's kind of bare."

When she returned, she passed Alex a fresh cup of water. Alex drained it, set the glass on her lone dresser, and plopped face-down onto the bed beside the captain.

"How can you listen to anything that woman has to say?" Alex asked once her heart slowed down enough for her to hear her own voice again.

Ghaoithe adjusted the strap of her eyepatch. It squeezed her head more than normal and made thinking uncomfortable. It happened around Alex more and more as time went on. She would never take it off around her crew, but for this conversation, it felt unnatural somehow.

"I don't know why, honestly. It's just a gut feeling that we need to hear her out," Ghaoithe said. She refit the band around her ear and covered it with a few short strands of hair.

Alex leaned up on one arm and pouted with an insulted look. "Even after she tried to kill me? Kill you?"

"If she really wanted you dead, you would be. I think there's more to her than you give her credit for," Ghaoithe replied. She leaned back on her elbows to meet Alex's eye level. "Something else tells me you aren't upset about Vargas at all."

Alex glowered for a brief second. She knew what scared her and the words she wanted to say. She'd needed to say them since they left China. Around her, the gentle sway of the ship provided a welcome catalyst, and her body's weariness took over. Before she could stop, she found herself in Ghaoithe's arms.

"I'm scared, Lynn. I don't want another Sorin," Alex cried.

Ghaoithe said nothing. She only held Alex, their thoughts in sync. She did not need to ask anything else.

In the wake of the crash, the two of them knew deep down that any distraction could only last for so long. Sorin's betrayal blindsided them and left them with the overwhelming sense of constantly playing catch-up with each new development. For the captain, she had to live with the knowledge that so much could have been avoided if she had rooted out the Osiris spy sooner. She would never know just how much information he fed to the organization or how many of their trials may have gone without incident had he been absent.

Alex sobbed again. "I keep seeing him laying on the floor. I can't get his eyes out of my head."

There was little doubt what she meant. Ghaoithe saw them, too: Ethan's eyes as he pleaded to Alex in his final moments before the explosive crack of a bullet deafened them. She saw his body go limp on the ground and Alex charge with rage before the *Cloudkicker* appeared in the nick of time. The captain sniffed and wiped her own eye.

"It's not your fault, Alex. It's mine," Ghaoithe said.

"Don't say that."

"It's the truth. I let Ethan go to Osiris. I kept Sorin aboard this ship. I should have been the one to know how far Deacon would go to get what he wants."

"I don't blame you. Even you couldn't have known about all of this."

Alex threw her arms around Ghaoithe and buried her face in the captain's armor. Ghaoithe leaned into Alex's curls and breathed in their slightly-sweet scent. Neither said a thing in their impasse.

"What if it happens again? What if it's you this time?" Alex said softly once her tears ran out. She kept a cheek against Ghaoithe's armor and soaked in the warm sigil light it emanated. The captain's deep breaths calmed her thoughts. Her eyelids drooped steadily with the rise and fall of Ghaoithe's chest.

"It won't happen again. I wouldn't leave you behind like that," Ghaoithe said.

"And Vargas?"

"You don't have to trust her. Just listen to what she has to say and we'll go from there."

Alex yawned and nodded. "Ok. I trust you. I'll always trust you."

Once Alex was fully asleep, Ghaoithe lifted her to lay properly on the bed. She pulled the sheets over Alex and began to make her way out of the room. At the last moment, she stopped, turned, and laid on the floor next to the bed. Soon after, sleep took her, too.

# XXI

If Vargas and Ghaoithe shared anything in common, it was their love of alcohol. When the captain came to wake the sniper, her captive proved less than receptive. The vulnerability shown the night before vanished in a display of verbal jabs, feigned ignorance, and a few lightning-quick snaps of the hands, like two mountain cats vying for the same territory. Once Ghaoithe managed to drag Vargas out of the cell, Jessie almost immediately demanded a proper breakfast, complete with the captain's apparently-famous Irish coffee. She refused to cooperate with the search for Osiris until then. Once it became clear that she could stick to her guns no matter what threats or intimidation Ghaoithe could throw at her, the captain relented and set to work to help Chef Richard in the galley.

Vargas was much more receptive to conversation once she had the coffee in her hands. She no longer leered at the captain as they sat across from each other.

"The rumors about your cocktail were true," Vargas said as they ate. She took a sip from her mug. Most of the food on her plate remained untouched.

"The secret is the cream. You can't just use any old carton. There's a lovely little village on the southern edge of the Kazakh Steppe that makes the best if you can get your hands on it," Ghaoithe said.

Her tone mirrored Jessie's. Alex noticed how uncomfortable the captain was at playing bad cop with Vargas. It was her hands that gave her away, always in nervous motion to fiddle with a mug or run through her hair. Normally, her size and husky tenor were enough to intimidate people into giving up information. She had precious little experience in dealing with someone truly fearless. Indeed, Vargas was not just brazen against the captain; she simply did not care. The dynamic threw Ghaoithe for a loop. A chat about fine liquors was much more suited to her speed.

When everyone finished breakfast, Vargas followed the crew with the sole demand of having a mug of coffee brought with her. Ghaoithe, given her own array of personal flasks, was in no position to debate and rushed off to brew one more pot as a string of curses trailed behind.

"We could have done this on the bridge," said Vargas once they arrived in the captain's quarters.

"I'm not letting you anywhere near the controls of my ship," replied Ghaoithe. She stood shoulder-to-shoulder with the sniper, two bronzed warriors unwilling to bend. Though neither could anyone else. Ghaoithe's cabin was larger than the others aboard the ship, but so many artifacts and memorabilia cluttered the room that the present company forcibly crammed themselves around her desk. Everyone from her inner circle waited eagerly for Jessie's information if for no other reason than to leave the overcrowded atmosphere.

"Where do we start?" Ghaoithe continued as she ignored her own discomfort.

"Western Gabon," said Jessie.

Ghaoithe squeezed past Alex and Kirk. Along the wall opposite her bed stood a tall, narrow cabinet. Once opened, it revealed dozens of rolls of parchment and maps. Ghaoithe picked one without hesitation, as though she had every scrap inside the cabinet memorized. The map was for everyone else in the meeting.

Alex knew very little about Gabon, only its general location in Central Africa and that it had monkeys. She imagined a trek through lush jungle, backpack in tow as she explored uncharted waters. Once the map was unfurled, the daydream kicked into overdrive as she looked at vast spaces of empty scroll among the topographical green. Named locations, even those of the Lost Earth variety, were few and far between.

After giving the map a once over, Vargas picked up a pencil from the desk and marked a cross on a section in the western area not far off from the Ogooue River.

"They've got a colony of some kind here. A lot of earthmovers and workers digging by hand day and night. A few buildings and a ton of security on the perimeter," Vargas said. She then made a rough circle around the cross. "The *Ascendant* patrols in a loop and never strays more than about thirty kilometers from the site in any direction."

"Have they found anything yet?" Fleet asked.

Jessie shook her head. "Not that I know of. If anything, he kept pulling in more workers."

Ghaoithe frowned at the news. She had little doubt that Osiris could move entire mountains when obsessed with something. She asked Jessie, "Is it the urn?"

"I have no idea. Neither did Sorin. Whatever Deacon's playing, he's keeping it close to the chest. The only people who know are him and that assistant of his."

"Assistant? I've never known Deacon to have a secretary."

Vargas shrugged. "Yeah, some young girl in over her head. Name's Rebecca or something."

Alex gasped. She slammed her hand down on the table to lean toward Vargas. "Becky?! Is she hurt? Is she ok?"

"She's fine, all right. She hardly leaves Deacon's side. Girl drank the Osiris punch and asked for seconds," Vargas said. At Alex's expression, she lowered her eyes back at the map.

Ghaoithe understood Alex's worry all too well. She wrapped an arm around the girl's shoulder with a gentle squeeze. Alex wanted no part of it. Her voice catching in her throat, she excused herself and ran out of the quarters. Everyone's eyes followed her without a word.

Fleet motioned to follow, but he instead hunched in defeat. He turned back to inspect the map. The strip mine was surrounded by dense forest on all sides. Only a few sparse villages dotted the map along the river some ways away, and Deacon no doubt cleared any other hidden settlements that dared to reside within his territory. Without a clear spot to land, the *Cloudkicker* would be fully exposed in any attempt to get near the dig.

Yet, the area looked familiar, and the answer Fleet needed stood on the tip of his tongue. When he found it, he pointed at the map with a little too much fervor. The rest of the team jumped back at his excited yawp.

"Lynn! Here!" he shouted.

The captain bent down. Fleet's finger rested on a patch of jungle about 100 kilometers west of the dig. When Ghaoithe scrunched her nose in confusion, Fleet rolled his eyes. "The doc!" he said.

At this, Ghaoithe guffawed. It lightened the tension in the room, though only she and Fleet understood the revelation.

"Finally a bit of good news," Ghaoithe said. She stood tall and faced her crew. "Everyone start packing for the jungle. We'll be there within a day. Damian, take Vargas and, I don't know, do crosswords or something."

Vargas glared at the young man, who shrunk under her gaze. "I've got a better idea. You know what horchata is?" she asked.

Damian returned a mischievous grin. "Sí. Ahora realmente podía tomar una copa. Con ron," he said. Vargas raised her brows, clearly impressed, and they walked towards the galley in a storm of Spanish.

"When you got time, let me know. We can discuss my little project," Kirk said to Ghaoithe. He left without another word. The others followed.

When only Ghaoithe and Fleet remained, the quartermaster gave a worried look to a spot below deck. "What about the lass? Is she gonna be alright?" he asked solemnly.

"I have no idea," Ghaoithe answered. She knew that Becky's capture by Osiris would not be taken well, but Jessie's intel proved worse than she imagined. "If Becky's working with Deacon willingly, the chances of getting her back are slim. You know how deep he can dig his claws into someone her age."

"You want me to go talk to her once she's calmed down?"

Ghaoithe waved off his suggestion. "No. I'll do it. Besides, that isn't the only thing about this missions she's not going to like."

Everything in the room hurt to look at. It was a perfect study in kitsch, with bright pink walls, an army of pastel-colored plush animals, and even a four-post bed with a sheer silk canopy. On top of the various hand-painted dressers, the likes of Sirs Kipling and Doyle mingled with Suess and Sendak. Only the door to the room stood out, its steel frame awkwardly painted pink to match the rest of the interior. In a corner near the bed, Ellie arranged a gaudy set of toy china for her guests. She poured a stream of invisible tea for her friends: a fluffy beige rabbit, a ferocious triceratops, and Raggedy Ann.

Footsteps approached the door. Even through the metal, Ellie heard them speak. She could hear voices from everywhere when she wanted to.

"I really don't mind staying. It makes me uncomfortable to leave you alone with her," said a feminine voice.

With precise enunciation, an older man replied, "I assure you we'll be fine, my dear. The girl won't cause any trouble."

One by one, a series of deadbolts rolled open from the other side of the door. In stepped Deacon. His suit of slick, dark green cashmere produced a void in the garish room. Behind him trailed Becky. As Ellie looked up, Deacon curtsied. The child nodded slightly in return. Becky, however, wore an expression somewhere between disgust and fear.

"Lady Elpis, I hope I have not interrupted your gathering," Deacon said.

Ellie shook her head. She reached over and removed the triceratops from its seat and placed it on the floor next to her. "No, it's ok. We have room," she said.

Deacon nodded and removed his overcoat. He handed it to Becky. "That will be all for now."

Becky frowned and gave one last glare in Ellie's direction. She folded the coat over her arm and said, "I'll be right outside."

Once the door shut, Deacon folded his grasshopper legs beneath the miniature chair. Ellie lifted her pinky as she sipped from her own teacup. The two said nothing as they enjoyed the imaginary tea party in silence. After Deacon observed the proper amount of respectful time, he lowered his drink and adjusted his spectacles. He placed his hands beneath his chin and leaned in to the table.

"I need your help, Elpis," Deacon said. "You are a very important little girl."

Ellie shrugged and said, "I know, but I can't help you. I keep telling you they won't let me."

"Who won't let you?"

Ellie pointed to the ceiling. "There are rules to this kind of thing. I can't break them."

Deacon sighed. He took his glasses off and polished them with a cloth from his pocket. "That's a shame, my dear. It would make it so much easier on your friends to be done with this business already," he said.

"I'm not worried. They'll find you," Ellie said.

At this, Deacon chuckled. It was low and hollow. He said, "Your confidence might sway others, Elpis, but not me. You can see a lot of things dealing with peoples' hopes, but you cannot tell the future. You are not a full-fledged god."

Ellie pouted and looked away. Reaching across the table, Deacon's hands found the plush triceratops and took it for his own. Ellie made a weak grab for it, but Deacon held it aloft and out of reach.

"Do you know why I am trying to find Pandora's Box? Why I even joined Osiris in the first place," he continued. His fingers toyed with the point of the dinosaur's felt nose horn.

"You want to rid the world of evil," Ellie said mechanically.

"Oh, come now. To be so basic is beneath you. Put some effort into it, dear."

Ellie stared at him with cold blue eyes. They pried him open with robotic efficiency and far less emotion than the stars inside them suggested. When she took what she wanted, she closed her eyes, lifted up her cup, and began with a sip of pretend oolong.

"You want people to listen to you. You want the bad, rich men to stop laughing. You tried to show them what you thought the world could be, but they never believed you. It hurt," Ellie said.

Deacon nodded as the crooks of his mouth slithered upward. "Ah, but I am not so worried about that now. Those men are dead now."

"You still hear them, though. In your head. You won't stop until you've proved them wrong for good."

"Maybe so, but I am about to do just that. You see everyone's hopes, but will you deny mine? I want this world to be safe, secure. It is what I want and my company wants, and it will be better for everyone in time. So what if I have a little personal vendetta to go along with that?"

Ellie tilted her head in confusion. "That's not what your people want, though. They don't trust you, you know. You make people afraid, so they listen, but that does not mean they want you to win. Even the people close to you follow because they are afraid. Many of them hope Ghaoithe stops you in time."

Deacon took Ellie's prophecy without a word of objection. He did not grin or frown or argue. When Ellie finished, he stood and turned to leave. Halfway to the door, he stopped and turned back to her. He

201

tossed the triceratops in his hands back to the young girl. The horn on its nose was ripped and hung only by a few thin stitches.

"One thing I have learned, Elpis, is that we mustn't take what we are given for granted. Humanity seems to have forgotten that. So have you," he said.

Ellie hugged her dinosaur, but her face betrayed no other thoughts. "I know what you're digging for. When you find it, do you really think it will work?" she asked.

Deacon bared his teeth in a wicked display. "Suspension of disbelief, my dear. Even dreams have a breaking point, and I know that captain's, if nothing else. It is time to bring her back to reality."

He knocked on the door. Becky entered, shot another accusatory look at Ellie, and closed the door behind them. Ellie was left to her tea party in the room made just for her.

# XXII

Alex swore with every curse at her disposal as another needle prodded her still-sore arm. The first one had not been so bad, but as they kept sticking her, she grew more and more agitated at the captain. Ghaoithe, for her part, remained insistent though her face paled with each poke. Knowledge of Ghaoithe's fear of needles was the only thing that kept Alex from slapping her friend. It was the captain's small penance for being the bearer of bad news.

"This can't be necessary. Once I can move my arm again, I'm paying you back," Alex said through grit teeth.

"Living in Lost Earth doesn't make you immune to disease. The moment we land, you'll be glad you had these instead of yellow fever," Ghaoithe said.

She pressed in the plug, removed the needle, and let out a long-held breath. She rarely made trips to the medical bay aboard the *Cloudkicker*, both out of discomfort and lack of need thanks to her armor. While most everything in the room was clean and sterile, the abundance of colored vials and bandages indicated she was not the only one to avoid the room for extended periods of time.

"At this point, I'd almost rather risk it," Alex huffed. She rolled down the sleeve of her light blue blouse over the large bandage that Ghaoithe placed on her shoulder. After a round of several shots, her arm swelled with red tenderness. She readied herself to stand up from the long patient's chair, but Ghaoithe's hand on her chest halted her.

"Something tells me it's not the vaccinations that you're mad about," Ghaoithe said. "We need to talk about Becky."

"There's nothing to talk about," Alex retorted.

Ghaoithe knelt and put her hands on Alex's knees. "You don't have to be stubborn around me. I know this isn't easy on you," she said.

"You dealt with Sorin just fine. I can deal with Becky."

"Sorin was a good crewman, yes, but he wasn't my best friend for almost two decades."

"What do you want me to say?" Alex yelled. She grew louder with each word. "How do we even know what that woman says is true, anyway? We don't know the whole story."

"You're right. We don't. But, Alex, we have to be ready for the worst," Ghaoithe said. She tried to maintain some air of stability and sense, but seeing Alex upset struck her harder than she anticipated. She was no longer sure if it was Alex's legs that were trembling or her own hands.

Alex lowered her head. Her curls covered her face as a way to hide. "I don't know if I can accept that," she said.

Ghaoithe reached up and lifted Alex's chin. "You may not have a choice. Our first priority has to be Ellie. You know that, don't you?"

The sigils that lined that walls lit up. A voice called to the two women through them. "Hate to interrupt yer chat, Captain, but we're almost there," said Fleet through the intercom.

"We're on our way," Ghaoithe replied. Then, to Alex, she whispered, "It's time."

Alex slowly nodded. She gave Ghaoithe's arm a squeeze before they left the med bay and made their way to the upper levels of the ship. As they walked in silence, the motion of the ship on its wind currents evened out. A slight pressure change in their ears indicated their descent. Soon enough, the ship turned port-side and came to a complete halt. Ghaoithe and Alex made their way outside alone; the captain insisted everyone else stay for the initial landing in case of trouble.

With Becky on her mind, Alex was wholly unprepared for Gabon when the door to the ship's deck opened. A blast of humid air splashed her face in welcome. She remembered their location and saw the jungle before her.

The *Cloudkicker* hovered among the treetops as thick mists rose off rain-cooled greenery. Dense foliage surrounded every inch of the ship except for a small walkway that wound away from the docking platform and into the canopy. She could not see much beyond the wide leaves and sturdy tree trunks. However, the cacophony of the rainforest called out, an orchestra of birds, insects, and the distant sound of voices just down the walkway. It reminded her of Roanoke, nestled among the Brazilian coastal forests, yet it was somehow just ever-so-slightly new, like the colors were more saturated and the trees the wrong size.

Alex walked to a railing that surrounded the deck and leaned over. They were several stories off the ground. Nothing but more leaves and darkness waited below. Looking up was more of the same. The canopy broke just enough for the ship to land. The limbs above curved inward, masking their location from every angle except from directly above. A skilled pilot could land, but only if they knew the exact location for it. She wondered how many other landing areas hid throughout the forest around them.

"How did you even park us here?" Alex asked.

"Thank our navigators. You didn't think I'd let novices pilot my ship, did you?" Ghaoithe said. She crossed her arms and waited as the voices in the brush grew louder.

Their dock was made of wood and twine, sturdy enough to hold but with enough give that they felt footsteps approach them from the path ahead well before they saw anyone. A few seconds later, a group of men entered the clearing. They were large and muscled, with dark skin that glistened with sweat underneath camo fatigues. Each of them grasped an assault rifle. The center man stood out with a red beret and impenetrable sunglasses. He stopped just short of the shore party. Once he sized up Ghaoithe in her blue armor, he removed his sunglasses and placed them in a shirt pocket.

"So, it has come to this," he said. Without his sunglasses, Alex saw that he was older, with small round eyes. "You are the Sky Thief, yes? I am General Zacharia Idesh, leader of this village. I take it you do not bring good news?"

Ghaoithe stepped forward and shook Zacharia's outstretched hand. He was one of the few people Alex knew to match the captain's height.

"We're here to see Doctor Lina and get some information. We'll be on our way after that," Ghaoithe said.

"I see you do not know the state of things. Come with me," he said with a frown. He waved his arm and motioned for the group to follow him into the jungle.

They entered the winding path through the trees. Alex's eyes rarely left the rifles carried by the men in front. They did not move as though Ghaoithe's team were under arrest, but the sight still made Alex uncomfortable. She stuck close to her captain's side.

"Are we safe?" Alex asked in a low breath. Not low enough, however, to escape Zacharia's hearing. He looked back at her from the corner of his eyes.

"Safe is relative in these parts, but my men will not harm you," he said.

Ghaoithe elbowed Alex's side to fuel her embarrassment. Alex said, "Sorry. It's just the guns. I'm not used to seeing them in Lost Earth."

"There are places in the world where war is a constant and the lines between old and new are thin. This is one of them," Zacharia explained. He said no more the rest of the trip.

Eventually, the path widened to expose a series of shelters built among the trees. Thatched walls with exposed doors and windows dotted the heavy trunks. A few rope ladders dangled towards the ground, but many more were rolled up along the rickety walkways that careened through the air. Most of the buildings were only large enough to house a few people. Only one building, a rectangular hall with a solid wooden skeleton, offered a communal space supported by the thicket. A few people milled about, many of whom wore similar fatigues as the greeting party, but only enough to suggest a few dozen families lived above the forest floor. Along some of the ropes, roving bands of monkeys played without care or fear of the humans that provided easy fruit for the taking.

Even by Lost Earth standards, the village seemed primitive at first. As they crossed the hanging pathways, though, Alex took note of the movements of the few citizens. They marched with purpose, like worker bees in a hive. While many previous stops in the *Cloudkicker's* journey invited stares at Ghaoithe, the people in fatigues paid her little notice. Alex knew those looks. She often did the same when her mind got tunnel-vision over a story she needed to write. Ghaoithe was the last thing on their minds.

The general led them to a hut not far from the communal hall. Through the mosquito netting that lined the interior, a bob of stark white hair noticed their approach. An elderly woman made of angles of bone stepped out, her mouth drawn in a thin, unamused line. She wore loose white robes that hung like a shower curtain over her tiny frame. Along her belt, several leather pouches were etched with small sigil light. She walked up to Ghaoithe and prodded the captain with a ragged finger.

"Same as usual. You come crawling back to me every time you've stirred up trouble," said the woman.

"Good to see you, too, Doc," said Ghaoithe.

The doctor stepped back and crossed her arms. "Real hornet's nest you've poked this time, missy. I suppose that's why I haven't heard from you in ages," she said. She finally noticed Alex as if the young woman had shimmered in from thin air. "Well now! Who's this young lady you've trapped in your web?"

Ghaoithe coughed. "This is Alex. Alex, this is Doctor Lina Staples. She's the one I told you about. With the frog dart," said the captain sheepishly.

Lina looked between Ghaoithe and Alex. A sly grin crossed her face, but she did not ask for any other details. Instead, she fumbled about her neck for a pair of glasses tied to a string, and she stepped towards Alex for inspection.

"You look a bit peckish. I'm guessing by that bandage on your arm that you got shot up before landing?" Lina asked.

"Yes, ma'am. Ghaoithe gave me the works," Alex said.

Lina removed her glasses and shook her head. She reached into one of her satchels and pressed two large pills into Alex's hands. "You're in for a rough night. Best keep hold of these. You'll know when to take them," Lina warned.

Alex accepted with a nod, though the doctor's words made little sense. Among the trees, Alex felt more alive than she did in the cramped quarters of the ship. She pocketed the medicine and thought nothing more of it.

General Idesh interrupted the chatter. "There will be time for catching up soon. For now, we should talk. There is extra space in one of the huts on the western end for you. The rest of your crew will need to stay on the ship. Meet me in the main hall at 1900," he said. With a nod to Ghaoithe, he walked off towards another group of soldiers inspecting their weapons nearby.

"We came to ask you about the Osiris camp nearby, but it seems things are further along than we thought," Ghaoithe noted to the doctor.

"Yes, they are. I made my way here to help with a nasty strain of fever that's hit the villages nearby. I did not expect to come to a warzone," Lina said. She placed her hands on Ghaoithe's arms. "I have work to do. After you are settled, get out of that armor and come see me. You cannot hide those stiff shoulders from me, girl."

Ghaoithe laughed and promised to meet the doctor before the commune with the general. They parted ways, and Alex and Ghaoithe began searching for the open hut promised to them.

As they walked, they crossed paths with a small family of locals. A mother herded her three children into the safety of their mosquito nets with little success. Upon seeing Alex and Ghaoithe, the youngest child ran up to them. He was no more than six or seven with bright eyes not yet tainted by the presence of the weapons around him.

"You're the Sky Thief!" he exclaimed to Ghaoithe. His hands prodded her armor without invitation. She lightly brushed it away with a smile. Alex giggled to herself as she recalled the captain's first meetings with Ellie. Ghaoithe and children did not typically mix well.

"Yes, I am," Ghaoithe said. She hovered just out of reaching distance of the child. Alex knelt down to meet his eyes.

"I'm Alex. Nice to meet you," Alex said. She extended a hand.

While he knew the stories of the Sky Thief, this second woman was new. He glanced at the shining sword on her back with no small sense of wonder. He reached into his pocket, pulled out a small cylindrical object, and placed it into Alex's outstretched hand.

"For you," he said and ran back to the protection of his mother, his eyes peering nervously at the two women from behind adult legs.

Alex looked at her new gift. It was a small, unused piece of black chalk. She stared curiously at it as she stood up and showed it to Ghaoithe. The captain's face was grim, though whether it was the chalk or the child, Alex did not know.

"It's a good luck charm," Ghaoithe said as she started across the bridge again.

"Odd kind of charm. Is it used for something?" Alex asked.

"Sometimes, when things get bad, people in Lost Earth use black chalk to write their sigils," Ghaoithe explained. "They're easier to hide that way. Spies can write unfinished runes in certain locations as markers or traps. When needed, just connect the swirls and the sigils activate."

"Kind of like what you did with the Library?" Alex asked.

"Exactly like that," Ghaoithe said. She eyed the chalk as Alex twirled it between her fingers. "Best hold on to that. You don't see them very often anymore. If a kid thinks we need a good luck charm, we probably do."

Alex survived about two hours before the doctor's prophecy came true. At first, she thought it was just the change in atmosphere, that her body was adjusting to the sticky heat of the jungle after so much time in the desert. As if to emphasize its point, her arm throbbed and burned soon after, and she ended up light-headed in a bed under a mosquito net while Ghaoithe gave her a few sarcastic pats on the leg.

"Just be thankful it's not the real deal," said Ghaoithe. "It'll burn through quick, so just get some rest until it does."

Alex, unable to argue otherwise as she could not longer stand, downed the pills Lina had given her and placed her head on her pillow. With the vibrant rhythm of the jungle outside as a soundtrack, she found sleep fairly quickly, though it was not a good sleep. The rainforest guided her with the same restless dynamic that it guided all lives within it. Alex tossed and turned in the heat, stuck somewhere halfway between dreams and hallucinations. Her room filled with all manner of creatures, including a rhino at one point, the Sky Thief calm as she rode on its back wearing little more than tribal skins.

As the fever burned through her, Alex did settle down, though her sleep was no less painless. She returned to the Osiris suite. Deacon bent over her with his cunning, collected smile. Beside him, Becky laughed and pointed at her old roommate. She stepped next to her employer, reached into his pockets, and pulled out a revolver. It was old, classic steel. No less would do for a refined man. Becky brought the barrel up to her mouth. She licked it, smiling the entire time, before she aimed straight at Alex.

Alex closed her eyes. She trembled violently on the ground. She thought she heard a voice, but it may have been her own cries for help.

"Alexandra Stirling! Wake the Hell up!"

Alex did so. Ghaoithe sat at her legs, shaking her. Outside, the sun had set over the jungle, but the forest was no less alive. Insects and darker creatures rumbled through the trees. A distant beat drummed through the village air accompanied by song in a language she did not know.

Ghaoithe offered a glass of water. "You were having a rough go of it for a while there," she said. "You look better, though. Doc knows her stuff."

Alex said nothing but gladly accepted the drink. She was no longer dizzy or feverish, though her arm still hummed with a dull pain. Her sheets were damp beneath her. The coming of night did little to affect the humidity and heat within the village. Africa's weather acted far differently than that in Roanoke, which at least had the coastal air to buffer some of the harsher climate of the inland.

Ghaoithe arched an eyebrow, viewing Alex with concern. "You sure you're up for a parlay?"

Alex closed her eyes, assessed her ability to move, and finally nodded.

Once Alex changed into dry clothes, she and Ghaoithe made their way to the large hall on the other side of the village. Most of the rope bridges were empty on their way. A few mothers with their children occupied the huts, but the village appeared deserted otherwise. Everyone else waited for the Sky Thief's arrival.

Sure enough, the community shelter was packed. A large bonfire lit the center of the hall, its flames nearly reaching the smoke release above. It dried the air inside, and Alex gladly accepted the respite from the soaked air outside. Nearby, a trio of drummers pounded their instruments with an occasional wail from their lungs. Along the walls, soldiers mingled with each other. A few talked quietly, cigarettes nearly down to stubs in their mouths. Others laughed with drinks in their hands. At the far end, sitting on plain straw chairs, were Lina and General Idesh. As he spotted the two women enter the hall, he stood and waved them over. The chatter in the hall lowered to a constant murmur.

"Some party you have going on here," Ghaoithe said as she shook hands with the general.

"They will not have many opportunities in the future," said Idesh. He motioned for the women to sit in extra chairs brought for them, and they did. On the floor between them all, a large map of the area was unfurled.

"I have the impression that you were not aware of us when you arrived," Idesh continued with a wry grin on his face.

"Honestly, we weren't. We came to meet with Lina and get information about the nearby digsite, but you beat us to the punch," Ghaoithe said.

Idesh nodded and leaned back in his chair. He removed his hat and rubbed a hand over his bald scalp. "The truth is, we did not expect to be here either. When word started to get out from Dilmun, though, I brought us all here in the hopes of doing something," the general said.

"You're pretty well-prepared for such short notice. Does Osiris know about this village?" Alex asked.

Idesh sensed her distrust and raised his hands in innocence. "Not that I know of. To them, we are just another band of rebels in an area clouded with strife. If the situation were not so dire, we would not choose to fight two wars at once."

"They're taking families," Lina said quietly from her seat. "I came to help with an outbreak of yellow fever some years ago, but the situation became so bad, I could not leave. This village is a hideaway."

"What do you mean they're taking people?" Ghaoithe asked.

"For their dig. They've got almost a whole army down there by now," said Idesh.

"I've been hearing from travelers that this isn't the only place, either," Lina added.

Ghaoithe's fists clenched white with pressure. Alex, too, felt a pull in her gut. The turmoils of the region were not unknown to her, even when she had lived in Missouri. In hindsight, Deacon's involvement behind the scenes of the conflicts that roiled Africa were almost predictable. But hearing it firsthand made the news no less easier to swallow. Even worse was the implication that their battle cry sent out from Dilmun had spread far too late. If Osiris already had a hold here, then what other areas could he claim? Even Idesh's rebellion sounded more a consequence of time and chance than anything. Alex worried that Lost Earth's insistence on a scattered, solitary lifestyle could become its own undoing. The crew had hoped for an army but found only a lone, ragtag group of fighters already entrenched in a different political conflict.

The captain stood and paced about her chair. Her shadow danced wickedly in the flickering bonfire light behind her. "One step at a time. Do we know what they're after? Is it Pandora's Box?" she asked.

General Idesh shrugged. He said, "We don't know the particulars. Our only goal has been to stop the dig and rescue those kept there. The relics are your territory."

"Then we need to find out, and quickly," said Ghaoithe.

"You are welcome to try. I do not think you will get far before that roaming skyship of theirs intercepts you."

Ghaoithe stopped in her tracks. "So you're not planning to help?"

Idesh removed his sunglasses and leaned forward in his seat. His face stonewalled any reading. He said, "Captain O'Loinsigh…"

"There's no 'O.' Just 'Captain' will do."

"Ok, Captain, I need to be clear on something. Against Osiris, we are one and the same. You are welcome to stay in port here however long you need and to act as you see fit."

Ghaoithe crossed her arms. The annoyance across her face threatened to turn ugly. "But?"

"This is my home, and in my home we only settle conflict in one way. My men are preparing to save my people. Everything else is secondary. You may have sparked the flames of war, but it will be finished by soldiers like mine. To me, Osiris is just another faction of many that have come to exploit my homeland, and they will be dealt with in the same way I have dealt with the others. I will not sit idly by while you try to fight a giant with sticks."

The tone in his voice irked Alex. As she looked at Ghaoithe, she knew she was not alone. The general's words lacked any interest in the fine details of Osiris' goals. Instead, they reflected the singular, mission-oriented mind of a trained strategist who sought his own ends. Idesh could certainly be counted on in the fight against Osiris, but the more the two women got to know him, they grew less sure of whether they would come to an agreement on how the upcoming conflict would be resolved. Even though she knew little of Ghaoithe's past, Alex knew that diplomacy was not the captain's strongest suit. Worried that Ghaoithe might very well walk over and clock the general in the jaw, Alex stood and joined and her captain.

"We appreciate whatever help you can give us," Alex said. "If anything, allow us a couple of days to find out what we can. That's all we ask."

Both Idesh and Ghaoithe stared at her in surprise with the outburst. The muscles in Ghaoithe's jaw clenched., but she thought better of whatever she had prepared to say.

Idesh mulled the offer and nodded. "We can do that. Like I said, you're welcome to stay as you need. However, if that ship of theirs gives us an opportunity to go in to that digsite, I'm going to take it."

"How very generous," Ghaoithe said through grit teeth.

"Captain, we may have different methods, but we are on the same side. If I find out anything to help your relic hunt, I will let you know. I hope you will do the same for me. If we are to beat Osiris, there are many facets to manage, and no one is an expert at all of them," said Idesh. He put his sunglasses back on, stood, and nodded once more in parting as he made his way out of the lodge.

Once he was gone, Ghaoithe turned and stared into the bonfire. Though it still burned brightly, the party had entered that quiet state of hushed chat and intimacy that came with passed hours. Alex looked up at Ghaoithe's sour expression.

"Are you mad because he won't help or because he has a point?" Alex asked.

"A bit of both," Ghaoithe responded.

Alex watched the fire for a few seconds and hoped their entrancing dance would soothe her friend. She said, "I know you're used to doing things by your own rules, but this is bigger than us. This won't be the only time we have to make compromises with our allies."

Ghaoithe snorted, half laugh and half indignation. "It's a good thing we have your experience in diplomacy."

"You can't be a good journalist without knowing what other people want," Alex said.

At this, Ghaoithe uncrossed her arms and sighed. Alex had a harder edge than her stature let on, and the captain too often forgot this fact. She looked down at Alex's resolute face and nodded. "You're right. I was out of line," she said. "I just need some rest."

Alex agreed, and the two departed. They would not join the remainder of the party. In retrospect, Alex wondered if maybe they should have. The crew followed much of the same path as Idesh's men, and there would be no telling when they could relax for a moment in the future. Ghaoithe was in no mood for pleasure, however, and they skipped their hut in the village for their own beds aboard the *Cloudkicker*.

# XXIII

The mess hall was busier than it had been in weeks, though the plates went mostly untouched. Ghaoithe rose well before dawn to continue her crusade against Osiris. By the time breakfast rolled around, she entered the eating area with an armful of papers and Dr. Staples at her side.

"She knows the area," Ghaoithe explained without fanfare before she dropped the parchments unceremoniously on top of everyone's meals.

"Dammit, woman, can't ya do this in yer own quarters?" Fleet cursed from across the table as he clutched his plate of hashbrowns and eggs.

"Hello to you, too, Fleet. I see your beard has taken on a bit of cotton," Lina said. She afforded the quartermaster a rare smile.

"No thanks to keepin' this whelp in check," Fleet replied. He eyed Ghaoithe warily as he picked up a spared biscuit. "Maybe ya should give her a sedative next time she gets wild ideas before breakfast."

"I teased the idea, but there's no telling what immunities she's built up over her years of recklessness." Lina lowered herself to a seat at the table like a spider on its thread.

217

Their comments fell on deaf ears as Ghaoithe unfurled the parchment. The map of the area was becoming such a common sight to Alex that she wondered if she was close to having it memorized. She silently sipped on her coffee, curious to know what plan Ghaoithe had cooked up overnight. It was entirely possible the captain had not even slept, though her font of energy was undiminished.

"I need to know where the other ruins are, however small," Ghaoithe told Lina.

"Here we go then," Fleet muttered. He crammed the rest of his food down and leaned in. Alex followed suit.

Doctor Staples glared at them in turn. Outnumbered, she folded her arms in defiance. "You know you may very well die at this rate?"

Ghaoithe scoffed, "If I do, it won't be at the hands of old ruins."

"How do you know there are other ruins," Alex asked, "or that Osiris hasn't taken them, too?"

"Come on, Alex. I thought I taught you better than that?" Ghaoithe joked with a teasing grin.

"Second entrance," Fleet interjected. He tugged at his beard as he searched the map. "Every underground ruin would have a second exit in case of emergencies during construction. That ain't something particular to Lost Earth, lass."

Alex shrunk. Her cheeks burned hot with embarrassment that she could make such a simple mistake. She was certain she just failed some basic lesson in Relic Hunting 101.

"It's ok, Stirling. You're right that we have no idea whether Osiris has already found it," Ghaoithe said to ease Alex's mistake. "It's a chance we'll have to take."

"They haven't found it," Lina said sharply. The others looked at her abruptly. She scowled and leaned over the map. Once she found what she was looking for, her finger landed at a point several miles east of their village, between them and the Osiris dig. "It's here. Small little man-made cave. No word on Osiris moving about the place, but you can be sure they'll be swarming the inside once you find the main tunnels."

The excitement on Ghaoithe's face radiated around the table. She slapped her hands down and let out a loud whoop. "We've gone through them before. We can do it again. This time, we're on my kind of turf," she shouted.

Though Doctor Staples's expression disapproved of Ghaoithe's intent, Fleet did not share her resentment. As he stared at the map, plans and preparation running through his head, his eye twinkled with a glint not seen since the *Cloudkicker* approached the hidden city beneath Bimini Road. Alex gently elbowed him in the ribs, caught up in the furor herself.

"Do I detect a bit of anticipation from our voice of reason?" she joked.

Fleet grumbled at being caught, but he did not deny his feelings. "If it means we can slow down Osiris and get back Ellie, it'll be worth the risk," he said.

"Ellie?" Lina asked. "You never mentioned a captive."

"Elpis, the hope that was left in Pandora's Box after the opening. We saved her from Osiris once, and we have to do it again," Ghaoithe explained.

At first, Lina struggled to make sense of the captain words, but once comprehension dawned on her, she softened. "Well, then. I suppose I'll have to help you plan," she said, the edge in her voice dulled.

Alex could not help but quietly rejoice. Finally, the roadblock in their journey had shown the cracks in its wall. She hated being helpless and stalled for progress in any aspect of her life, and the stakes were far higher now than they were when she struggled to earn a compelling story to write for her local newspaper. The warnings of Doctor Staples paled next to the brief glimmer of hope that they could stop the Osiris march.

All they had to do was step into the unknown once again.

Within the belly of the *Cloudkicker*, other voices shouted in excitement. Damian and Vargas sat across from each other, cards splayed out across the floor. Though bars separated Jessie from her guard, she acted quite at home with her game, a mug, and a large pitcher to split between the two of them. As Damian turned over the final card in their poker match, Jessie cackled in earnest and pulled a scant few coins through the bars. Undeterred, Damian threw his hair behind his shoulders and piled the disheveled playing field.

"If you don't let me win a couple, we'll be out of chips," Damian said. He shuffled with a crisp flutter of paper.

"It's all worthless junk anyway. Our clothes are probably worth more in Lost Earth than these things are," Jessie said. She lifted up the pitcher and refilled her mug in a clean swoop.

"Moving on to clothes now? Please don't tease like that," Damian joked.

"You'd have to win for me to be teasing you. At this rate, you'd be the one handing over the fabric," Jessie said. The way her voice purred made Damian's cheeks grow warm, and he struggled not to look at her for fear of lingering too long in all the wrong places.

He passed out another hand. As he looked at his five of clubs and ace of hearts, he said casually, "You're a lot different than I expected."

"You had expectations, did you?"

"Of course. My mother was a huge fan of yours before you disappeared."

Jessie's legs tensed. The mention of her old life always triggered such a reaction. She wanted to run, but locked in the cage of the brig, she had nowhere to go. She lifted up her mug and chugged it down.

"That was a time in my life best left buried," said Jessie.

"Your fans didn't think so. After that incident at your last premiere, you just vanished. Some thought you retired, but a lot of people worried about you. I think my mother even wrote a letter to the studio, but she never heard anything back," Damian said.

Jessie hummed in reply. She looked down at her hands, but instead of cards, she saw a contract. The thick paper nearly blended in with the rest of the countertop of her kitchen island. It was morning. Soft light poured through the large picture windows along the wall. White marble and stainless steel around her glowed as if conjured by the dreams of entitled homemakers everywhere. By many standards, she did live in a dream.

She could see into the next room, a cheerful space of color and life. A young girl in pastel pajamas watched cartoons on a large television screen. A commercial break cut in. A preview of the upcoming news hour started. Jessie saw herself, with wild hair and tangled clothes, erupt out of a bar. She raised a blurry hand at the camera as she hastily entered a black stretch limousine. Two men in clothes that reeked of loose morality and ill-gotten riches climbed in after her. She remembered their names: Javier and Daniel. They were not her friends.

Her phone had buzzed continuously since then. It sat, silenced, on the counter next to the papers. Already, its screen flashed with a stream of voicemails from the people she had once made very rich.

Picking up her pen, Jessie rushed a signature onto the contract. She could still feel the plush bathrobe along her arm as a children's theme song returned in the background.

"I don't blame you," Damian said. Jessie snapped back to her cell. She looked away, briefly, and hoped she had not cried all while knowing it would probably be best for her if she did.

"Your mother would have if she knew all I left behind," Jessie said in a salty, cracked voice.

Damian laid down the pile of cards. He let out a long breath. "I don't think she would have. If anything, she knew exactly why you left. Maybe more than anybody."

Jessie scoffed.

"It's true," Damian said. "My mom was not from the States, but she had me there anyway. She worked long hours for barely any pay so I could go to school and do something better. She wouldn't even let me speak Spanish in the house most of the time. 'Successful kids speak English,' she would always tell me."

Jessie sat back up and leaned in to the bars. "Yeah, and how'd that work out?" she said with more acid than she intended. It did not faze Damian.

He said, "Fine for a bit. But Osiris controlled the power, and power fluxes with demand. When the world no longer demanded my mother's help, they came for her and left me. I didn't know about Osiris then, but I learned by following the trail. I came here." He stopped and scanned the sigil-touched walls around them. "On the whole, I think I did alright. I think she'd be proud of me fighting the good fight with friends."

Jessie expected his eyes to go dim as he talked, as she knew hers did when she tried to paint a happier picture than she was capable of feeling. However, Damian's face showed no touch of regret or lack of conviction. He was truly happy. It was like seeing him for the first time. He sparked something in Jessie she never acknowledged.

People crossed to Lost Earth, but it it was a rare occasion. Scientists, explorers, and scholars made the bulk of foreign newcomers. Solitary in her mercenary work, Jessie never figured she would find someone else like her, someone that came to Lost Earth by falling through the cracks or by forging themselves through a crucible. Yet, there on that impossible ship, Damian waited for her.

His companionship did not make her feel better. That was a job for time. But, he did help take the bitterness out, like just a dab of cream in a too-strong coffee. Maybe that would be good enough for now.

Jessie's chest tightened. She stood up, stretched, and shook off her oncoming pangs. A flood threatened to drown her, and she decided to hold it at bay with beer and games for the time being. There would be time for introspection afterward, when she could crawl into the darkness.

"You know, you're a pain in the ass," Jessie said.

Damian shrugged and swirled the cup in his hand. "That's what Ghaoithe tells me, but I'm still here," he said.

"Deal me in and I'll see about taking you down a notch."

Another round of cards went out. Jessie tossed her hat onto the pot.

# XXIV

Moving along the forest floor proved more difficult than Alex anticipated. She, Ghaoithe, and Fleet had embarked early in the morning before the first rays of sun charged over the canopy. As the day wore on, however, very little of the light penetrated the dense foliage above, giving the forest an otherwordly hue of shadow. Not long after their departure, Alex's legs burned as she navigated the thick roots hidden on the ground. Her arms ached, too, as she slashed through tangles of vines with Excalibur only for more to appear to block the travelers' paths a few steps later.

When they stopped for a moment's rest, Alex plunked down on the nearest root. Sweat soaked through her clothes, but she no longer cared for appearances. She just wanted air—cool, fresh air—to enter her lungs.

Fleet cleared his throat in an attempt to stifle a laugh. He pointed at a spot beside Alex. "Ya may wanna watch where ya sit."

Without even looking, Alex felt the tickling presence of far too many tiny legs cross over her hand. She shot up with a shriek. "I am so over this jungle already! We were better off in the desert!" she yelled as she whipped her arm back and forth through the air.

"Don't tell me a tough country lass like yerself can't handle a little walk in the woods after all we've been through!" Fleet roared.

Alex grumbled a halfhearted excuse, but Fleet was right. After so much recent time in cities and aboard the *Cloudkicker*, she must have gone soft toward wild exploration. She resolved to act more stoic toward the next over-sized insect that crossed her path. She looked to Ghaoithe for guidance, but if the captain noticed Alex's discomfort, she made no sign of it.

"Quiet down, you two," Ghaoithe said. Her tone surprised both Fleet and Alex, and they hung their heads in passiveness. "We're not far. Don't let Osiris know our whereabouts before we arrive."

Alex cautiously peeked around Ghaoithe's shoulder to glance at the map in the captain's hands. She tried to make out anything in the direction the captain faced, but there was nothing but more vines and the squawks of unseen birds.

"What are we looking for? It'll be hard to find heads or tails of things with all these trees," Alex asked.

"It could be anything. A back entrance won't be very ornate. Just keep your eyes peeled for anything out of place," Ghaoithe said.

After a quick round of water, they continued their hunt in the unforgiving terrain. Ghaoithe offered to take Excalibur off Alex's hands for a while, its undullable blade far better for hacking through the jungle than her own rapier. Alex refused. She was hellbent on proving her worth. The short woman's curls tossed drops of sweat about with every strike, but she persisted without assistance. Ghaoithe shot Fleet a thumbs up as they followed.

They continued in silence until Alex came to a halt in midswing. She wasn't sure exactly what caught her eye, only that something was out of place among the trees. Something about the landscape was awkward and artificial despite no change in the vines or roots that surrounded the trio. As she knelt closer to the ground, Alex found what set off her intuition: a rock no larger than a backpack. It was covered in lichen from the forest, but it was topped with a sphere a little too perfectly round to be found in such a wilderness.

Ghaoithe knelt beside Alex. "Good eye, Stirling. Fleet and I would have passed right over that."

"Sometimes being closer to the ground gives you perspective," Alex beamed.

Fleet pulled off handfuls of vines and moss from the base of the rock. "It's a bloody statue. We're on the right track," he said.

Without the plants, the figure was much clearer. It was certainly a head, blank-faced and solid, with the rest of its figure buried in the ground below the shoulders. Time and moss had worn it smooth. There were no sigil markings that Alex could see of to mark it as a product of Lost Earth.

"Is it another golem?" Alex asked. She thought with a rush of excitement of her first battle with stone automations in Eden.

"If it is, it's not digging itself out anytime soon," Ghaoithe said.

They decided to split up to circle the area. Alex did not know what she was looking for, but the presence of something amiss continued. As she cut through the brush, she found three more half-buried statues, their arrangement in no particular pattern that might help discern the entrance she sought.

A sharp whistle sounded to Alex's left. She ran as swiftly as she could among the brush. Another whistle shot out and, a few moments later, Fleet appeared through the foliage. Ghaoithe crashed in shortly after Alex arrived.

"Found it," Fleet said.

Alex looked around. Another statue waved to them from the ground not far from where they stood, but she could not see anything remotely resembling a tomb entrance. She looked at Fleet, his face wide with a joker's grin. He turned and pointed to two massive trees just behind him. They were a few feet apart and thick even among their rainforest peers, but nothing about them suggested anything other than normal trees.

"Take a look at the bark, lass," was all Fleet said.

Both Alex and Ghaoithe stepped up to the tree trunks. When Alex got close, she let out a gasp. Along a portion of the tree about her eye-level, the grains in the bark twisted and wove in on itself in an unnatural fashion. They did not shift like Ghaoihe's armor did, nor did they glow, but there was no mistaking the sigils etched into the tree trunk.

"That's a good eye, Fleet. Not bad for an old-timer," Alex said.

"Never too old to show up a greenback who's a bit full of herself," Fleet joked. He stepped up and placed a wide palm on top of Alex's head. He turned to Ghaoithe and, in a more serious manner, asked, "What do ya think? Will we be stuck here all night or ya gonna work fer once?"

Ghaoithe leaned in to inspect the runes. She rubbed her chin with her fingers. "I could open it in a few seconds, but I may take my sweet time. You don't seem to mind the heat out here that much," she said.

Fleet waved a dismissive hand at her. "Oh, just open it, ya blue witch."

While they bickered, Alex was content to enjoy the brief respite between the harsh jungle and whatever dangers waited for them in the hidden ruins. She reached into her side pouch and munched on what little rations she brought with her. Once the squabble between her superiors stopped, Ghaoithe pulled a piece of chalk from the ruby sash at her waist and went to work on the trees. She wrote swiftly, connecting broken runes and adding swirls where they needed to be.

"Easy. Whoever hid this must have been in a rush," she said. Her face scrunched in concentration as she looped patterns across the trees' trunks.

She finished scrawling on the second tree. The bark and chalk lit up with blue light as the sigils activated. As they gained life, the space between the two trees shimmered as if the crew was looking through warped glass. Slowly, a small doorway appeared, its entrance a black hole in the middle of the rainforest. Time-stained and cracked marble blocks lined the door. Just inside, rough stairs indicated a pathway immediately down. The stone was old and covered in mossy green like the area's statues. The two trees had absorbed the corners of the entryway into their bark and created a natural frame.

Ghaoithe poked her head in. She placed a foot on the first step and tested its construction.

"Don't just go in like that!" Alex warned. "What if it's trapped?"

Ghaoithe climbed down a few more steps. She turned and waved her hands at Alex. "So scary!" she cackled. "We're fine for now, Alex. What's gotten into you?"

"I just want you to be careful. That's all," Alex stammered. She wanted to say something else, but the words stuck in her throat. Grasping Excalibur firmly, she followed the captain inside. Fleet guarded the rear.

Inside, stale air choked them as they entered, but the heat from the jungle immediately cooled. The steps were wide and easy to navigate behind the light of Ghaoithe's armor. As they continued, the sound of rushing water welcomed them from far below. It grew louder with each step until the stairwell ended, and the crew stood at the opening of a gigantic cavern. Ghaoithe's low sigil light glistened off wet stalactites above. A wide river cut across the center of the cave. On the other side, another doorway continued onward into their ruins.

Alex knelt at the edge of the river. Its water was clear and cool, flecked only with bits of foam as it rushed by. By her estimate, they would have to cross fifty meters to reach the other side. She eyed the current warily as she hearkened back to warnings from her days growing up near the Mississippi River.

"We'll need some rope, I expect. There's no bridge in sight around here unless you can find another hidden one like down in Bimini," Alex declared.

The captain stepped beside Alex. She stood with her hands on her hips as she judged the river. After a moment, she waded in.

"Ghaoithe! Don't!" Alex cried out. She tried to pull the captain back to the shoreline, but Ghaoithe was already too far out. Alex turned to Fleet for help. Fleet scratched his beard, his eyes narrowed in curiosity, but he stayed put.

When Ghaoithe reached the middle of the river, she stopped. She waved back at the shoreline. The water only touched her knees. "What are you waiting for? Afraid you'll melt?" she called back.

Fleet waded into the water. He motioned to his back. "Need a lift? Water'll come up a bit higher on yer frame," he said.

Alex brushed him off and placed her feet in the river. It soaked into her shoes, and she acknowledged her squishy socks as worthy punishment for her mood. In her overzealousness, she was certain a nefarious trap had been laid beneath the current for wayward explorers like Ghaoithe. Even with the captain safely on the other side, Alex shuffled her feet through the riverbed as she crossed, a trick she once read about to avoid buried stingrays and poisonous rockfish. She did not think stingrays or rockfish lived in such an underground stream, but one could never be too careful with ancient places.

The river did, in fact, come up higher on Alex. Though the current was slow and fairly easy to navigate, she reached the other shore drenched to her chest once again. She shivered and cursed her destiny to never be dry ever again. Fleet and Ghaoithe chuckled between themselves at first but quieted after they saw the warning in Alex's eyes.

They inspected the tunnel. It was clearly man-made, with smooth walls and bright sigil light along the ceiling. It was only wide enough for one person at a time but just tall enough that Ghaoithe managed to fit in without crouching. It shot straight through the rock without turns or corners. Several hundred meters away, the exit was nothing more than an illegible darkened space. They entered, single file, into the walkway, their shoulders brushing lightly against the sides as the music of the river behind them echoed softly off the stone.

Ghaoithe barely slowed as she walked, much to Alex's worry. Alex surveyed the floor before she rushed to catch up to the captain. She followed in silence, but that did not stop her eyes from twitching with each uneven footstep on the stone path. She peered along the walls for any breaks, any openings for hidden darts or swarms of deadly insects. She found none.

Alex felt Fleet's hand on her shoulder. She slowed down as the captain continued ahead.

"Ya ain't gotta protect her," Fleet said.

"I don't know what you mean," Alex lied.

Fleet grunted a dismissal and said, "Ever since Dilmun, ya keep hoverin' over her every step. She's a professional, lass. Let her do her job."

"I'm just trying to watch her back. She's not invincible."

"Yer treatin' her like a child," Fleet said, his voice sharp with reprimand. "Look, the captain don't let people in very often. Not because she's afraid of them knowin', mind ya, but because they look at her different after. People start thinkin' she's some deeply wounded animal that needs cared fer, and it annoys the hell outta her. Don't go thinkin' she needs fixin' or ya might end up snuffin' out whatever this is growin' between ya before it takes off."

Alex pursed her lips, somewhat annoyed herself. She almost told Fleet that she knew all of those things, that Ghaoithe was the most incredible person she knew. She held her tongue, however, and focused on the words that really bothered her.

"This isn't right," she said. "I know Ghaoithe can hold her own, but I can't shake this itch that something really bad is waiting around the corner."

"Bit heavy on the foreshadowin', eh?"

"Can you blame me?"

Fleet shook his head. "No. It ain't my right to. Still, we've been a thumbnail away from the dragon's mouth since Roanoke burned down. No sense in gettin' nerves this late in the game. Where we're standin', trouble is always around the corner."

Fleet patted both of Alex's shoulders and nudged her onward.

They caught up with Ghaoithe at the end of the tunnel. Blocking their path was a solid and unadorned wall. The captain prodded it in a few places to no avail. Then, she inspected the nearby walls. Nothing indicated a way through the passage.

"Could the builders have closed the path once they left for good?" Alex asked.

"It's possible, but not very likely. We must have missed something. Back we go," Ghaoithe said.

They turned awkwardly around in the narrow space and made their way back down the path. Fleet led the way, slowly this time so they could stop every few meters to take another look around. They saw nothing in the smooth stone on either side. The floor was also flat and devoid of any triggers to the naked eye, a point Alex emphasized loudly after her own search for traps.

Just as they were about halfway back, Ghaoithe called out, "Hold up! I think I found it."

The others turned and saw Ghaoithe stopped in the distance behind them. She stared intently at the ceiling. As they approached, they figured out what caught her eye. The sigils along the ceiling looped about like normal but one bit was cut off as it vanished through the corner above. Only Ghaoithe, her hair already close to brushing the top of the passage, could have noticed it so easily. She looked at the runes on the ceiling, then the wall, then back to the ceiling. Slowly, she reached out to touch the wall. Alex yelped as Ghaoithe's hand went right through it.

Even Fleet was taken aback by the illusion. "Well, ain't that a right trick," he said.

"So do we just waltz on through or what?" Alex asked.

Ghaoithe reached through the wall once more. She moved her arm back and forth. When she pulled it back, she shook her head. "It's a tight fit. We'll have to turn sideways to get through. Fleet, this may be a bit much for you," she said.

"I'll be the judge of that," Fleet said. He reached in with his own arm and tested the hidden crevice. With a disapproving rumble, he said, "Guess not. Don't go gettin' yerselves killed. It'd be hard to reach yer bodies fer a proper burial."

"We'll try our best," said Ghaoithe. She squeezed Fleet's arm and went through the wall. Alex followed.

The chasm was no joke. Ghaoithe was thin enough, but her armor made for a tight squeeze nonetheless. Alex had to remove Excalibur from its scabbard in order to fit through. Though she was not normally scared of tight spaces, she worried about their ability to backtrack should anything go wrong. She was already using muscles that were not used to such minuscule, precise motions. Her legs pushed just to get to the end of the rift, let alone return. Worse yet, she could not see around Ghaoithe to judge the remaining distance under the sigil light.

"Guess it's a good thing not many things can get through solid rock, eh Stirling? We could be swimming through centipedes right now in other places," Ghaoithe said.

"Oh, that just makes it so much better," Alex grunted. The balls of her feet began to ache.

"We're almost there. It opens up in about a dozen meters."

They pushed through the last portion of the tunnel. As Alex popped out, she fell to the ground. She stretched and swung Excalibur over her head and reveled in the freedom of open spaces. Though more subdued, Ghaoithe was not above loosening her arms and legs a bit, too.

When they were finished with their stretches and their lungs had room to expand again, the women looked about. They stood in a wide chamber, all white stone and tall columns. The chamber was circular and built as a theater-in-the-round, with stairwells circling a flat, open area in the center below. A high wall barred viewers except for openings for the stairwells spread along its length. The amphitheater showed little signs of wear. The steps were free of cracks or chipping, and the columns sturdily handled their forgotten task. Nothing moved other than the two explorers.

"Well, we made it," Ghaoithe said.

Alex had trouble seeing at first. The chamber was dim with only a few pillars of light in dramatic ensemble around the upper ring where they stood. As her eyes focused, she jumped from a figure to her left, lurking in the shadow of a column. She prepared her sword. The figure froze in place.

After a moment of standstill, Alex lowered Excalibur. She approached the figure only to discover it was a statue. It looked much like the ones outside, featureless and worn with moss, though this one was not buried. It stood as a regular man would, posed in heroic display.

"Ghaoithe, I found one of those statues in here," Alex called.

The captain appeared behind Alex. She knocked on the statue lightly with her knuckles. Then, she scanned the upper concourse of the theater. "There are others placed around the ring," she said.

"Think they're golems?" asked Alex.

"They'd be pretty poor guardians if they haven't activated yet, but stay alert anyway."

As her eyes adjusted, Alex saw the other statues. More than that, she saw faces along the inner wall. Large carvings in grotesque display of comedia and tragedy stared at the two trespassers wherever they walked. The faces leered at them, stuck their tongues out, taunted them. They forced shivers up Alex's spine more than any automated golem could.

Finally, Alex and Ghaoithe reached a staircase with a clear view into the stage. A flat pedestal rose from the center of the earthen floor. At the sight of it, Ghaoithe cursed and flew down the steps. Alex called out for her to stop but the captain was too far gone. The Sky Thief reached the pedestal with a flurry of obscenities. She circled the pedestal, ran her hands along the base in search of a clue, and cursed again.

Only after she calmed down did she notice a slip of paper on the ground half-covered in dirt and footprints. She picked it up, her face flush at the neatly defined cursive written on it:

*I expected more of you. Best not to linger. -Richard Deacon IV*

# XXV

Everything in the air was wrong. None of the usual chatter amongst the trees welcomed the explorers as they left the ruins empty-handed. The faint smell of cigarette smoke lingered. Fleet knelt and moved his hands along the earth.

"Footsteps. All headed back west to the camp," he said.

"How many?" Ghaoithe asked.

"A lot. Hard to get an accurate count."

Alex knelt down to see for herself. The footsteps overlapped each other and trampled the ground below. She searched the nearby plants for signs, as well. Broken branches, snapped flowers, scuffed bark. Anything to get a better idea of their numbers. She eventually had to admit defeat. Her training as an explorer had not advanced far enough for her to make out anything among the jungle greenery.

In the distance, the silence broke. A loud rapping sound like a woodpecker shot out from the direction of the village. It took Alex back to memories on her uncle's farm where entertainment was made, not packaged.

"Assault rifles," Alex said. "We need to get back."

Ghaoithe nodded. She pulled her rapier from her sash. "Go around from the south."

They took off. The journey back to the village was no easier in the forest terrain, but adrenaline and urgency overrode a few bruises to the legs. The gunshots increased steadily as fighters joined the fray. The cigarette smoke in the air eventually mingled with heavier smoke and gun oil. When Ghaoithe was close enough to hear shouting, she waved back to her companions and they cut sharply left. Any closer and they would step right into the heart of the fight with only Ghaoithe's armor offering any protection among the three.

Alex scanned the branches in the hopes of spotting the village safe and sound. She found out she did not need to search; the village was easy to spot as they walked below it. Bucket lifts lowered residents to the ground, where most began an escape to the west. Soldiers called from above to raise the empty elevators and make way for the next groups. Given the chaos sounding from the battle just a short distance away, the entire process was incredibly efficient.

Ghaoithe, Fleet, and Alex hopped into an empty elevator. The solider above stared down at the sudden weight and, at the sight of Ghaoithe's armor, turned a crank to lift the bucket skyward. Once the group was squarely on the landing platform, the young soldier saluted the Sky Thief. She returned with an awkward imitation.

"Where's your general?" Ghaoithe asked.

"In the main hall, ma'am. He asked us to send you his way immediately if you came back in time," said the soldier.

"Sounds like we just made the cut. Thank you," Ghaoithe said. The soldier saluted once more before he returned his attention to the remaining villagers near the lift.

The lines for the lifts were not long, which eased Alex's mind. Most of the remaining figures wore military fatigues, their faces drawn tight as sweat beaded on their foreheads. They rushed about the treetops as they counted weapons, readied supplies, and prepared for a skirmish with Osiris. A few carried cylindrical canisters and hefty amounts of rope to battlements along the edges of the sturdier platforms.

Inside the village hall, the furor only grew. Where the bonfire flickered during the celebration, a table now stood. Idesh huddled over several maps laid about it. He pointed hurriedly at a few markers as he spoke with the trusted men by his side. Along the walls, guns and stacks of even more dangerous crates were being inventoried. Dr. Staples doled out emergency kits to those willing to carry them. New creases stretched from the corners of her eyes. The smallest of relieved smiles touched the corners of her lips when she noticed the captain.

Idesh beckoned the returning party to his table. He said, "It's good to see you're still alive. Did you find what you needed?"

"No. Deacon beat us to the punch," Ghaoithe said.

"Unfortunate, but not entirely unexpected," said the general. He lifted his sunglasses to rub his eyes. "As you can see, they are wasting no time in cleaning up after themselves."

"How are things down there? We almost ended up right on top of them when we left."

"Our main force is still here. The men fighting below are buying us time to put up sight wards around the base of the trees. It's not likely to help much if they were already coming for us, but they will buy us some time to see the civilians to safety."

"What about the canisters your men are carrying?" Alex asked. "You can't mean to hole up here forever."

At her question, Idesh grinned. There was a touch of irony in his expression. "If they make it to the scaffolds, we intend to bring the trees down on top of them."

Everyone at the table understood what he meant. "You can't..." squeaked Alex.

"It's only a last resort. My men can hold Osiris long enough to allow us a retreat once the civilians are safe," said the general.

Both Fleet and Ghaoithe were of the same mind. The quartermaster whispered in the captain's ear, and she nodded. "Let us take the remaining evacuees. The *Cloudkicker*'s more than big enough," she told General Idesh.

"No!" said Idesh. The force of the word startled those around him. Even Fleet jumped in his skin. "If Osiris got what they were after, your ship may be the only damn hope left around here. You need to be getting skyward as soon as possible. Find a way to stop whatever it is they are doing and leave the fighting to those of us who know how to do it."

Ghaoithe's face twisted as she rolled arguments through her head. Unable to find a suitable retort, she leaned onto the table to look at the maps. She asked, "What about that big Osiris ship? The *Ascendant?*"

"Probably loading its newest haul. It hasn't been spotted in the air today."

"Then we've got a chance," Fleet said. He stepped up to the map and pounded a finger on the Osiris excavation marker. "If they're fightin' us here, then it's easier fer the *'kicker* to get in there. Deacon's probably usin' that distraction below to make the same escape plans we are."

"All the more reason for you to leave. That means you, too, Doctor Staples," Idesh barked to the physician.

Lina refused to move from her huddle near the kits. "You'll need help after this fight," she said.

"I have field medics. You'll be of more use to the captain and her crew," said Idesh.

Lina huffed and pouted. Eventually, she strode to Ghaoithe's side. "I will be watching like a hawk," she said.

"I would hope for nothing less," Ghaoithe replied. She looked about the hut as the *ratt-a-tatt* of gunfire edged ever closer. "I suppose this is it. We need to go."

Idesh stood tall. He reached out a calloused hand to the Ghaoithe, which she returned. They nodded at each other in understanding, two different ideologies within the same war but ultimately of the same side. When they released each other, Ghaoithe made her way to the front of the hall with her crew in tow.

"Captain," Idesh called out as she stepped through the door. She stopped and turned. "Finish that bastard off for good."

Ghaoithe grinned and shot a thumbs up his way before she left.

Alex, Fleet, and Lina followed as she raced to the airship. When they reached the landing platform, they stopped. Ghaoithe stood with Roy at the base of the on-ramp. Their discussion was low but heated as each took turns gesturing wildly.

"He's leaving us," explained Ghaoithe as the group neared.

"I'm just taking a bit of a detour," Roy said, his voice strained. "The Table needs a runner, and the general's known to cover a lot of ground. I'll be better down here getting information and spreading the word than I would be weighing you down in a fight. I'll meet back with you as soon as I can."

"Are you sure? There may not be much of a war after this," Alex said.

"I'm placing my bets with this ship. This is far from over."

Alex ran forward and threw her arms around Roy's waist. "Don't stay down here for too long," she said.

"I won't. Captain needs someone with street wisdom around here," Roy said. "Now go on. Ship's waiting."

With a final pat on Alex's shoulder and a curt nod to the rest of the crew, Roy ran toward the gunfire beyond the village. Ghaoithe waited until he was out of sight then made her way aboard her ship. She shouted orders to the crew standing by before she even reached the top of the loading ramp.

"Start the engine! Keep her wings folded until we clear the tree line. And someone drag Kirk into the bridge!" her voice roared as she entered.

Once the others were inside, the ramp retracted. The *Cloudkicker* dipped as it broke away from the landing pad. Once clear, the sigils within the bridge hummed to life. The ship lurched upward and rose unsteadily above the forest canopy. Alex could no longer see the landing or any other hint of the village through the bridge's window.

"Not too high! We need to stay just above clearance," Ghaoithe said.

Fleet sat in his seat beside the captain's chair. His brows lowered over his eyes as he anticipated Ghaoithe's next move. "Where we headin', Captain?"

"Three degrees southeast. As fast as we can without making too much noise."

"That's..."

"Yup. We're going to cut Deacon off while we can."

The last time Ghaoithe made a direct course for an Osiris operation ended with everyone captured under Deacon's eye. Alex worried for a moment that the captain was being rash again, but the more she mulled the possibilities, the more she came to terms with the decision.

"We don't know what they found," Alex hesitantly said her thoughts aloud as they came to her. "If it is Pandora's Box, we can't let them take off with it. If not, it's still our best chance of getting Ellie back while Osiris is distracted down below."

"I ain't arguin' that, but we still need a plan. That ship of his is huge," Fleet cautioned.

"I'm working on that," said Ghaoithe. "Someone find Kirk!"

A tired voice called back from below the captain's rise on the bridge, "Quit yelling or you'll let the whole jungle know we're coming!"

Kirk entered the room. He started up the ramp to the captain's chair but thought better of it and leaned on the rail instead. The cigarette in his mouth was almost as ashen as the bags under his eyes.

"We need your little project before we land," Ghaoithe said.

"It's not ready," Kirk said. "Still needs testing."

"This will be the test. Don't tell me the world's best runic scientist isn't confident in his work?"

"If it doesn't work, we're dead."

"We'll be dead anyway."

Kirk stared the captain down. He ashed his cigarette on the floor and disappeared.

The *Cloudkicker*'s runes sang as it barreled toward the Osiris dig. Alex's fingers drummed the armrests of her seat. Since their arrival in the jungle, she could not shake the queasy pit that roiled her insides. The closer they got to Deacon, the larger and more frightening his image grew in her imagination. She did not know she was shaking until the captain's voice whispered in her ear.

"Be strong, Alex. We're in this together," Ghaoithe said.

Alex tried to strengthen her resolve but cracked with her words. "I'm scared."

Ghaoithe bent down and embraced Alex. Her arms were calm as stone. "I know you are. So am I. Whatever happens, keep going. Get Ellie back. You are stronger than you think."

"Please tell me your idea will work."

Ghaoithe did not answer immediately. She released Alex from her arms. "We don't have much time."

Alex rubbed her palm across her eyes to brush away the wet. She breathed deep, stilled her heart, and placed her faith in the Sky Thief.

# XXVI

The *Cloudkicker* slowed for nothing. It stayed on its low path to Osiris as though the hounds of Hell chased it. Sometimes the hull shook as it clipped the tops of trees with enough force to shear them clean off. Such a stealthy approach was not part of the ship's usual repertoire, but it was more than up for the task. What the *Cloudkicker* lacked in size and firepower was more than made up for in sleek agility.

For the *Cloudkicker*'s inhabitants, they needed every edge they could find.

The Osiris dig appeared in the distance, a dead patch of brown within an emerald sea. Alex scanned the horizon in search of any sign of activity. A few ramshackle huts dotted the landscape from afar, but very little moved around them. Whatever Osiris forces occupied the space had long since gone.

Alex spotted something within the trees to their port side. It was nearly invisible to her at first but radiated an unnatural presence just like the statues in the forest. Then, it moved.

"Pull up hard to starboard!" Alex yelled.

The crew wasted no time with her warning. The *Cloudkicker* rocked as it tilted into the sky. Outside, the trees whirred to life. A low hum emanated from below the ship as a monstrous object began to climb. Its black hull flashed as red neon sigils lit up the hard angles of its exterior. A machine of incredible technology filled the window as the *Cloudkicker* tried to dodge its surprise launch. The *Ascendant* was waiting for them.

Alex had only seen the Osiris airship once, when it left them behind in Eden, and she gawked at its size next to the *Cloudkicker*. They may as well have been a canoe against an aircraft carrier. Still, Ghaoithe would not be shaken. She barked orders to her crew with the conviction only a seasoned captain could muster.

The *Cloudkicker* obeyed. It bucked away from the *Ascendant* and put a clear distance between them. With its superior speed, it cruised forward in an attempt to head off Deacon's monstrosity. More than that, its sigils wards could protect it from any attempt to shoot it down.

A large hole opened on the side of the *Ascendant* as the relic ship passed. A coil shot out. As it flew through the air, it unraveled to become a network of mesh in front of the *Cloudkicker*. Ghaoithe ordered a hard dive, but it was too late. Her ship ran straight into the net like salmon in a stream. The crew fell to the floor as the *Cloudkicker* abruptly halted against the fine steel wires. It struggled for a moment, but the mesh tightened around the *Cloudkicker*'s wings and folded them out of commission. It hovered, inert, within striking distance of the *Ascendant*.

All eyes turned to the Sky Thief.

"Shut everything down. Those able to fight, stay. Everyone else head below until we can chase wind," Ghaoithe said.

No one moved.

A piercing screech cut through the air from the direction of the *Ascendant*, like a high school PA system right before the class president makes an announcement. In fact, had she not been terrified of the near future, Alex might have remembered that Becky actually was the class president a lifetime ago.

"*Alex... is this thing working?... ALEXANDRA STIRLING! You and your friends come out to the deck. We won't fire*," Becky's voice blared.

The sound of her voice triggered a flood within Alex. She missed that voice, but it also enraged her. How could she? How could her best friend stand on top of an Osiris ship and promise not to harm anyone? Will Not Shoot Friends should have been somewhere near the top of universal truths of kinship. Alex clenched her fist as Becky made the announcement a second time.

Ghaoithe turned to Tory, the stalwart commander of the *Cloudkicker* in times of Ghaoithe's absence. "Stay back and keep her warm," Ghaoithe said.

Tory nodded. Her dreadlocks swirled about like a miniature brown tornado as she checked the systems in the bridge.

Ghaoithe led her crew to the deck. With Alex and Fleet at hand they commanded only about twenty people total. No doubt Roy and Kirk were whipping up the others below deck with armaments in case of a full-scale invasion of the ship. Alex believed it might come to that.

The *Ascendant* hovered beside the *Cloudkicker* in defiance of physics. A ramp connected its bridge with that of Ghaoithe's ship just to the left of the cannon that held the netting securely in place with a solid disk of bolts. Countless Osiris soldiers lined the railing, their guns waving testily at the sky. In the distance, thunderclouds boiled in warning to all those in its path. They rumbled and shook the air, the only sound aside from the tense breaths of those caught in the standoff. Near the top of the ramp stood Becky, megaphone in hand. Beside her, Sorin stared down with his modern garments and stone-faced demeanor.

Becky spotted Alex as she left the *Cloudkicker* cabin, a fair dwarf among swarthy giants. She smiled briefly, an unconscious reaction to Alex's wellbeing. Then, she returned to her business-like state and raised her megaphone again.

"It's over, Alex. Please turn yourselves in," Becky called.

"Over?! You barely know how it all started and you want to claim it's over?" Alex bellowed. Such was her fury that even Ghaoithe remained silent. This was a fight much older than and beyond the captain's ability.

Becky continued, "This is for your own safety. Sir Deacon promises to see you all safe until the opening of the Box. He rather likes you all!"

Alex placed a foot onto the ramp. The Osiris guns wagged in threat or fear, but Alex knew they could not do a thing so long as she stood on the *Cloudkicker*'s deck. "Tell that Bono wanna-be that the only box he'll be opening is a juice box to drink out of after I'm done with him!" Alex yelled.

"Please, Alex. You don't want to…"

"Don't tell me what I do and don't want! After all we've been through, you choose to side with the traitors? You were supposed to me there for me!"

At this, it was Becky's turn to lash out. She straightened up and gripped her perfectly-manicured hands around the megaphone. "It's always about you, isn't it, Alex? How I've always been there for you? How Becky always protects poor, fragile Alex from the big, mean world? When did you ever support me? When did you ever do a single thing to pay back all that I gave you over the years? The one time I was finally able to do something for myself, it turns out you still had your lousy hands in it! Well, I'm making my first choice for me, and I'm not one bit sorry about it!"

Alex wanted to cry. She never knew. All she could think about was her best friend, there for her after her parents were gone. Always there to offer up ice cream or a movie or makeovers when Alex desired to stay shut up in her room the most. Had Alex really been so ungrateful in all that? In hindsight, she supposed she could have been more open about her appreciation, but surely she had let Becky know how much she cared, right?

Hadn't she?

"Becky, I'm sorry! I didn't know!" Alex called out through her tears. "I was ungrateful, but you were always there for me. Please, don't do this. Let me be there for you this time"

From her perch, Becky's eyes watered at the sight of a pleading Alex. Her best friend for most of her life. The one who knew her inside and out.

The one who stole her best years.

No, Becky thought, she would not ruin her mascara today. She said, "I don't need you anymore, Alex, but you still need me. The best way to keep you safe from what's ahead is by coming on board this ship. If you won't come on your own, we'll drag you. Go ahead, Sorin!"

At the order, Sorin moved onto the ramp. Along the length of the deck, other ramps extended as Osiris soldiers invaded the *Cloudkicker*. Rain loomed above.

Now it was Ghaoithe's turn to be angry. She glowered at Sorin as he made his way down the ramp. She remembered the last time she saw him as he revealed himself as a turncoat. She'd suspected a leak on board her ship, of course, but knowing it was someone she held so close to her still stung. Yet there he walked, smug in his new clothes and life away from the *Cloudkicker*. Sorin made his choice, and it was time to deal with the consequences.

The captain drew her rapier and ordered the crew to form a line. They did so along the length of the deck, each crewman carefully placed through hours of training for this moment. There were far too many Osiris troops to stop the assault entirely, but the *Cloudkicker* had some advantage while Sorin's team struggled along the thin walkways.

"Was it worth it?" Ghaoithe snarled. "Was it worth turning on your friends for a set of modern clothes?"

Sorin's face flickered with a trace of anger before it fell back to its usual expressionless facade. "You do not have a family. You would not understand," he said.

He drew his own saber as he neared the deck of the *Cloudkicker*.

As his men stepped onto the ship's polished wood, Ghaoithe raised her rapier high.

"Alex! Now!" she yelled.

Alex dropped to the deck. From the sash at her belt, she pulled out a stick of black chalk. Only then did Sorin notice the dark sigils that lined the deck of Ghaoithe's ship. They blended in with the wood and shadows of the oncoming clouds. Alex hastily drew a connection in an empty space between two tendrils of runes. Sorin rushed towards Ghaoithe.

The entire crew of the *Cloudkicker* disappeared.

Behind the wall of invisibility runes, Ghaoithe's crew went to work. The distraction only lasted a few seconds as Osiris processed what happened, but it was enough to throw them off their balance. Sorin stepped through the runes, like stepping into a dim room after spending all day in the sun, and only got his bearings in time to block a charging Ghaoithe. He threw up his saber to hear it sing against Ghaoithe's rapier. Around them, the Osiris troops looked about in confusion, unable to see the wave of armed relic hunters heading their way.

Chaos erupted, and the fight began.

Damian held tight to Jessie's hand as they made their way through the *Ascendant*. Running through the halls, they passed scores of Osiris troops on the move, none of which paid the two any mind. Jessie rarely hesitated in her hunt, but Damian's chest felt ready to burst every time they pressed against the airship walls and waited for the soldiers to pass by. With his right hand, the one not sweatily gripping Jessie, he held a pendant. A gift from Kirk.

In the scant few minutes before the *Cloudkicker* became netted, Ghaoithe had explained her plan. The captain and any able-bodied fighters would hold the deck. Damian, the young wharf-rat who only managed to join the crew because he somehow sneaked aboard the ship as a stowaway, would use his skills to infiltrate the Osiris ship.

Enter Kirk.

"They aren't ready yet," Kirk told Ghaoithe. The tattooed scientist held two black disks in his hand, each the size of a silver dollar. Sigils wrapped around each one like a spider's web, but they were inert and dark. "They haven't been tested thoroughly."

"We're putting them through a field test right now. Damian just needs a crash course on them," Ghaoithe said.

Kirk grimaced. He raised a skeletal hand up to puff on his cigarette while he mulled his options. Seeing none, he handed the disks over to Damian.

"They work like the big invisibility runes, but they're portable. When you need, just connect these two sections," Kirk pointed at an empty space on the coins while smoke billowed into Damian's face, "and you should disappear. You can move about in broad daylight and no one'll see. Least, that's how they are supposed to work."

Damian flipped the smooth objects through his fingers as he observed them. "So, what's wrong with them?"

"I got them to work. I just don't know for how long. Could be until you toss it, could be you'll appear stark naked in the middle of the Osiris barracks. I got no way of knowing."

Ghaoithe knelt down to face Damian. He was not nervous until she did so, her humble acknowledgment of him almost unprecedented.

"I need you to find Ellie. She trusts you more than anyone on this ship, and you want her back just as much. I know it's a big ask," Ghaoithe said.

Damian shook his head and flashed his goofy, nonchalant grin. Inside, his guts squirmed with restless unease, but he couldn't let that show. "Wait until everyone hears that the Sky Thief couldn't sneak in somewhere. They'll be so disappointed," he said.

He did not mention a thing about Jessie, of course. He did not really consider her until he ran below deck to gather a few things from his quarters. In his pockets, he stashed a switchblade, a small plastic container that held a pristine set of stainless steel lockpicking tools, and a handgun he squirreled away from the jungle camp. He did not have much ammunition, but it was better than his fists.

On his way to depart, he passed by the brig. He wasn't sure why. Neither of them were much for goodbyes, but something nagged at him that it would be the right thing to do. When he got there, he saw Jessie sitting on the edge of her bed with her hands between her knees and a taught expression on her face. Even out of the loop, she had some sense of the urgency in the situation panning out above.

"Let me have my rifle," she pleaded.

Damian had to make a judgment call then. He knew the others' opinions of Vargas, their lack of trust. Though he spent time as Jessie's prison escort, his devotion to his captain remained unbroken, and he would have to decide if he could see enough in Jessie to warrant the risk of setting her free in such a crucial moment. Armed, no less.

He decided he did.

As the events between Alex and Becky unfolded above, Damian and Jessie waited within the *Cloudkicker*'s deck. As Sorin started to make his way down the ramp, they each struck Kirk's disks with chalk and connected the sigils. They flashed blue, and the two disappeared. Jessie pocketed hers and reached for Damian's hand.

"I can't see you, and I'm hoping you can't see me. Don't let go," Jessie said.

They did not, at least for the most part. While the Osiris troops were caught by Ghaoithe's parlor trick, Damian and Jessie climbed the netting that surrounded the *Cloudkicker* and used it to cross to where it connected with the *Ascendant*. They fumbled about for each other and made their way inside with Jessie at the helm.

As it turned out, the decision to bring Jessie along was justified the moment they stepped into the ship. Damian was used to the simple layout of the *Cloudkicker*. The *Ascendant* was an entirely other beast that he could not possibly navigate in the time they had. Jessie pulled him along the bright, cold hallways almost as if by instinct. With the arrays of holographic videos and drone of chipper female voices relaying the current Osiris news, Damian could almost pretend he was being dragged through an upscale shopping mall rather than an air fortress. He did not complain.

They came to a four-way intersection. A group of soldiers rounded the corner to Damian's right. Jessie pulled him against the wall where they flattened as best they could until the soldiers passed. Though he could not see the sniper, Damian somehow knew Jessie's free hand was poised to shoot should anything should Kirk's disks go wrong at an inopportune moment.

Damian almost spoke but remembered at the last moment that though his body was hidden, his voice was not. He wanted to ask Jessie why she offered to come along, to go back into the maw of the dragon she wanted so desperately to escape from. Maybe it was her chance at atonement, he wondered. Or, worst-case scenario, maybe he had been mistaken in bringing her, that Ghaoithe was right about Jessie being a possible spy under duress to do Deacon's bidding.

Once the soldiers passed, they both let out a long-held breath. *No,* Damian thought, *this is her personal mission now.*

As they twisted through the airship halls, the white-noise voices started to disappear. The video feeds quieted, replaced with little more than the Osiris logo of a tree within a green circle. The soldiers disappeared almost altogether. What few people they came across were dressed in casual clothes, their doors open to show beds, desks, and what few personal items they could fit in.

"Residence hall," Jessie whispered carefully after she slowed to ensure no one could overhear. Damian nodded in understanding. Then, feeling foolish, he squeezed her hand tightly.

Jessie beelined for a door within the residence block. From the outside, it looked no different than the other thin, steel entries in the other dorms. An electronic pad on the wall next to it blinked threateningly. Damian pulled out his lockpicking tools. He looked through the set with their intricate handles and hooked ends. Finally, he closed it and pulled out his handgun instead. He used it to bash in the control panel. It shattered with a cloud of sparks, and the door opened.

"You didn't have to do that. It's always unlocked from the outside now," a small voice giggled.

Damian and Jessie entered and blinked. Their eyes took a moment to adjust to the bright pink of the walls. In front of them, grinning and wide-eyed, stood Ellie. She ran up to Damian and wrapped her arms around him.

"You made it!" she squealed.

Damian laughed and knelt down. "I did! And you can see me!"

"Of course I can see you! I can see people here and way far away and sometimes people who don't think they can be seen," Ellie said. She looked up at Jessie. "Thank you. I know it was hard."

Jessie turned away to escape the gaze of those stardust eyes. She looked out into the hall. "We need to hurry," Jessie said.

Damian held on to Ellie's hand. He held out the black disk of sigils. "I need you to hold this for me, El. It'll keep people from seeing you," he said.

At this, Jessie whipped around. "No. Let her take mine," she said.

"I'll find some way to get around. You can get her back easier and safer."

"Just follow me. I'll be less suspicious on the ship if people see me. They'll just think I'm hitting one of the tanks again."

Jessie pulled her disk out of her shirt pocket and tossed it at Ellie. The girl caught it with a grin and promptly vanished. Damian opened his mouth to argue until he looked up at Jessie. She nearly filled the frame of the open doorway. She did not hide behind a glass bottle or slink like a rat through forgotten crevices. She was the Jessie Vargas she used to be, and no amount of debate could douse that fire. All Damian could do was pray that she did not scorch all of Osiris on their way out or, worse yet, turn that blaze on the *Cloudkicker*.

"Just stay close and hope the *Cloudkicker* keeps Sorin occupied for a while," Jessie said. She slung her rifle casually over her back and stepped out. It was a long shot, but hopefully the rank-and-file kept their distance from her just as they did while she was lounging about in the bars of the ship.

Damian pawed at the air to find Ellie's hand. She reached out and took his, small and soft in his palm. Together, they trailed Jessie through the ship.

In the residence area, Jessie stopped every few moments to look back only to see an empty hall. She adjusted the strap holding her gun around her shoulder and continued on. She would have to trust that Damian and Ellie were on her tail, just as she would have to trust that the *Cloudkicker* team could find a way to undo the net trapping them and just as she would have to trust that she would not run into anyone on the Osiris ship that would question her sudden reemergence after a few days away. She did her best to look annoyed, her face curled as if she'd tried to start a car only to discover the battery had died.

As it turned out, pretending to be upset at everything and everyone was the easiest part of the plan. No one bothered her as she strode through the residence halls. Even as she passed into the busier wards, she received hardly a bat of an eye. A single soldier looked as though he was about to speak to her as she passed, but she looked at him with all the distasteful fury she could muster, and he continued briskly on his way.

Jessie's insides turned to jello with each encounter. She glanced at the overhead cameras, wondering if Deacon watched over her, waiting until the last moment to strike her down. She shook the thought out of her head. It was too late to worry about it now. She had to get Ellie back to the *Cloudkicker*.

She turned into a wide area and stopped. Soldiers filed out in practiced efficiency through large bay doors. Streaks of lightning flashed overhead as the outside world readied for a storm. Yells and clashes of battle rang out of sight from below.

Jessie looked back. Though she could not see Damian, she could almost feel him nodding her on, sharing with her some small bit of confidence. Jessie swallowed her fear and silently turned left, away from the doors and into a separate hallway. More soldiers clamored to the front lines, but she was out of sight of the fight below. She tugged the brim of her hat down low, hoisted her rifle into the crook of her elbow, and steadily advanced. Even then, none of the Osiris goons bothered her, too lost in their own heads as they ran to battle against a bulletproof ship. Soon, Jessie was past the brunt of the forces and on her way to the bow of the *Ascendant*, closer to where the net held Ghaoithe's ship in place.

The exit to the deck was loosely guarded with most of the soldiers either keeping the ship running or assigned to keep watch over the fight below. Only two men stood beside the small, open doorway that led outside. Their black helmets obscured their faces, but there was no mistaking they recognized Jessie. They turned her way, tips of their rifles pointed in her direction.

"How did you get...," the left one yelled before he fell to the ground with a muffled oomph. Another thump hit the back of the second soldier's helmet, and he fell beside his partner. A moment later, they were both out cold.

"Oh no, it appears the ship is haunted," said Damian's voice from the open doorway.

Jessie could not help herself. A laugh caught in her throat, and she found herself snickering despite her best intentions. She'd forgotten what laughing felt like. She missed it.

"Let's just finish this," she said between breaths.

Outside, the humid air clung to her skin like a damp blanket. The clouds were nearly over them, ready to unleash a torrent over anyone caught below their rage. Jessie took it as a blessing; there was no wind to knock her about as she grasped the first rung of the net.

"You go first," Damian ordered. "I'll keep watch just in case. Take Ellie with you."

Jessie nodded. "Ellie, honey, you want a piggyback ride? We need to get you across as fast as we can."

Jessie felt the weight of Ellie as the young girl's arms wrapped around her neck, a feeling that was familiar as though in a dream from long ago. A twang hit Jessie's heart, and she gripped the net firmly to keep her knees from going weak.

"She's ok," Ellie whispered into Jessie's ear. "You don't have to be sad for her."

Jessie let out a breath and nodded. She found her well of strength, placed her feet into the rungs of the net, and began to scale across.

As she climbed, Jessie became acutely aware that she was no longer invisible. She made her way swiftly across as steadily as she could. Though she had no fear of heights, she judged the drop into the jungle below and both the literal and figurative weight of the child on her back. By the time she landed on the deck of the *Cloudkicker*, her legs crumpled underneath her.

Shouts clamored through the air. At first, Jessie thought it was the fighting on the deck around the side of the bridge. Then she realized they were far too loud and clear in her direction. She shot up.

"Ellie, go get inside," Jessie ordered. She could not see the child, but she knew Ellie was already gone.

On the other side of the netting, Damian stood in plain sight aboard the *Ascendant*, the disk of runes dark in his hand.

# XXVII

Once the invasion of the *Cloudkicker* began, time blurred. Slowing the Osiris march proved harder than the crew expected. Alex could not be sure how the fight started once Sorin stepped onto Ghaoithe's ship, only that cries from both sides went up simultaneously as fighters crashed into each other like ocean waves against a bluff.

Alex drew Excalibur and swung at the first soldier she could see. It was more of a reaction than a conscious decision on her part. The blow landed with a soft squish. The man, obscured behind his helmet, let out a cry as he grabbed his arm and fell to the ground. Alex had no time to linger on him. More came behind him. Had she looked about, Alex may have noticed Ghaoithe beside her. Her own movements mirrored the captain's. Perhaps Alex was not quite as clean as Ghaoithe's practiced strokes, but they moved in lockstep nonetheless as Alex's training kicked in.

Maybe she would have noticed, but she did not look, and she was far too frightened to find any kind of beauty in an old-fashioned brawl.

At first, the *Cloudkicker* had some advantage. The Osiris fighters had to traverse narrow ramps and were easily blocked or even shoved into the jungle below. Their guns offered little aid against the hazard of the *Cloudkicker*, and most held swords and bludgeons awkwardly in their hands as they crossed. All, of course, but Sorin. A gun would never fit well in his paws.

His team gained ground eventually. While he vied for Ghaoithe's attention, soldiers slipped past the human barricade and onto the deck. Even without practice, most were large mercenaries in thick armor and their weapons no less deadly for lack of experience.

For a brief moment as Sorin clashed with Ghaoithe, Alex saw an opportunity to come to her captain's side. By the end of the first swing, she knew it was folly to try. She had never seen the two fight—truly fight—until then. Ghaoithe had taken out a few inexperienced freebooters in Roanoake, sure, and a robotic drone or two in China. Here, against a skilled opponent and former friend, a different woman emerged.

Sorin gravitated to Ghaoithe through the crowd, his eyes never leaving the bright blue armor amid throngs of white and black. When he finally came within striking distance, he wasted no time bringing his saber down upon her. It was not a strong swing, more of a test than anything, but Ghaoithe reacted all the same. She brushed his arm aside with her left wrist and planted her other fist squarely across his jaw. The blow came so quickly and precisely that Alex would have missed it had she blinked. Sorin recoiled, a trickle of blood forming on his lip. He smiled.

"You never were one for grace," Sorin said.

"You're one to talk," Ghaoithe replied.

The captain aimed her rapier and released a flurry of jabs at his chest. A lesser man might have fallen then and there, but Sorin was built of brick and oil, a honed machine of his own making. He stepped back and parried each with an ease of motion hidden by his brutish figure. They continued, back and forth like two tigers over a feeding ground, with neither giving way to the other, each landing blows where they could.

A figure blocked Alex's view, and she raised Excalibur up in response. As much as she wanted to gawk and worry over her captain, she had her own fights to win.

Through the furor, Becky's voice screeched from the deck of the *Ascendant*. "Don't *kill* them, for God's sake!"

Alex ducked below a flying arm. She swept Excalibur through the legs of the faceless thug, knocking him off balance with a thud. She thought briefly of plunging the sword through his side while he was prone, but she could not bring herself to do it. She could fight, yes, but there was a line she was not yet ready to cross. At least not knowingly. So, she ran.

She wasn't afraid; the adrenaline coursing through her drowned her fear, turned everything into the pulse in her ears. Still, she knew her limits, and she was not built for such a grand melee. Instead, she needed to find a better position. She needed to be useful to herself and her crewmates beyond just another flashy sword against an overwhelming tide. So she weaved through the crowd in search of a vantage point where she could make out the lay of the land.

Her search ended futilely. When she looked back, another wave of soldiers crossed the ramps. The *Cloudkicker* was soon to be overrun.

To her right, near the far edge of the scene, Fleet fought a small crowd that threatened to overtake him. His face was red from a cut above his left eyebrow, but he stood no more willing to fall than the Acropolis. He, too, understood their dire situation.

"Captain! We need to fall back!" he called out as he planted a bear's fist into the stomach of the nearest soldier.

Ghaoithe did not yell back any acknowledgment. She faced Sorin with the look of a tempest, apprehensive of the idea of retreat. She charged. Sorin brought up his arms in a boxer's guard and steeled himself against the captain. At the last moment, Ghaoithe shifted her weight and planted a booted foot squarely at his stomach. The air left him as he fell to the ground gasping.

"Into the ship! Everyone off the deck!" Ghaoithe yelled. She lingered on Sorin's form for a split second before she turned and ran to the main door.

Those remaining in the fight fell back as best they could while locked in close combat. Ghaoithe waited by the door, her rapier singing at any Osiris trooper that dared come close. Alex dashed inside. A moment later, Fleet. Once the last member of her team passed the frame, Ghaoithe shut the door with a heavy slam. As her eyes adjusted, Alex saw those around her. Most were fine, if somewhat bruised and bloody, but a handful had more serious wounds that soaked through their clothes. The crowd was smaller than the one that started the fight.

"Get downstairs and tend the wounded," Ghaoithe ordered. "Any extra hands follow me to the bridge."

Ghaoithe marched to the bridge, any number of escape plans cycling through her head, none of which sounded any more viable than the last so long as the net held her ship in place. She hated the term "miracle," but silently she wished Ellie would come up with some of her magic. From the captain's perspective, things certainly looked hopeless and more than worth divine intervention from the child. If Damian had succeeded, that is.

Alex knew something was wrong the moment she turned the corner into the control room. It was quiet, for one. Tory's abrasive commands were nowhere to be heard. No one milled about in efficient calamity to keep the ship afloat. The only movement came from a tall, slender figure at the base of the ramp leading up to Ghaoithe's seat. Behind him, several members of the *Cloudkicker* team, including Tory, were bound and gagged or knocked out cold.

Deacon smiled as he saw the captain, a cunning fox's grin too certain of itself to be any good. He held a white sphere in his hands. A mass of writhing stone tendrils capped it like a helm of seaweed, all still except for one. The green appendage shot at Ghaoithe. It hissed and its eyes flashed red before it joined its brethren, inert forevermore.

Ghaoithe tried to jump back, but her legs held to the floor. Her bronze skin cracked and marbled as it turned to stone until all that remained was a sculptor's image of what the Sky Thief may once have been. It happened so quickly that Alex had no time to register what had happened or cry out.

"Marvelous! Absolutely fantastic!" Deacon said in greeting. His voice cut through stunned air to send prickles down the spines of his audience. "You can never really know how much of those old myths are really true. Much gets lost in rumor and fable, but this... this was just as advertised, I dare say!"

He admired the head in his arms. It's mutated face was locked in an angry scream as the snakes on its head roiled with fury. He passed the dead Gorgon to one of the several men flanking him. Tracing the frozen stone face of Ghaoithe with the tip of his cane, he admired her with a scientist's curiosity.

"Ah, to see it end like this," Deacon continued. "I would have preferred that we ended as friends, like minds in research and study of the old tales. At the very least, you could have told me the secret of that incredible armor of yours. Alas! Pandora's Box is far too important to have you nipping at my heels at every turn. It's truly for the best this way. And to think you would have beat me to Medusa's resting place if you'd gone into that crypt half a day earlier!"

Everything swirled in Alex's head. The bridge, Deacon's voice, her comrades... they all nauseated her. The only stillness she could grasp was Ghaoithe's form. She begged for the captain to respond, to make some quip about their predicament. Her knees buckled.

Deacon knelt down to Alex. He pretended to look empathetic behind his purple-tinted pince-nez. He even took off his top hat in a rare show of respect.

"My dear Alex. This would have been so much easier had you just died and broken the poor captain's spirit," he said. He reached out with a skeletal finger to lift Alex's chin. "Now I have both your captain and your childhood friend. Perhaps it's best if you stop trying to act so special for such an overwhelmingly average little girl."

Alex barely noticed Deacon's touch. She was lost, floating in her own dismay. The edges of her vision darkened as she fell further and further into the pit. She liked it there. It was quiet and simple and lonely. Nothing could bother her there. After all that she'd gone through, the despair was easier to handle. Closed off from the world, nothing could hurt her again.

Yet, somewhere at the far end of her vision, a pinprick of light appeared. It gained form, first as Deacon's wretched face, and then as the window of the bridge behind him. Outside, she saw the netting holding the *Cloudkicker* in place. At the other end, where the net was locked to the side of Deacon's ship, a figure clung to the wire with a workman's intent. Alex recognized his thin frame and long hair, and she knew what he meant to her and the crew. Damian returned. Ellie was safe. Hope lived.

The blackness at the edge of her vision tinged red.

"I'll stop when you're dead," Alex growled. She grabbed the finger at her chin and twisted with all her strength.

Deacon howled and clutched his left hand. The soldiers behind him moved into action. They pushed against Fleet and the others, bludgeoned weapons swinging without care.

As Deacon moved backward through the swarm, Alex refused to let him out of her sight. She trailed him, his violet coat jacket a spotlight in the crowd as he turned the corner and into the entry hall of the ship. She gripped Excalibur and gave chase as fast as her legs could take her.

Outside, the sky opened its maw and brought down a torrential wall. Deacon, in his designer shoes and heavy garb, slipped about the deck unsteadily with Alex hot on his heels. Osiris soldiers milled about, checking on the wounded and dead scattered across the deck. They turned at the appearance of Alex and, far more frightening, the head of Osiris. The soldiers looked at each other, unsure of whether to jump. They ultimately settled on waiting for a direct order.

Alex caught Deacon in the open air. Once she was close enough to reach him, she leapt and tackled Deacon around his legs. They hit the deck together with a thud. Alex bounced back up and jabbed at Deacon with her sword. He spun, and her sword glanced off the ship in a narrow miss. He kicked at her legs and forced her back just enough to right himself.

Alex came at Deacon with another flurry of swings. This time, he raised his cane with his right hand for each blow. Alex expected her sword to slice through it cleanly, but it held without so much as a scratch. That only frustrated her more, and she continued her barrage until she had to step back and take a breath.

Deacon clicked his tongue. "I have been at this game far longer than you have, girl," he chided.

Grunting, Alex made another swing. Without gloves or true fighting experience, her hands started to slip in the downpour. Deacon tossed the blade aside with a snap of his wrist. Excalibur fell with a clang upon the deck. Deacon's cane fell beside it. Alex regained her balance to find the barrel of a pistol aimed squarely at her head.

"Fire. I dare you," Alex snarled.

Deacon turned the gun to his side and let off a succession of shots that left Alex's ears pounding. The bullets cut cleanly through the air.

"Well, that's a fine experiment. We could have saved so much time earlier had we known only the ship was protected," Deacon said. He pointed to Alex again. "That's science for you, I suppose."

Another shot exploded. Hot pain burst through the top of Alex's shoulder. She cried out only to realize that so, too, did Deacon. His gun clattered to the deck. Alex grabbed her shoulder and felt the heat of blood mix with the rain soaking into her shirt. She turned to see Jessie's sniper rifle aimed in her direction. Her skin was pale, but her hands did not waver on the trigger. Behind her, Osiris soldiers flooded out of the ship, chased by Fleet and the remaining crew.

Deacon knocked Alex down. Jessie aimed her rifle once more, but the steady stream of new bodies to the deck kept her from finding a clear shot at the Osiris leader. The Osiris soldiers escorted him up the ramp and back onto the *Ascendant*.

New shouts came from the Osiris ship. Someone fired their gun. It was not aimed at the *Cloudkicker*, but the side of Deacon's ship. Alex and the rest ignored the fleeing troopers to focus their attention on the new target: Damian. He still clung to the wire mesh, sparks flying as he hacked at the thin line keeping the net secured in place with his tiny switchblade. The net groaned as he made progress, but the Osiris soldiers above threatened to fall upon him in a few short moments.

"Damian! There's no time! Come back!" Jessie yelled. She rushed to the railing along the side of the *Cloudkicker*'s deck.

Damian looked back to her, then down at the frayed wire. It wasn't clear if he heard Jessie's voice, but his intent was clear all the same. Jessie shook her head. He nodded back, solemn and resolute.

Jessie raised her sniper rifle but refused to pull the trigger. Damian nodded again.

She fired.

Her bullet ripped through the remainder of the wiring. The *Cloudkicker* groaned as it came loose from its captor and the net slid off its prow.

Damian, with a victorious grin, flipped two fingers at the Osiris ship as he fell with the net to the ground below.

# XXVIII

Free from its shackle, the *Cloudkicker* dove away from Deacon's ship. The steel planks that crossed the two gave way, sending the last vestiges of Osiris soldiers overboard as they clamored after their leader. Those from Ghaoithe's crew that remained on the deck scrambled to get back inside, as well. Only Alex remained. She sat on her knees as rain splashed over the boards around her and stared at the spot Damian had been moments ago.

"Up ya go, lass! We don't have time fer that quite yet," Fleet shouted over the storm. He came to her side and knelt down. He picked up Excalibur as it started to slide across the deck and, with his other hand, lifted Alex to her feet.

Her legs moved, but she did not comprehend where they took her. Only when they entered the bridge did Alex show any sign of alertness. There, still at the bottom of the ramp, was Ghaoithe's solid form. Alex gagged at the image. Fleet spun Alex around, their noses almost touching.

"I know. There'll be time for that later. Right now, we need to get ya strapped in," he said.

He took Alex to her seat on the observation area and sat her down. Then, he began to shout orders to what little crew remained. In the absence of their captain, they looked to anyone willing to take initiative, and Fleet's experienced frame was more than up to the task. Though the blood caked on his brow grew more worrisome by the second, he showed no sign of weakening.

Through the bridge window, the *Ascendant* loomed. The *Cloudkicker* unfurled its wings in a dazzling spark of light. The entire ship lurched forward and forced everyone against the back of their seats. All around the bridge, sigils flashed as the ship kicked into high gear. Like a winged valkyrie called to battle, it took flight in a race against the leviathan at its side. It bolted forward, passed the prow of the *Ascendant*, and left Deacon middling about in its wake.

They did not stop. The sped onward without any precise destination. Their only goal was to escape. Soon, the canopy of the jungle was out of sight below. Next, the desert. Finally, endless ocean on all sides. Only then did Fleet dare to slow their sprint. How long it took, Alex did not know. Minutes at their speed, maybe. Perhaps hours. She had trouble concentrating on anything other than the statue below.

"You've lost a lotta blood. We need to get ya downstairs," Fleet said once they'd fully stopped. He did not look or feel so great himself.

Alex carefully rose from her seat. Her legs warbled as she did so. She grasped the railing of the captain's platform. Looking over the balcony, she saw the scarce crew milling about. Most had dark circles under their eyes from fatigue. A few even worse. One person in particular stood out among the crowd to Alex's hazy vision. Jessie sat along the wall, just under the port side of the window, her hands entangled in her long hair. Even from the distance, Alex could see the sniper's eyes were red. Her rifle was slumped over her legs.

At the sight of Vargas, Alex took off. She ran unsteadily down the platform, careful not to look at Ghaoithe as she passed.

"Where's Ellie?" Alex demanded. When Jessie looked up without responding, Alex bent over and pulled Jessie by the collar of her shirt.

Vargas stared back, dead-eyed and barely able to comprehend Alex's question. "I'm sorry, Alex. I'm so sorry. It was your shoulder or... or..." Jessie could not finish the sentence.

"WHERE THE HELL IS ELPIS?"

A small voice chimed in, "I'm right here, Alex."

Ellie stood beside the two women, though she had not been anywhere on the bridge a moment ago. Alex dropped Vargas and threw her arms around the child.

"You're safe. It wasn't for nothing," Alex choked out. She repeated herself several times, as though the more she said it the more real it became.

Ellie hugged Alex back and patiently waited for her sobs to quiet. When Alex slumped in her arms, Ellie kissed her on her cheek. Alex felt a faint breeze, and then she slept.

Alex woke up in her room to the sound of crinkling paper. She stared at the ceiling for a moment as it swam above and gained form. When she sat up, she felt a tug at her arm. Someone had bandaged her shoulder, and she could not move it enough to even lift the sheets off her bed.

"Hewwo," said Ellie. She sat in the chair next to Alex's vanity. Her face was smeared with chocolate from a Snickers bar she eagerly unwrapped and crammed into her mouth. The sight was so preposterous that Alex rubbed her eyes to make sure she wasn't still dreaming. She could not remember the last time she even saw a Snickers bar, let alone on the *Cloudkicker*.

"Can I have a bite?" Alex croaked.

Ellie nodded. She took out the last chunk of the candy and passed it over. Alex nibbled at it, the sweet sugar a godsend to her desperate insides.

"Fleet wanted me to watch you," Ellie said. "They are moving the captain to her room. It's taking six people so they don't break her. She's heavy!"

The mention of Ghaoithe pierced Alex's heart. She looked despondently down at her hands.

"The captain. Is she...?" Alex started. She did not want to finish the sentence. Ellie picked up on the rest.

"I can't hear her, but that can mean lots of things," Ellie said. "Sometimes I can't hear flowers, but that just means they're sleeping."

"Can we save her?" Alex asked against her better judgment. She was afraid of the answer.

Ellie only shrugged.

Alex looked at the child, her cheeks hot. "Ellie, if you know anything that can save Ghaoithe, you need to tell me."

"I can't! There are rules," Ellie said. She shifted uncomfortably in her seat and refused to meet Alex's eyes.

Pangs of guilt tugged at Alex, and she chided herself for getting angry at Ellie. When she looked at Ellie again, she saw sparkling blue eyes and a petite frame no different than any other child. How easy it was to forget that she was not a child at all. Alex decided to drop the subject. There were other avenues to explore.

"It's ok. We'll figure something out," Alex said. She swung her feet around the side of the bed. "Would you like to help me get dressed?"

Ellie's face lit up, and she bounced on her toes enthusiastically.

"Pick out some clothes in that dresser there. Make sure they're good ones," Alex said.

Ellie chose a pair of soft gray breeches and a cream-colored blouse, both in that flexible, airy style of Lost Earth. Jessie's gunshot wound was clean and shallow, but it made Alex's arm terribly sore. She needed Ellie's help to pull on the blouse. The shirt fit awkwardly over the bandages wrapped around her shoulder. It reminded Alex of her mother's suit jackets from the 80's with their pointed shoulder pads. She wondered what her mother would think to see her now, injured so far from home and vastly out of her element.

Afterward, Ellie sat Alex down at the vanity and played a handmaid's game in which she tried to comb Alex's curls under playful direction. Ellie's joy at helping a real adult was contagious, and Alex was able to laugh. Even if just for a little while, she was able to forget what awaited the moment she left her room. Perhaps that was Ellie's grand intent all along. Or maybe Ellie really did just want to play House.

Once her hair was tidied (and Ellie's, too, for good measure), Alex hugged Ellie with her good arm. Up close, the child smelled like grass after a spring rain. It gave Alex a surprising peace-of-mind.

"I'm so glad you're back," Alex said.

"Me, too. You should go now. Fleet's waiting," Ellie giggled. It didn't sound so hard to do when she did it.

Fleet was, in fact, waiting when Alex arrived on the bridge. He sat at a folding table with Kirk on the observation balcony. Alex's eyes flickered to the empty captain's chair. Fleet had apparently rejected the notion of taking it over any time soon. At Alex's arrival, the old quartermaster stood and placed his knuckles on his hips. His head featured a new gash held tightly by three staples, but he otherwise seemed healthy, a least in body.

"How're ya feelin', lass? You was out fer a good while there," Fleet asked as Alex pulled up her own chair.

"Ellie kept good care of me," Alex said.

"Good to hear. Lina worked hard on the lot of us, so be thankful when ya see her next. She said ya won't be able to move yer arm fer a week or so but you'll live."

Alex was silent for a moment. Eventually, she asked, "Any word about... about..."

Fleet cut her off with a wave of his hand. He sounded as reluctant to talk about the elephant in the room as she was. "No. No word about the captain yet."

Alex looked toward Kirk. He sat with his head down, staring at a full ashtray before him. The cigarette in his mouth burned listlessly as it hung from his lips.

"What about you? Surely there's some kind of word, some sigil that can undo it?" Alex asked. Her voice rose more than she intended.

Kirk massaged his bald head with his fingers. "Not that I've found.

With Osiris on our tail from here on out, it's going to be tough finding a way to research anything."

"So make more of that bulletproof armor or whatever! Then we don't have to worry about Osiris!" Alex shrieked.

"I can't! I don't know how!" Kirk replied. His fingers nervously traced the lines of the tattoos on his dome. The cigarette rolled from side-to-side between his lips.

"What do you mean 'you don't know how?' Aren't you supposed to be Kirk Langley, the world-renowned runesmith? The man who made the *Cloudkicker* fly?" asked Alex.

Kirk took the cigarette between his fingers and spit on the ground. "For someone so bright, you sure don't have much upstairs do you? I can make ships fly. I can work their interior dimensions to make things a bit more comfortable. I don't know how to craft the armor the *Cloudkicker* has."

Alex stared at Kirk in shock. She didn't believe him at first, but he refused to meet her eyes. Even through the tough exterior, his loyalty to Ghaoithe shone through. Not even Kirk could escape their situation unfazed.

"Then how...?" Alex started.

"Look around, kid," Kirk said. "How many other things have you seen in Lost Earth like the *Cloudkicker* or Ghaoithe's armor? Or in Osiris, for that matter? If making those kinds of things was common knowledge, don't you think Deacon would have decked out everything he owns with it?"

Alex blinked and tried to comprehend what Kirk said. All this time, she thought Ghaoithe's armor was a rarity, but the scope of it never occurred to her. She knew very little about the limits of the sigils that powered Lost Earth. Yet, looking back, Kirk was right. Osiris guards wore armor, sure, but they were no different than the SWAT teams back home with Kevlar and ceramic plates. No one wore what Ghaoithe shrouded herself in, her yellow sigils unique when all of the other natural sigils Alex knew of glowed blue. Then, Alex remembered the other incidents. Osiris holding Ghaoithe's armor in their R&D lab with Ellie. The *Cloudkicker* brushing off military weapons after Alex was kidnapped. The dogtag that protected Alex during their escape from China. They all circled back to the Sky Thief and that azure leather armor.

Alex rubbed her burning eyes. Once her mind processed the new information, she said, "I didn't know Ghaoithe knew that much about sigils."

Kirk grunted. He pulled out the stub of cigarette from his mouth and used it to light a fresh one. After taking a puff, he said, "She doesn't. Not really more than basics anyway. I don't know if she learned the protection runes herself or just found someone who does. Either way, she's the only one that knows it these days, and it's worth a hell of a lot more than all of the other knowledge about runes combined."

Alex's chest tightened. Without Ghaoithe, she failed to see a way to beat Osiris to Pandora's Box. Not only did the captain always seem to have the answers, but she also had the resources to see them through. What chance did the crew have without her? Did Alex even want to continue without the captain?

"So that's it, then?" she said. Her jaw trembled. "We're just screwed and Deacon gets to erase whatever he wants? He'll find Pandora's Box before us, and then it's just matter of time until he tracks us down, too."

"NO!"

Kirk's fist slammed onto the table. Startled, Alex jumped in her seat and looked up. Kirk's face darkened, and his scowl made him no prettier than usual, but his eyes locked onto Alex's with a conviction that had remained hidden within him until that point.

"We are not done," Kirk hissed. "We may be set back, but we still have this ship and her crew. We have Roy on the ground working people up against Osiris. We still have you. We have Elpis. Until those are gone, we have a chance."

Alex shook her head. "Me? What can I do?"

"You can fight," Kirk said. He pointed a craggy finger at Alex. "I've never seen Captain Loinsigh take to anyone like she's taken to you. Not me, not Fleet... no one. You might not know how yet, but if there's anyone that's going to get Ghaoithe back, you're our best hope."

Kirk leaned back into his seat, crossed his arms, and turned away. Though she couldn't help but appreciate his begrudging compliments, Alex failed to agree with them. Despite her adventures aboard the *Cloudkicker*, she was still a Missourian at heart and knew so little about the world that accepted her without question. She did not know how to build protective armor or read lost coded directions. If anyone could heal Ghaoithe, it needed to be someone who grew up in their world, not a farm-girl-turned-failed-journalist.

"There's something else, lass."

Fleet stood, his voice raspy and raw. His eyes sagged over his cheeks. He shifted on sore legs before moving to stand beside Alex. With a topic to distract him from his emotions, Kirk returned to his usual self. He placed his boots on the table and took a drag of his cigarette.

"We could use some good news. Whatcha got?" he said.

"Lynn told me that if anything ever... ever," Fleet started. He closed his eyes to settle himself before continuing, "If anything ever happened to her, we were to go to her home. She didn't say what's there, only that it would help if we was outta options."

At this, Kirk's eyes widened in surprise. He took the cigarette from his mouth to let out a low whistle. "You're telling me you actually know where she's from?"

Alex looked back and forth between the two men. "I thought she was Scots-Irish? From some island?"

"She is, but she's kept the exact location as much a secret as her armor. More than a few people have wondered why," Kirk said.

Fleet cleared his throat. "I've known that girl since she was barely out of her knickers. We shared a few things between us. I think this is the kinda thing she was talkin' about when she told me the location."

Kirk rubbed his chin. "We'll lose a few days looking for Pandora's Box at best. Who knows at worst. That's a lot of time for Deacon to put between us."

"If ya can come up with a plan in less time, I'd love to hear it," snapped Fleet. Without another word, they both looked at Alex.

She did not like being asked. Through her head ran thoughts of her simple Missouri home, of a time when her biggest worry meant calling a few real estate agents for an interview. Her town carried little opportunity, but also little trouble. Nothing changed or needed to.

Alex also knew none of that mattered anymore. Things did change for her. She did join the *Cloudkicker*. She did meet Ghaoithe. She lost her best friend and gained new ones. She discovered so much more of the world than she knew even existed. Their current situation was bad no matter which way they looked at it, but that was the risk in trying to achieve a lot of good. Alex could not change the past nor would she. She could not forget where she came from, but the present was where she belonged.

And perhaps that was the point. Deep within her head, Alex heard Ghaoithe's laughter, as though the captain had been waiting inside all this time for Alex to figure out some great puzzle. Even as a stone figure, Ghaoithe's ability to inspire lived on.

Despite the loss and the pain of the past few hours, Alex found herself holding her face in her hands, not to hide away tears but to stifle the inappropriate smile that invaded her lips at the prospect of a new adventure. When she pulled her hands away, she bore into Fleet with wide, cobalt eyes and said, "Get those coordinates to the rest of the bridge, Fleet. Whatever Ghaoithe wanted us to find is going to be important."

In the quiet of night, the *Cloudkicker* made the exchange.

It landed on a bed of sand, far from the prying glances of city lights. As an extra precaution, Captain Fleet ordered its flight crystal be removed from its chamber to dim the sigils along its hull. After a few silent moments scanning the area, the crew went into action.

Alex left the ship and wandered into the desert. She opened the small black box in her hands and pulled out the cell phone gifted to her by Samir. It took her a few minutes to wander out of range of the *Cloudkicker*, which scrambled signals. Soon, a single bar popped into the corner of the screen. It was not much, but it was enough, and she made the call. A few hours later, the *Cloudkicker* was surrounded by several jet black SUVs and one hooded cargo truck. Samir stepped out of the lead car and aimed straight for the young blonde woman alone in the desert. He hugged her, as was his custom, but it lacked the strength of their last meeting.

"Where is she?" Samir asked.

"They're bringing her down now. It'll take a few minutes. So they don't chip anything," Alex replied.

Fleet and his men appeared over the deck of the airship. In their arms, they hoisted Ghaoithe. Carefully, they descended the boarding ramp with her until they felt sand at their feet. They laid her down, and Samir's men took over.

Samir fell to his knees at the sight of her, cold and dark under the desert stars. He whispered something into the wind as his arms went to the sky. Alex did not need to understand Arabic to know they were a prayer. Once Samir finished, she rushed to help him to his feet. Several men in dark suits lifted Ghaoithe and carried her towards the cargo van.

"Will she be safe? I know you have men, but there's no telling what Osiris might do," Alex asked.

"What you saw was my house. Where I am taking my child is a fortress," Samir said dryly.

Once Ghaoithe reached the truck, the men lifted her into its bed. They strapped her down with enough thick cable ties and belts that she would not move an inch when they nudged her. Alex reached out and placed a hand on Ghaoithe's boot. She closed her eyes, unsure of what to say or who to say it to. So, she turned and let the men close the van's hood instead.

"We will keep her safe. However, you must return. Where are you going?" Samir asked.

Alex shook her head. "I can't say. Fleet's orders and, to be honest, I'm not even sure myself."

"That is good," Samir nodded. "Fleet is a sharp man. You have my blessings, wherever they may take you."

With those blessings in her mind, Alex returned to the *Cloudkicker* and watched the black cars disappear into the desert. She never had an innate ability with directions, but she swore they veered south instead of beelining to Cairo. Once Samir was out of sight, Fleet waited another half an hour before ordering a launch.

"She'll be safer with him. Samir's got assets we don't," Fleet reassured once he saw Alex's troubled face enter the bridge.

Alex nodded dutifully. She did not disagree with Fleet, but she felt as though a piece of her soul had been taken on that cargo truck. She would continue to worry until they were reunited and made whole again.

She viewed the horizon outside the windows. It was still dark, but the first shades of dawn approached from over the dunes. The ship turned away from it and sped off.

"Do you know anything about where we're going?" Alex asked. Maybe, if she tried hard enough, she could let her imagination bring some solace to their circumstances. After so many struggles, new worlds and hidden locations did not have quite the same ring they did when she first boarded the ship. However, none of those other secrets were tied so intimately to the captain. Alex wondered what kind of home could raise such a woman. That, in turn, gave her some break from the shadow that chased her thoughts.

Fleet rumbled, "Not much. She only mentioned it once or twice in passin' outside of when she gave me the secret to finding it. Truth be told, half of it sounded made up."

"Made up? How so?" The shadow receded, albeit cautiously.

Fleet plopped into his chair, the legs creaking as he did so. He eyed

Ghaoithe's beside his and squinted, as if it might reveal the words he needed to him.

"There's something ya gotta understand. Maybe ya already figured it out," Fleet said. "Most of Lost Earth ain't all that strange or special. Homes are older, clothes are plainer, but most life gets on same as yers. We got some magic, in the runes and sometimes from a relic we dig up, but that's about it."

Alex nodded. "Right. I mean, it's all new to me, but there haven't been any ghosts or magic fireballs thrown about, I guess."

"Well, Ghaoithe always told me that there are certain places that hold power. Not just sigils and artifacts, but the land itself is sort of a wellspring. And we found some, sure enough. Atlantis, even Dilmun has a bit of that. Still, they had buildings and people and all that just like anywhere else, right? They were just hidden from yer side of the fence."

Alex scrunched her nose as she thought. She thought back to a similar conversation not long after she first agreed to be in the ship. Ghaoithe had mentioned places with power before. To hear the captain speak it, they were a sort of magnet to the human psyche, places people were drawn to without ever really knowing why. Alex's first thought came to Stonehenge at the time, and that power was affirmed through their travels. Places like Cairo and Dilmun did feel different in a way though Alex could never quite put her finger on it. It was like they were cities born because the earth itself said they should be born, and humanity simply answered the call to gather there. It would have felt wrong not to have cities in those places.

Still, Alex's question remained unanswered. She said, "I get that, but what's this have to do with Ghaoithe's home?"

Fleet shifted in his seat. He tugged at his full beard, almost as though he were nervous that Alex would laugh at him. He eventually relented.

"Now, I ain't got proper words for it. It was just something in the way she mentioned it, but it sounded like her home's got a power beyond even what we know. Like time stopped somewhere along the way," he said.

"Like time stopped?"

"Aye. It sounds silly. Maybe she had too much to drink. But that's what it sounded like when she told it. She said that even though Lost Earth is old, it still evolves and people move forward like the modern world, just at a different pace. She said her home hasn't moved forward, that it contained some primal and real force that kept itself sheltered away there."

They both sank into the back of their seats. Alex became aware that her heart was racing.

"Did she say anything else," Alex asked after a moment.

"Only that it's beautiful and that we should never fer a second let our guard down if we find ourselves there."

Alex mulled over the description. To her, Excalibur was magic enough. The *Cloudkicker* was magic enough. What could Ghaoithe possibly hide that was more magical than a flying, bulletproof airship? A thousand more questions needed to be asked, and Alex pondered all of them at once. Deep down, there was also the slightest tinge of another thing, something she did not want to say out loud: some of those possibilities scared the daylights out of her. If even Fleet did not know the answers after years beside the captain, Alex feared she may run into something about Ghaoithe she didn't want to know.

Alex stood and stretched her legs. She stared through the window and out into the night sky.

"There's only one way to find out," she said. Then, nearly at a whisper, "I'm not leaving without a way to help Ghaoithe."

Where they flew, Alex didn't know. All she understood was that it was away from Osiris, away from Lost Earth, and towards something new.

# EPILOGUE

Behind the girl, the door to the house slammed shut. "House" was a generous term, of course. They lived there, but there wasn't much to the building. It contained only one room with a small loft area overhead for their thin beds. The storm shook its warped frame and wind whistled as it slipped through the cracks of ancient boards. Firelight glowed through the windows, beckoned the child back to its warmth.

She ignored its call.

She pulled her hood down tight over her forehead as the wind dared her to venture forth. She loved the challenge. Storms like this one made her feel alive. The air had a certain vibe to it that kept her from sleep no matter how much she desired it. She was certain the man inside the house would not approve of her leaving, as he never did, but he had long since stopped arguing.

Through the rain and into the fields surrounding her home, the girl ran. If it were daylight, she would see nothing but grass and gentle slopes in three directions. As it was, she could not see more than a few feet through the downpour.

She turned and made her way past the side of her house, bare feet splashing joyously through the puddles they found there. She wanted to see the other side, the direction that did not have endless fields.

There, she found the ocean.

She made her way to the low wooden fence that marked the edge of her land. She never understood why it was there, only that it was and that it was a part of her home like the stone fireplace or the uncomfortable chairs that wobbled on uneven legs. She hopped over the fence like a cat in hot pursuit of unseen prey.

Not far beyond, she arrived at the cliffs. She heard them well before she could see them as the waves roiled below in a thundering symphony. Sometimes on nights like this, she could see tiny pricks of light pass by on the horizon, ships in need of refuge. There were no lighthouses nearby, though. The ships, more often than not, would live forever in the deep sea. It was the way of things, a law meant to pacify what lie beneath. There could be lighthouses anywhere but here.

The girl threw off her cloak. It flapped in the wind, whipped about before it landed soaking on the ground. She held her arms wide as if in sacrifice to whatever may take her, though nothing ever did. It was her cry of freedom, of bliss among the raw elements and their gifts.

As the rain drenched her sheer nightgown and made it stick to her skin, a shiver crept up her spine. Not out of cold, oh no.

She could feel it out there, past the cresting waves and the tiny lights and the storm itself.

She sensed the world beyond her world.

One day soon, she would chase it.

# ACKNOWLEDGMENTS

To be completely honest, finishing the first book was enough of a surprise. To be wrapping up a second feels no less special and, in many ways, is even more surreal than the first time. Just as with "The Sky Thief," I would not have finished this project without the help of some wonderful people who have supported and advised me to help make this the best it could be.

To my parents for again providing a cheering squad and acting as some of my most fervent sales people.

To Hannah Gathman for taking the time out of her busy schedule to read over some very early work and provide incredibly insightful notes. Your feedback changed how I approached thinking about these characters I hold so dear for the better.

To my professors and classmates at Southeast Missouri State University for providing an open platform to improve and continue this journey into professional writing. Many of our workshops have proved invaluable, and I can't wait to see what else you all create after you have so patiently done the same for me.

To all my fans, friends, and family that have cheered on this book, showed up to my first signing, and helped me realize how great it is to reach others with a goofy little fantasy story. A story without readers is not a story worth telling. Thank you for making it worth it.

To Alexis, for all of your love and time enjoying each other's company. This book would not have been possible without your support and patience while I scrambled to finish this. I love you.

Finally, to Brad, Kayla, Davis, and Josh for always being there.